C

Thomas Elphinstone Hamb the police.

Chief-Inspector Bagshott. Of New Scotland Yard, a friend of Tommy's.

Deputy-Inspector Ennis. Also of New Scotland Yard.

Cobden. Hambledon's fellow escapee, that's not his real name. He's a crook but a decent sort.

Salvation Savory. That isn't his real name either and he runs an gang of crooks who eschew violence and aren't above acting a bit like Robin Hood.

Dick. Sal's butler. A good man when he can find his teeth.

David Arnott. A possible jewel thief, a more likely corpse.

Mary Gregory. His unfortunate girlfriend.

Daniel Deacon. In spite of the name, he's no pillar of the church.

The Masked Fiddler. He plays his violin for a few bob. But is he who he seems to be?

Robinson, Morgan, Parker, Tetlow, Sam & Ginger. Crooks, of the bad sort.

Peter, Bob, Bill & Johnny. Rather nicer crooks.

Mr. and Mrs. Bates. Not the most honest of landlords.

Prof. Jeremy Carnoustie. Perhaps he's not a mild-mannered retired teacher.

Henry Billing. No one can remember why he was nicknamed Oscar. He's small time in the crook game but has aspirations.

Plus assorted crooks, neighbors, shopkeepers, and police personnel.

Books by Manning Coles

The Tommy Hambledon Spy Novels
Drink to Yesterday, 1940
A Toast to Tomorrow (English title: *Pray Silence*), 1940
They Tell No Tales, 1941
Without Lawful Authority, 1943
Green Hazard, 1945
The Fifth Man, 1946
With Intent to Deceive (English title: *A Brother for Hugh*), 1947
Let the Tiger Die, 1947
Among Those Absent, 1948
Diamonds to Amsterdam, 1949
Not Negotiable, 1949
Dangerous by Nature, 1950
Now or Never, 1951
Alias Uncle Hugo (Reprint: *Operation Manhunt*), 1952
Night Train to Paris, 1952
A Knife for the Juggler (Reprint: *The Vengeance Man*), 1953
All that Glitters (English title: *Not for Export*;
Reprint: *The Mystery of the Stolen Plans*), 1954
The Man in the Green Hat, 1955
Basle Express, 1956
Birdwatcher's Quarry (English title: *The Three Beans*), 1956
Death of an Ambassador, 1957
No Entry, 1958
Concrete Crime (English title: *Crime in Concrete*), 1960
Search for a Sultan, 1961
The House at Pluck's Gutter, 1963

Ghost Books
Brief Candles, 1954
Happy Returns (English title: *A Family Matter*), 1955
The Far Traveller (non-series),1956
Come and Go, 1958

Non-Series
This Fortress, 1942
Duty Free, 1959

Short Story Collection
Nothing to Declare, 1960

Young Adult
Great Caesar's Ghost (English title: *The Emperor's Bracelet*), 1943

* Reprinted by Rue Morgue Press as of July 2011

Among Those Absent

A Tommy Hambledon novel

Manning Coles

Rue Morgue Press
Lyons

ISBN: 978-1-60187-058-2

Rue Morgue Press
87 Lone Tree Lane
Lyons CO 80540
www.ruemorguepress.com
800-699-6214

Printed by Pioneer Printing
Cheyenne, Wyoming

PRINTED IN THE UNITED STATES OF AMERICA

About Manning Coles

Manning Coles was the pseudonym of two Hampshire neighbors who collaborated on a long series of entertaining spy novels featuring Thomas Elphinstone Hambledon, a modern-language instructor turned British secret agent. Hambledon was based on a teacher of Cyril Henry Coles (1895-1965). This same teacher encouraged the teenage Coles to study modern languages, German and French in particular, having recognized Coles' extraordinary ability to learn languages. When World War I broke out Coles lied about his age and enlisted. His native speaker ability in German prompted him to be pulled off the front lines and he soon became the youngest intelligence agent in British history and spent the rest of the war working behind enemy lines in Cologne.

The books came to be written thanks to a fortuitous meeting in 1938. After Adelaide Frances Oke Manning (1891-1959), rented a flat from Cyril's father in East Meon, Hampshire, she and Cyril became neighbors and friends. Educated at the High School for Girls in Tunbridge Wells, Kent, Adelaide, who was eight years Cyril's senior, worked in a munitions factory and later at the War Office during World War I. She already had published one novel, *Half Valdez*, about a search for buried Spanish treasure. *Drink to Yesterday,* loosely based on Cyril's own adventures, was an immediate hit and the authors were besieged to write a sequel, no mean feat given the ending to that novel. That sequel, *A Toast to Tomorrow*, and its prequel were heralded as the birth of the modern espionage novel with Anthony Boucher terming them "a single long and magnificent novel of drama and intrigue and humor." The Manning Coles collaboration ended when Adelaide died of throat cancer in 1959. During those twenty years the two worked together almost daily, although Cyril's continuing activities with the Foreign Intelligence Branch, now known as the Secret Intelligence Service or, more commonly, MI6, often required that he be out of the country, especially during World War II. Cyril wrote *Concrete Crime* on his own but the final two books in the series were the work of a ghostwriter, Cyril not wanting to go on with the series without Adelaide. While the earliest books had shown flashes of humor, it would not be until *Without Lawful Authority*, published in 1943 but set in 1938, that the collaborators first embraced the almost farcical humor that would come to be their hallmark. For more details on their collaboration and Cyril's activities in British intelligence see Tom & Enid Schantz' introduction to the Rue Morgue Press edition of *Drink to Yesterday*.

Among Those Absent

I

OPERATION STONEWALL

Down the middle of the room there was a long, polished table, furnished as for a Board Meeting with blotting-paper, ink-pots, ashtrays and notepaper arranged with geometrical precision. The Detective-Superintendent responsible for the arrangements gave one more critical look at the table, moved one blotting-pad a quarter of an inch to the left and went out of the room, shutting the door behind him. Five minutes later the door opened again, a dozen men came in together and stood about talking quietly until a tall grey-haired man entered and went straight to the armchair at the head of the table.

"Please be seated, gentlemen. Thank you. Now, I think you all know that this rather unusual meeting has been called at the express desire of the Home Secretary in order that we may consult together about what steps can be taken to deal with those to whom—er—'Stone walls do not a prison make nor iron bars a cage.' In fact, any course of action upon which we decide might well be called, in the jargon of the day, 'Operation Stonewall.'"

The Commissioner paused, looked at some notes he held in his hand, and went on in a more businesslike tone.

"Every one of you here knows some part of this story, but not many of you, I think, know it as a whole. It will be as well, perhaps, if I run through it as briefly as possible so that we may all have an equal knowledge of the essential facts. Here they are.

"For just over two years there has been a series of daring and successful prison breaks. Disquietingly successful. Those of you present here who are Prison Governors have had personal experience of them. What is so particularly—er—disquieting about it is a thing which is bound to happen occasionally now that we no longer manacle our charges and confine them in dungeons. It is the fact that they are not recaptured, at least, not at once. They are diligently sought for, but not found brought them within reach of the law. In most cases—in all cases, in fact—they have either been apprehended abroad, or they have spent some time abroad and have been arrested

9

on their return to this country. That is correct, Chief-Inspector Bagshott?"

"That is so, sir, in every case we have dealt with so far."

"It follows," went on the Commissioner, "that behind these escapes there is an extremely efficient organization which not only gets the men out of prison but conceals them afterwards and conveys them away to a place of safety. Now for a few figures. It is difficult to say exactly where to begin, since the organization does not advertise its successes, but we have agreed to take as the start the escape of the forger Greenwall from Parkhurst Prison just over two years ago. He escaped from a working-party, evaded his pursuers, and was not seen again until he was arrested in Paris on a similar charge eighteen months later. We applied for his extradition and he was handed back to us by the courtesy of the French authorities. Since then—that is, within the space of twenty-six months—there have been no less than nineteen successful prison-breaks, counting as two the case of the coiner Mankatell who has escaped twice."

The Commissioner paused to blow his nose, rearranged his notes and continued.

"The methods employed have varied in each case to suit the difficulties encountered. In the majority of cases we have a fairly clear idea of how the scheme was worked, in two or three cases—two certainly—we have none at all. The prisoner was there and then he was not."

One of the Prison Governors previously referred to sighed suddenly and then looked round to see if anyone had noticed it.

"The obvious conclusion," went on the Commissioner, "is that in these cases someone has bribed a warder. Such a thing is commendably rare but it would be absurd to regard it as impossible. No amount of inquiry has, however, enabled us to identify the warder, or warders, responsible. It follows, therefore, that if a warder was guilty, that warder is still employed. A disquieting thought."

He followed his general remarks by giving a short account of each of the nineteen cases and of the prisoner concerned, referring every time to one or other of the men at the table for confirmation or fuller details. One of the escaped prisoners was a foreigner named Vissek.

"An expert housebreaker," said the Commissioner. "He is a national of a friendly Power, and when we applied to the Police of the Power for news of him, they found him for us and very courteously sent him back. It is in regard to this man that Mr. Hambledon, of Foreign Office Intelligence, is with us. Can you tell us anything interesting about him, Hambledon?"

"I knew him," said Hambledon. "He was—we are all discreet here—working for the Intelligence Service of the Power to which the Commissioner has just referred. Why not? We all do it, friendly or no. He was an extremely able burglar, but as an Intelligence Agent he wasn't so bright. He would get in anywhere, even into the most impossible places, and I wish I knew how he did it. I would back him to break into the Tower of London and steal the Crown Jewels. Only—if the Crown Jewels had been replaced by replicas in paste, he would have brought them away quite happily. That is a metaphor, he may have been an expert about jewels for all I know. I only know that in the case of documents of any kind he was singularly easily foxed. I don't wish to say anything unkind about a poor man in trouble, but I must admit I found him very useful on at least three occasions. Eventually, of course, this Government got tired of paying him for things like breaking into the Chinese Embassy for a list of the Chinese troops in Upper Burma and coming away with a Chinese laundry bill—"

"Oh, really, Hambledon!" said the Commissioner across the laughter.

"It's a fact," said Hambledon seriously. "I put it there for him myself. You couldn't expect him to read Chinese. So his Government sacked him and he took to ordinary burglary for a living. When he bolted back home they naturally didn't want him starting in business over there, so they made a magnificent gesture and handed him back. Sensible people, the—the Power in question."

"These international courtesies," murmured one of the Prison Governors.

"Quite, quite," said the Commissioner hastily. "The next case, gentlemen—"

At the end of the discussion the Commissioner put down his notes and leaned back in his chair.

"Has anyone anything further to add? No? Very well. Full minutes of this meeting have, as you noticed, been taken, and a practically verbatim report will be sent to the Home Secretary. I thank you all for your attendance."

Ten days later Hambledon received, to his surprise, a summons to an interview with the Home Secretary himself. In accordance with instructions Hambledon said nothing about it to anybody, not even to Chief-Inspector Bagshott of Scotland Yard who usually knew as much about his doings as anyone. At the appointed hour Tommy Hambledon arrived at the Home Office and was not kept waiting more than ten minutes.

"The subject I wanted to talk to you about," said the Minister, "or rather, the subject I wanted you to advise me about, if you will, is all this prison-breaking business. Will you have a cigar?"

"Thank you," said Tommy.

"I had a very full account of that meeting you attended the other day and I read it very carefully, but I can't say that I found it very helpful."

"No?"

"I was hoping that some fresh and ingenious method would have been put forward for preventing escapes, but I must admit I found none. More careful checking and counter-checking, greater vigilance—the treatment as before only stronger, in short. That was all. Do you agree?"

"Yes," said Hambledon frankly, "I do. But one should remember that they were all policemen—even the Prison Governors in a sense—and their actions are all laid down for them in Regulations. I think that's an excellent thing, mind you; unregulated police are the devil, I've met them in Germany and didn't like them a bit. But you can't have strict Regulations *and* sparkling initiative."

The Home Secretary nodded. "That's perfectly true, but what I was thinking was this. They all look at the problem from the inside, as it were. Escapes must be prevented: double the warders, build another six feet on the walls, frame better regulations for working parties, all that sort of thing. Now I was wondering whether escapes couldn't be forestalled."

Hambledon nodded. "It's exasperating to consider that you could probably open up the whole thing by giving one man five hundred pounds and a free passage to the Argentine, if only you knew whom to give it to."

"You have done as I knew you would," said the Minister. "You have put your finger on the spot, and that brings us to the reason why I sent for you, Mr. Hambledon, and not for a policeman. You have spent years of your valuable life finding out what people were going to do before they did it. Can you advise me how to find the man for the five hundred pounds?"

"When I received your letter making this appointment," said Hambledon slowly, "I guessed it would be this which you wanted to discuss, and I spent the intervening three days thinking it over. There isn't much doing in my Department at the moment. If you agree, I think I'd better go to jail myself."

"Good gracious—"

"With a very carefully arranged background, sir, and nobody must know. Nobody. Well, I suppose somebody must know, because I can't expect you to fix up identity papers, fingerprints on documents, official transfers and so on with your own hands. What I mean is that the police mustn't know, nor the warders, not even the Prison Governor of wherever I go. By the way, the prisons from which escapes are made are always convict prisons, aren't they? Not local prisons."

"That is so, yes. Local prisons are only used for short sentences up to two years and in the great majority of cases much less. Six months, that sort of thing. It wouldn't be worth while staging an expensive jailbreak for a short sentence. When it comes to five or seven years or even longer, it's another story."

"Yes. Haven't you got a nice middle-aged prisoner with a five-year sentence of smuggling diamonds or something like that, who could be moved from his present abode to another? *En route* he could be switched off to the docks, shipped to the Argentine and told never to come back, while I take his place, name and record? Surely you could spare one prisoner in a good cause," said Tommy, and stubbed out the end of his cigar.

The Home Secretary laughed. "A good example of the sort of sparkling initiative you spoke of just now, which one couldn't expect from the police. Just a moment, though, you've given me an idea. Excuse me a minute while I turn something up." He rang the bell and sent the clerk who answered it for a certain file.

"There was one thing which I noticed about these escapes," said Hambledon, while they were waiting. "They seemed to me to fall into two very different classes. Either they were the sort of men to be useful to a criminal organization if there is such a thing—expert forgers, coiners, housebreakers and so forth—or else they were rich men who could afford to pay for freedom."

"You're quite right, I noticed that myself."

"So if I were a comfortable City man of no use to anybody but myself," went on Tommy, "I should be less likely to be lured into a life of crime as the price of liberty, which is a nice thought. I don't, of course," he added more seriously, "really expect to be involved in an escape myself, I only hope to get some news of one."

The clerk came into the room, handed a file of papers to the Home Secretary, and went out again.

"I shouldn't like to take the responsibility for your being lured into a life of crime," said the Minister, untying the traditional red tape which is really pink, "we might be out of the frying-pan into the fire as we said in the nursery. Well, here we are. Edwin Vincent Hawkley, aged 49—in 1945 that was—convicted at the Old Bailey of fraudulent misrepresentation in connection with the issue to the public of shares in a company called the Beauty House Replacement Corporation. He headed his notepaper," said the Minister indignantly, "'To give unto them beauty for ashes,' the sacrilegious dog! The idea was to buy up the sites of completely demolished houses by a small cash payment to the owner plus some shares in the business, and sell more shares to the gullible public. By this means money would be available to rebuild houses on the bombed sites. The shareholders were to have the first option on the new houses when they were built. That's what he said. Of course it transpired at the trial that he'd only bought three sites and was twisted over one of those, the seller didn't own it. It had occurred to Hawkley that there was no need to buy properties to show his clients, any property would do, and copies of the title-deeds were readily available. The originals, he said, were deposited in his bank at Llandudno for safety. The properties were all small lots in the poorer parts of London and the cheaper suburbs, thus tapping a class of customer unlikely to be familiar with the laws of property and so forth. He collected about fifteen thousand pounds, and then somebody smelt a rat and the whole thing blew up. He tried to bolt, signing on as a steward on a liner for South America, and the police collected him ten minutes before she sailed. He got seven years."

"And rightly, in my opinion," said Tommy. "Did they get the money back?"

"No. He was convicted in December 1945, and served thirteen months of his sentence. He then escaped from prison—that was in January this year. He had a brother who was a pilot in a firm of private passenger aircraft, on charter, you know. The brother faked an order to fly a passenger to Glasgow, picked up Edwin Vincent Hawkley and started off with him across the North Sea. They were reported crossing the coast and again about forty-five miles out, but the weather turned bad, strong northeasterly winds—a head-wind, naturally—snow, sleet and so forth. They did not arrive so far anyone can discover. What is more, wreckage was picked up by a fishing-boat on the Dogger and considered by experts to be part of the missing aircraft. So that was probably that."

"He'd have done better to stay in jail," said Tommy. "Better for himself, I mean."

"Yes, quite. Well, there you are. If he wasn't drowned after all, and the police got their claws on him, he'd go back to serve the remainder of his sentence. Suit you? I should like to point out that this isn't one of the series of escapes which we are investigating, though it occurred during that period. There was no mystery about this one, the police traced it all out. The brother worked it. So if you should contact any of the people we want there is no fear of their saying, 'This isn't the man we got out before.'"

"What about his past?" asked Hambledon. "Had he been associated with criminals before?"

"No. He was a clerk in a solicitor's office for some years, then he was employed by two or three City companies in succession, with gaps between jobs. But he'd never been what they call 'in trouble' before."

"I see. And what about his family, any more brothers or sisters? Was he married?"

"One other brother was killed in the war and their parents are both dead. Hawkley was a widower, no wife, no children."

"I always prefer, on these occasions," said Hambledon, "not to have a wife."

II

UNWILLING GUESTS

The nine hours of silence was broken by the clanging of a large handbell, four hand-bells at once, in fact, one on each of the three galleries and one on the ground floor. The sound passed along the landings as the warders walked fast from end to end; behind every door a man awoke, stretched himself, and tumbled out of bed to wash and dress. The water was cold, but cold water is wholesome, they say. Beds were hastily but accurately tidied up and arranged for the day in the prescribed pattern; by the time all this was done another bell rang and cell doors were unlocked and opened. This was the moment of the day when all the prisoners were housemaids, every man his own domestic, and the prison officers were more critical than any modern housewife dares to be. The prisoners scrubbed, swept and polished as for dear life, not only from fear of caustic comment but because, if you castle is only seven-foot-six by nine, it may as well be clean.

There followed next a noisy clatter of boots on the iron staircases as all the prisoners assembled in the hall below to be sorted out into parties for exercise or Swedish drill. The elder men were usually given what was called exercise, which meant walking round and round in concentric rings and occasionally trotting for a change. The prisoner called Hawkley was set among these at first, but he found it intolerably monotonous. He applied, therefore, for permission to see the Medical Officer.

"Well, my man? What's the matter with you?"

"Nothing, sir. I only want to ask permission to have physical drill instead of 'exercise.'"

"Oh. Well, we usually give that to the younger men only. It's pretty strenuous, you know. Why do you want to change?"

"I'm doing sedentary work, sir, sewing mailbags all day, and I rather think"—the prisoner's voice dropped a tone and he patted his front reproachfully—"I think I'm getting a tendency to middle-age spread."

The M.O. smiled. "Getting too much to eat, are you?"

"No, sir, by no means. But the diet is rather starchy, perhaps."

"Oh. Well, you can try it if you like. Application granted."

The prisoner called Hawkley told his next neighbor in the workroom about this arrangement, and the prisoner Cobden scoffed.

"Dam' silly idea," he said. "Next week or the week after we'll be put on outside jobs. Digging drains, or digging post-holes or—or just digging. You won't have to worry about your figure then, it'll just go back by itself. You'll get more than enough without physical jerks too. You wait and see."

"Then I'll change back again," said Hawkley.

"Of course," said Cobden, "it may be that they won't put you on outside work, at least, not so soon as they generally do."

"Why not?"

"Well, you got away before, didn't you? Or so they say."

"I haven't got a brother now," said Hawkley.

Cobden merely nodded. The murmur of talk all over the long room had risen to a buzz and prison officers on duty checked it. "Too much talking." There was silence for a few minutes and then the low murmur started again. Hawkley's fingers slipped on the coarse needle and he jabbed himself painfully in the left thumb. He muttered something under his breath and sucked the wound.

"You aren't very expert, are you?" said Cobden.

"Needlework has never been one of my accomplishments," said Hawkley.

Cobden said nothing and went on sewing his mailbag, he was very much quicker and neater at his work than Hawkley. He was a tall slim young man with dark hair, quite unusually good-looking and with considerable charm of manner. He had evidently been well educated, he spoke with a cultured voice and was serving a three-year sentence for working an ingenious form of confidence trick. He and Hawkley had arrived at Northern Moor prison together, travelling in the same party from Crewe where Hawkley had been added to the collection.

When Hawkley and Cobden had been for five weeks at Northern Moor they were drafted to outside work in the fields surrounding the prison. It was a fine September and there was little hardship in the weather, it was pleasant, too, to be beyond those grim stone walls and to look at green things and far horizons instead of those monotonous grey buildings with rows of barred windows exactly nine feet apart. Northern Moor is the newest prison in England and is laid out upon the most enlightened plan, but a prison is still a prison and walls and bars are its natural skeleton. You cannot fillet a jail.

When he had been at Northern Moor for nine weeks and never a whisper of an escape in prospect his spirits sank. This was the silliest idea he had ever entertained in a life distinguished for ideas which have often looked sillier than they actually were. This one was even sillier than it looked, which was saying a lot. What guarantee was there that an escape would ever be attempted from this place? None, except the Home Secretary's opinion that there were several prisoners there of the type which might be thought to be worth rescuing. That fat slug of a man nicknamed The Bishop, for example, rolling in money and disliking the life intensely. But even he showed no signs of illicit activity.

Hawkley straightened his aching rubbed his stiff knees, called himself insulting names in every language he could remember, which were many, and made up his mind. He would give this place another week, if nothing happened in that time he would throw his hand in.

There was a stand-easy for ten minutes in the middle of the morning's work, and since the prisoners were more or less loose in a large field they naturally drifted together into congenial groups. Hawkley and Cobden sat down together on the grass strip at the edge of the field, the Bishop and a long-nosed man named Brooks lay down a little further along and stared at the sky. A group of half a dozen men were squatting in a circle apparently engaged in some game with small pebbles; two moonfaced fellows of great strength and slow intelligence, who answered to the names of Mutt and Jeff, sat on the opposite sides of a wheelbarrow, back to back, and obviously were not talking. They seldom did, having nothing to say.

"Funny mixture, aren't we?" said Cobden.

"Well, we're a mixture anyway," agreed Hawkley.

"I'd like to know why The Bish and the fellow Brooks are palling up like that," went on Cobden. "Quite new. The Bish used to be just as sarcastic to him as he is to everyone else, and now look at them. Buddies, real buddies."

"I suppose they've found something in common. Both got aunts at Clacton-on-Sea, or collected matchbox covers or trained performing fleas. Could I care less? I shouldn't think so."

Cobden looked at him and laughed. "You've got the needle today, haven't you? Novelty worn off and not yet got used to the life?"

"Novelty?" said Hawkley. "Novelty, after serving—"

"Don't tell me fairy stories about serving thirteen months at Parkhurst, when anyone with eyes in his head could see you'd never been inside till the day you came here," said Cobden frankly. "Why, even now you don't know how to scrounge a cigarette and you told me you couldn't sew, and—"

"I am, perhaps, not a very observant person," said Hawkley mildly.

"You know, you do puzzle me. What are you doing in here?"

"Penal servitude," said Hawkley blandly. "Aren't you?"

"Are you serving somebody else's sentence for twenty pounds a week?"

"I wouldn't serve anybody else's sentence for twenty pounds a day," said Hawkley, with so much emphasis that Cobden believed him at once.

"There's only one thing I am sure of about you and that is that you're not

Edwin Vincent Hawkley."

"What gives you that idea?"

"You remember the other day when we were talking about William the Third and you said you'd never been to Brixham? Well, Hawkley was born and brought up there."

"I am trying to forget my past," said Hawkley, "don't remind me. The small grey house with wistaria over the porch, my little bedroom with the sloping ceiling and the rocking-horse in the corner, the smell of paraffin lamps and fried herrings rising up the stairs, the cracked bell ringing for Sunday chapel, the black cat with white whiskers—"

"And the little girl in a pink frock who lived next door," prompted Cobden.

"Blue. Her frock I mean. She had a doll called Angeline—"

"And you threw it down a well. Now tell me the name of that steep street which runs up from the harbor, it has a pub called the William of Orange on the corner?"

The prison officer in charge blew a whistle and Hawkley sighed with relief.

"I'll tell you some other time," he said, and returned to his kale plants which at least did not ask questions.

To his relief Cobden did not return to the subject of his identity when they met again in the afternoon break. He said instead that Hawkley looked a good deal more cheerful but that he himself had caught the complaint.

"Your hump," he explained. "I'm sick to death of this place."

"Let's leave," said Hawkley. "Any ideas?"

"Not at present. Look here, if I can think of any scheme, are you on?"

"Of course. That's why I asked to be transferred to physical jerks. Nothing like keeping fit."

"Oh, was that why? I thought you were just bats."

Mutt and Jeff came mooning along together and it was plain that Jeff had a grievance.

"What's the matter?" asked Hawkley.

"That—so-and-so—Mister Blooming Bishop,"—only the adjective was not flowery.

"Been annoying you again?"

"Markham said as we'd be 'oein' turnips next' week and I says good, I likes 'oein' turnips, and Bish 'e turns round and says, 'Mind your 'ead then, don't 'oe it by mistake,' 'e says, 'quite easy mistake,' 'e says, 'nobody'd blame you.'"

"One o' these days," said Mutt darkly, "somebody'll 'oe 'im. An' no loss."

"I am inclined to agree with you," said Cobden.

Hawkley found it difficult to go to sleep that night. If Cobden were in touch with escape organization, life looked a lot more hopeful. The hopes were dashed by Cobden's first remarks the next day.

"If I knew who it is gets these fellows out," he said, "I'd put in a claim for assistance."

"What fellows?"

"All these jailbreaks they've had the last couple of years. Somebody works it, they don't just happen."

"Oh, that," said Hawkley. "No, I suppose not. Does anyone here know anything about it, do you think?"

"I don't know, but I should think it's more than likely."

"How does one get in touch with these people?" asked Hawkley sleepily, for the sun was warm. "Put an advertisement in *Exchange and Mart*? 'Gentleman bored with monotonous employment desires change to sparkling variety, risky if possible.'"

"You want *The Stage* for that," said Cobden.

Two days later he told Hawkley that there was a rumor going round the prison.

"What is it?"

"That The Bishop and Brooks are going to be got out."

Hawkley nearly said: "At last," and just changed it in time.

"Not really? When? And how?"

"I don't know yet, but I'm going to cultivate Brooks."

"But surely he won't talk?"

"I think he might. I wasn't a con man for nothing, you know. Besides, haven't you noticed an odd thing about convicts, if they talk at all they must boast? And the conceited ones are the worst. Brooks is the real smart-Alec type and thinks himself such a clever boy. In the meantime, I think you and I had better cool off a bit. It's definite blast, but there you are."

"We'll have a thundering row in public if you like," suggested Hawkley, who was wondering whether Cobden really meant to transfer his allegiance to the Bishop-Brooks party. One could hardly blame him if there was a chance of their getting him out.

"No, that wouldn't do all," said Cobden. "How am I to tell you what's going on if we're not on speaking terms?"

"You're right, of course. Go to it."

"Watch me," said Cobden, and laughed.

Hawkley watched with fascinated interest the undoing of Brooks. Cobden started off by being surprised into laughter at one of his jokes, and gave the impression of discovering suddenly that there was more in Brooks than he had thought. Brooks's line of business had been to enter small branch post offices run by women and persuade them, by pointing a pistol at them, to hand over the contents of the till. He did fairly well until one evening when a constable happened to want a twopenny-half-penny stamp at the critical moment, after which it was explained to Brooks that this was called Robbery with Violence and that it was no defence to say the pistol wasn't loaded. He served a sentence, came out, and did it again. This time he got five years, which he considered unfair. He told Cobden all about it.

"It'll pass," said Cobden cheerfully, "there's nothing to stop it. If you behave yourself you'll be out in a little more than four years."

"Four years?" Suppose I'm goin' to stop in this 'ole for four years?"

"Yes," said Cobden simply.

"Not me. Not—something—likely. They can't keep me in 'ere."

"They all talk like that," said Cobden, yawning. "But they stay."

"But I'm different. You ain't seen nuffin' yet."

"Huh," said Cobden.

"I tell you, as you're a pal, I shan't be 'ere more'n anuver fortnight. If that."

"Says you. Being transferred to Dartmoor?"

"Transferred nuffin'. I'm goin' out, I tell you. Me an' The Bishop. We're leavin'."

"What, that fat old cow? He'd fall down dead if he ran fifty yards."

"Not 'e. He's tougher than you'd think. 'Sides, 'e'll 'ave me to 'elp 'im."

Cobden laughed scornfully.

"You laugh," said the baited Brooks. "You wait till one of these days when the fog comes down sudden, like it does."

"That's when you throw down your spades and run, I suppose. Fine. You running and The Bish puffing behind till you wind up sitting up to your necks in a bog howling for somebody to come and pull you out. There are bogs on these hills, you know, one step on them and they catch your feet and suck you in."

"Sucker yourself," said Brooks rudely. "We ain't goin' on so silly. We goes straight as a die to where there's some'un waitin' for us."

"You can't run straight as a die in a fog. You run round in circles, you can't help it. Everybody does. Besides, fancy expecting to meet somebody you can't see in a place you can't find—"

"Ever 'eard of direction-finding wireless receivers?"

"Not in jail," said Cobden firmly.

"Well, there's one 'ere. Ah, that surprises you, don't it?"

"I've seen them," admitted Cobden, "and even used one during the War. But d'you mean to tell me the warders are going to stand round sucking their thumbs while you go and strap on your front a box a foot square—"

"Foot square! Mister, it's no bigger than a box of a 'undred Players."

"Now that I do not believe," said Cobden with conviction.

"Look 'ere. Termorrer, when we goes to get the tools out, you and me 'angs back last an' I'll show you somefink. Seein's believin', ain't it?"

"Not this time," said Cobden. "You and your wireless cigarette-boxes!"

"You wait," said Brooks.

The wireless receiving set was in a tin box painted black, it contained a marvelously compact apparatus with tiny valves no bigger than the first joint of one's fingers. It was actuated by a dry battery and there was one small earphone with connecting flex.

"I was a foreman electrician in a wireless factory once," said Brooks. "We got the set in in bits an' I assembled it. Old Guffey in the tinsmith shop made the box for me, I told 'im I was goin' in for collectin' beetles. An' 'e wore it, silly old—!"

Guffey was serving a life sentence and had learned in ten years of it how the silliest craze will spread. When Cobden asked him to make another box for beetles like the one he'd made for Brooks he agreed at once. Cobden took it out in the field with him and showed it to Hawkley.

"I'll weight it with earth wrapped in a bit of rag," he said, "and hope I get the weight about right. Then I'll swop it for their some night when we come in. I think they take theirs out every day now, hoping the fog will come down."

"Suppose they open it," said Hawkley.

"Not with Mutt and Jeff looking on. You've noticed that, of course I told them carefully several times over in words of one syllable that The Bish and Brooks were going to get out. If Mutt and Jeff hung around and waited for B. and B. to start running and then clouted them good and hearty it would be Assisting the Authorities to Maintain Order and they'd probably get remission of sentence. I don't know if they would really, but it doesn't matter because they weren't a bit interested in that. The clout or clouts would be, apparently, their own reward. So now they don't so much hang around as haunt them, and in the meantime I'll have their set."

"Splendid," said Hawkley, "absolutely. Besides, a good scrap will cause a diversion. Couldn't be better. I wonder when it will come off."

"When this fine spell breaks," said Cobden. "It can't last much longer at this time of year, it's nearly November."

Two days later the prisoners were out again, clearing a bean-field and piling the rubbish into heaps for burning. The day was cold and clammy, a heavy dew lay upon every twig and blade of grass, soaking the prisoners' legs to the knees and their arms to the elbows. The sky was lowering and seemed almost to touch the tops of the hills round the high moors where they lived and worked; Hawkley noticed the prison officers in charge watching the weather. Two of them came together within earshot of Hawkley and one suggested taking the party in.

"Not just yet," said the other. "There's only half an hour to go. We'll watch it, though."

Cobden brought a load of rubbish to Hawkley's pile and muttered: "Look out," in passing.

Ten minutes later there came one of those sudden shifts of wind the high moors know so well. Hawkley happened to be looking towards the prison at the moment and it was as though a veil had slid across the tall buildings, the next moment they weren't there. It was like magic. At once the warder in charge signalled to his assistants, blew his whistle and shouted an order for the men to cease work and fall in. Hawkley looked round for Cobden and walked towards him, he was on one knee tying up his bootlace.

"Steady now," said Cobden, "don't press, keep your eye on the ball."

The fog surged up to the turf wall surrounding the field, paused like a breaking wave and poured over; instantly everything became indistinct and figures moved like ghosts in the mist. The warders were shouting orders and rounding the men up, Cobden stood up and he and Hawkley moved slowly forward.

"They'll never get another chance like this," muttered Cobden, "if they don't go now they never—"

There was a series of yells from the fog ahead of them. "Hi! Stop that!" and less articulate sounds suggestive of battle. Cobden grabbed Hawkley's arm, wheeled and made a dash for the turf dike.

"Give me a leg up—I'll pull—that's right, come on—"

They dropped down the other side and ran at top speed till their lungs were laboring, over drystone wall they hardly saw before they touched it, and on till the shouting died in the distance while the fog wrapped them round and hid them away.

III

ROPE TRICK

Cobden stopped, panting, in a tangle of dead bracken up to his thighs, Hambledon came up behind him and instantly sat down. Cobden looked at him and grinned.

"That's right," he said, undoing his coat to get at the precious tin box which was inside his shirt, "take it easy while you may. I must say you can run."

"Had to," gasped Tommy. "'Fraid of losing you."

"I'm glad to get this box off my chest, the corners have been digging holes in my ribs every day since I had it. Now then."

He opened the box, turned a switch, drew out the single earphone on its length of flex and held it to his ear while Tommy watched him anxiously.

"I hope it works," he said.

"So do I. Brooks said he'd tried it out and it was all right." He sat down beside Hambledon, made a small adjustment and swivelled slowly on his axis. "Wait a minute—what's that? That's him and that's the direction," he said, pointing the way he was facing. "Come on, we'd better not hang about or somebody might come to look for us. Mutt and Jeff must have put up a good scrap," he added, as they hurried across the rough moorland, "we haven't been reported missing yet."

"How do you know?" asked Hambledon, tearing himself free from some affectionate brambles.

"No bell," explained Cobden. "That big bell on the top of the main block."

"Should we hear it up here?"

"Lord, yes. Hear it for miles, especially downwind. Listen, what's that?"

There came a dull booming sound which seemed to Tommy to make the fog quiver; again and again repeated, not very regular but persistent, ringing on and on.

"Not a very expert campanologist," said Hambledon, but he quickened his pace and Cobden kept level with him.

23

"Better not talk," he said in a low voice, "every soul within a three-mile radius is listening now. Left a bit, we're getting off the line."

"What are we going to find when we get to the transmitter?" murmured Hambledon. "Any idea?"

"None. Car of some kind, I suppose."

They plodded steadily on in a silence broken only by an occasional direction from Cobden till they found themselves walking on a road; a rough road, stony and pot-holed but still a road.

"I don't like this," said Hambledon.

"Nor I, but I think he's very near now. Walk on the grass at the side. We're pretty well on top of whatever it is. This fog's getting thicker. Look, what's that?"

Something large loomed up ahead, looking enormous in the fog, a big covered lorry painted grey. Cobden dropped the wireless set inside his shirt and advanced boldly towards the lorry. A man came forward at the sound of their footsteps and peered at them, or rather, as Hambledon noticed with relief, at their clothes. This, evidently and happily, was someone who did not know Messrs. Bishop and Brooks by sight, though the escapers were not very likely to be the wrong convicts. Even in a dense fog escaped prisoners are not dispersed over all the countryside like spilt ball-bearings on the workshop floor.

"Come on," said the man, and led the way to the back of the lorry. As they passed along the side Hambledon glanced up and recognized a familiar monogram made up from the letters I.G.A.

"Industrial Gas Association," he said thoughtfully.

"Don't you go writin' them no letters of thanks," said the man swiftly. "We 'ad to put I.G.A. on it so's nobody should arst questions about the cylinders."

"Cylinders?"

There was a second man inside the lorry who put his head out between the rear curtains and said: "Is that you? Good. Take your boots off."

Hambledon was so surprised that he said: "Boots? Why?" but Cobden was already untying his laces.

"Boots," said the man in an impatient voice. "Boots, nails, sparks, hydrogen, bang. What did you expect? Bastinado? Get a move on."

"That accounts for the cylinders," said Tommy, and tore off his boots. A hydrogen fire was a thing he had learned to respect years before.

"Got any matches?" asked the same man. When they said they had not he told them to get into the lorry. "Clothes," he said, pointing to two neat piles, "yours," to Hambledon "and yours," to Cobden. "Change Quick. There are three sets of underclothes each, put them all on." He swung himself up to where the roof of the lorry should have been, and Hambledon noticed that the cover had been rolled back. The man disappeared upwards and there were creaking sounds as of ropes in tension. The escaped convicts changed into clothes provided as quickly as possible under the circumstances; it was growing dark, they stumbled and slipped because the floor was covered with heavy tubular objects with a tendency to roll and pinch their toes, and hurry made them fumble-fisted.

"What is all this, do you think?" asked Cobden in a low tone. "And why three sets of underwear?"

"Indian rope trick." said Tommy instantly. "We climb up it and disappear, and it will be cold up there."

A voice overhead said something to the man outside about "pressure nearly O.K.," and the man outside opened the car bonnet and appeared to be brooding over it, for they did not hear him doing anything. Hambledon and Cobden were changing their dark grey socks with the telltale red lines at toe and calf for the subdued stripes of civilian life, and there was a silence in which a quiet hissing sound made itself heard. Cobden said: "What's that?"

"Nothing," said Hambledon. "Only the characteristic hiss of a king cobra about to attack us."

Cobden leapt to his feet, staring about him, and Tommy apologized. "It's only gas passing up that tube from one of these cylinders."

"Sorry," said Cobden awkwardly, "but I do hate snakes. Where's the gas going?"

"I don't really know, but I imagine it's filling a balloon."

"Is that what you meant just now when you talked about the Indian Rope trick?"

Tommy nodded. Creaking sounds from overhead announced the return of the man who had gone aloft, a pair of long legs waved between them and he dropped silently to the floor. He looked critically from one to the other and went out without speaking. Outside in the road they could hear him ask his mate some question about "the Met. report," the answer was inaudible and a murmured conversation followed. In a few minutes he returned.

"Ready? Here," to Hambledon, "here's wristwatch for you, put it on. This is a pocket altimeter, don't believe all it says but it will at least tell you whether you're going up or down. Put it in your pocket. Here is a wallet for each of you, they contain your identity cards, ration books, money, a few letters addressed to you and so forth. Don't lose them. Here is also an electric torch, don't drop it. Now these are parachute packs, I'll put them on you to make sure they're on the right way up." He fitted them on, adjusting the harness with some care. "This is the release-cord, pull it *after* you jump, not before. Got that? Ever made a parachute jump before? No, well, you're going to tonight. Now listen carefully. Ten hours after the moment when you start, that will be at about 4 a.m., climb over the side of the basket and let yourself fall. Count five and pull the release-cord. Repeat that."

They repeated it unwillingly.

"Don't jump both together, you may get tangled up. I don't care which jumps first, the second must wait ten seconds. Got that? Don't forget it. You should then be just north of London. Endeavour not to break your ankles when you land, let yourself roll. Pick yourselves up, roll up your parachutes—having first divested yourselves of the harness—and hide them. Then go to the address which you will find written in pencil on the back—the back, mind—of one of the letters in your wallets. You have the wallets in an inside pocket, have you not? That's right. Otherwise you may lose it when you jump. Now, have you taken all that in or shall I repeat it again?"

"You do take us for idiots, don't you?" said Cobden angrily.

"You got yourselves jailed, didn't you?" He paused for a reply but there was none. "Now come up this way. Once you're on the roof there's rope ladder."

He climbed up the side of the lorry, Hambledon and Cobden followed. They were urged and pushed up a rope ladder, at the top there was a round basket, bobbing and tilting as they climbed in. Their adviser followed them up far enough to put his head over the edge.

"What's the time?" he asked, and Hambledon told him.

"Right. Add on ten hours and that's when you jump." He climbed down without another word and they saw him drop off the end and disappear into the lorry.

"How old would you reckon that man to be?" asked Cobden.

"How old? Oh, about thirty-five. Why?"

"It says a lot for human nature that he's lived on earth for thirty-five years and nobody's hit him on the head with a blunt instrument."

"Contemptuous blighter," agreed Tommy. "Irritating manner, very. Now I suppose he cuts us loose."

There was a pause during which nothing happened.

"Are you enjoying this?" said Cobden suddenly.

"Not particularly. Are you?"

"No. You know, there was one thing to be said for my private room over there"—he jerked his head towards Northern Moor Prison—"my old 'flowery dell'—"

"What's that?"

"Nobody threw me out of the window at 4 a.m. with an umbrella tied to my shoulderblades. I rather—gosh!"

The basket appeared to kick the soles of their feet with such violence that Tommy staggered and sat down abruptly. There was for a short time the sensation of rising in a lift, but even that eased off and ceased and only a faint rocking suggested that they were airborne. There was nothing to see but fog. It was some time before Cobden exclaimed and pointed. There before them hung the rising moon.

"How long have we been—been here?" asked Cobden.

Tommy looked at the watch, it had a luminous dial.

"Seventeen minutes."

"Is that all?"

"It does, doesn't it?" said Hambledon, answering the thought behind the words. "If we had a pack of cards we could play solo or animal grab."

"If we had a piece of string," said Cobden, "we could play at cat's cradle."

"If we had a few mailbags, we could—"

"Shut up! Do you know what we're missing?"

"Supper", said Tommy without hesitation. "And tonight's dripping night, too."

The moon, which had remained steadily in one place as is customary, suddenly began to move. It slid very slowly round them horizontally till it returned to its starting point and began another circuit. As they were not conscious of motion the effect was eerie.

"We are spinning," said Hambledon.

"I didn't really believe the moon had broken loose," said Cobden, "but—d'you know, if this keeps on I shall be sick."

"Come and sit down where you can't see it, on the floor. There isn't much room, but if I curl my legs round one side you can have the other. That's better, isn't it?"

Cobden sat down, coiling his long legs into little space, and said: "What will you do when we get out of this?"

"I shall have my hands full keeping out of the way of the police, I think. What about you?"

"Like you, lie low for a bit and then get a little place in the country somewhere and go in for dog-breeding. At least, that's what I think now. But I suppose some mug will come along with more money than scene and I shan't be able to resist it. The things people will believe! Even the Spanish Prisoner trick that's as old as the Napoleonic Wars works just as well with Franco. Well, I ought not to talk, I was a mug once myself."

"And now you're the bitten biting, eh?" said Tommy. "What bit you, if it's not an intrusion?"

"I came out of the Army with over a thousand pounds in the bank; gratuity, pay saved up and so on. You don't spend money in the desert. I met such a nice man with a keen sense of what he personally owed to the Service Man who had saved him from etc., etc., etc. Lord, I was green. He said it would be a mere repayment of a debt if I would allow him to make my fortune. He introduced me to some friends of his, they were going to let me in on the ground floor in a new company that was going to make us all rich men in two or three years. You can guess the rest. I put in all the money I'd got plus a

mortgage on my mother's house—she had just died. So then they got out
from under and left me with the lot to carry, and of course I lost every bean
and the house was sold and that was that. Sure you're not bored?"

"Not a bit. We have another eight hours and fifty minutes."

"Sure the watch hasn't stopped? No, I was afraid not. Well, I said to myself that what man had done man could do. I sat down and thought out a few
simple schemes. As everybody knows, the con man's standby is the violent
objection people feel to admitting they've been stung, and the simpler the
trick the less they wish to admit it. Especially the hardheaded business man,
so-called. I went for the City guinea-pig type, like the one who'd stung me,
and did very well out of it till I was silly enough to tackle a Yorkshireman.
He didn't mind what he looked like in court. I'd gotten t'brass and he wasn't
going to stand for it. He went to the police and then some of the others
plucked up courage and joined in the chase. I was sunk. Northern Moor. End
of anecdote."

"Pity," said Hambledon thoughtfully. "An awful pity."

"Yes, wasn't it?" said Cobden brightly. "Well, that's the story of my young
life. Now it's your turn. Not that I really expect you to unroll the pageant of
your days for my benefit, but I should like to know what you're doing in this
balloon."

"Escaping," said Tommy innocently.

"All right," said Cobden amiably. "Funny thing, isn't it, I wish I had a
cigarette. I thought the craving had passed, it must be the air of freedom
acting upon me."

"Listen," said Hambledon. "I see no reason why you should go through
with this. I mean, wait the specified time, jump at the appointed spot or as
near it as this heavenly chariot takes us, and present yourself at the address
on the back of the envelope whatever it is. Why don't you hop over earlier
and make yourself scarce? I suppose you've got somewhere to go."

"Why don't you?"

Hambledon hesitated. "Yes, why not? If we dropped out separately we
should stand a better chance—"

"Look here," said Cobden. "I don't know what you're doing here but you're
no convict. You were far too new, you'd never done the six week's trial trip
in a local jail, let alone a year at wherever-it-was. I really thought you were
serving somebody else's term for him, but if that's so, why are you escaping?"

Hambledon did not answer at once and Cobden went on: "Listen, if you'll
jump first, I'll jump later. That's fair offer."

Hambledon made up his mind. "I can't do that," he said. "You are quite
right, I'm note quite a convict. I went there to try to get to the bottom of all
this escape business. So I must go through with it, go to that address and all.

I'm rather ashamed you saw through me so easily."

"So that's it," said Cobden softly. "Now I'll tell you something. I was transferred to Northern Moor from Portland because two men escaped from there and one of them was a friend of mine. He was a good chap, he clouted a man who'd been running round with his wife, only he hit him rather too hard. I heard later what had happened, news does filter even into prisons, you know. He had been approached by this organization you're looking for and asked to help a forger to get out, an oldish man, not very active. He agreed and they got out. Then this crowd, whoever they are, wanted him to do some job for them, don't know what it was. Something pretty foul, presumably, because Ted dug his toes in and refused. Apparently they said in effect, 'Do what you're bid or we'll put the police on to you,' and he told them not to bother, he'd go to the police himself."

"Rather unwise, to be so frank," murmured Hambledon.

"Yes, but he was like that. Then he was found dead in a lane a few miles out of Southampton, he'd been shot. I imagine he was going that way with some idea of getting on a ship and going abroad, but they got him first. No arrest was made."

"That's not to say that none ever will be," said Hambledon quietly. "How long ago was this?"

"About six months. Oh, the police may get 'em for it yet, but I doubt it. Anyway, what I was going to say was that if you're after this crowd, so am I. No doubt yours is business, but my share will be a pleasure."

"I shall be very glad of your help," said Tommy frankly. "I think you'll be very useful. There's a certain amount of risk, of course, but I doubt if you'd be any safer trying to dodge them. I much prefer having a partner," he added, "it's always so difficult when one has to be in two places at once."

Cobden laughed. "That's what people come up against when they try to establish an alibi, isn't it? I must move, I'm getting so cramped. Let's see if the moon is behaving itself." He stood up and stretched, holding on to the guy-ropes. "I think the moon's gone home again, it's very dark now."

"Overcast, I expect," said Tommy, struggling to his feet. "I don't know anything about ballooning, but don't you think the wind's getting up? I feel more as though we were being pulled along instead of floating. Any lighted cities below?"

"There's a sort of glow over there, but it's still foggy at ground level, we've got into a higher current of air. I hope those blighters who set us off knew their job, they ought to have told us what altitude to keep," said Cobden, rather anxiously. "We don't want to drift out to sea, there's no future in that."

"What an unspeakably repulsive prospect. We have now been airborne for just over three hours."

"If only we could see the stars we could get some idea of which way we're going. Listen. I thought so, aircraft. Sounds like a Dakota."

"Oh dear," said Tommy Hambledon. "Which way's he going? You know, I don't like this particularly."

"He's not coming straight at us, I think—is he? No, I don't think so. We must wait, that's all."

The Dakota passed by upon its lawful occasions and Hambledon looked at it enviously.

"I wish I were there instead of here," he said. "'Lights are burnin' brightly, sir, an' all's well.' Warmed, steered, powered and under control, how lovely."

"'How different from us, Miss Beale and Miss Buss,'" quoted Cobden. "It's getting frightfully cold, too." He flapped his arms to warm himself.

"You know, this was a very brilliant idea," said Hambledon. "This balloon would pack down on its basket in the lorry and nobody would see anything. When they reached their destination all they had to do was to roll back the roof cover, connect a tube or tubes from the hydrogen cylinders to the appointed spot on this blister above us, and the specific gravity of hydrogen would do the rest."

"Suppose somebody'd come along just when the egg was rising from the nest. A bit of a risk, wasn't it?"

"I expect they chose a pretty lonely spot, and as soon as the balloon rose it would disappear into the fog, leaving only connecting ropes and the aforementioned tube. Besides, people don't look up as a rule, especially if they're afraid of losing their way. An Industrial Gas Association's lorry is not such a novelty, I wonder whether they stole a real one or faked one up."

"Very interesting," said Cobden absently. "Where's that pocket altimeter he gave you? I think we're dropping."

Hambledon confirmed this. "We are, slowly but steadily. Why is that? The increasing cold?"

"I don't know. There may be ice forming on the envelope, or she may be leaking. It doesn't look as though we'll stay up for ten hours, does it? What's the time?"

"A quarter-past ten—nearly. The fog's getting thicker."

"Yes," said Cobden. "We're getting down into it again. How high are we according to that gadget?"

"Eleven hundred feet, but he said it wasn't reliable."

"Margin of error unknown. I wish we could see something."

The time dragged on as they drifted helplessly. Half-past ten, a quarter to eleven. Just as Hambledon said: "Eleven o'clock. Seven hundred feet," Cobden said: "Hush!" There drifted up to them through the murk the distant sound of a church clock chiming the hour.

"Did you say seven hundred feet?" asked Cobden.

"The church may be on a hill."

"There is that, yes."

Tommy Hambledon turned his torch upon the balloon envelope above his head, examined it carefully and then laid his hand upon a thin cord tied to one of the guy-ropes.

"This is it."

"What?"

"The rip-cord. When you pull it it rips out that panel and we descend."

"You don't want to do that too high up, do you? I mean, she won't turn into a parachute for two?"

"I wish I'd studied aeronautics, if that's the right term for ballooning," said Tommy. "Even a short correspondence course would have been a help. I do know you mustn't bail out with a parachute from too low down or you'll break you bones. Or get spiked on a church steeple as in the comic pictures."

"Too high, too low," said Cobden, "which are we?"

"You know," said Hambledon thoughtfully, "I can't help feeling that our well-intentioned rescuers didn't think out this scheme carefully enough. Too many adverse possibilities."

Just before twelve another sound floated up to them, a familiar sound near to the kindly earth, it was the bark of a dog.

"That makes me feel homesick," said Hambledon. "If I were sitting firmly on the ground within ten yards of him I'd be so happy I'd bark back. Do you think—Good Lord, look at that!"

Something loomed up out of the fog so close that it seemed they must brush against it—it was a factory chimney. Tommy turned his torch on it and they could even distinguish the brickwork.

"This won't do," he said, and leaped at the rip-cord. "Hang on, Cobden, I'm going to bring her down."

There was a tearing sound as he pulled with all his strength, and a long narrow strip tore out of the fabric of the balloon. The envelope tilted and swung them, the basket dropped beneath their feet with a sickening sensation of weakness. Tree branches slewed them round and released them, spinning. They dropped again and were dragged, clinging like monkeys, through a screen of thin trees and then, with a sound of breaking sticks, through a rose pergola and across a lawn. The balloon ahead of them settled, sank and billowed to rest as Tommy rolled out among vegetables.

"I always did like brussels sprouts," he said.

IV

THE COLONEL HAS VISITORS

Tommy Hambledon rose to his feet, brushing mud from himself, replaced his hat which had been crushed over his nose and called: "Cobden! Are you all right?"

"Quite, thank you. I am among, I think, raspberry canes. I say, do you feel as though you were still floating? How wonderful—show a light, I can't see you—how wonderful to know it's only an illusion. Hullo, there's a house here and lights are going on. What do we do, run?"

"Certainly not, I'm surprised at you. Leave it to me."

In the silence they heard distinctly the sound of bolts being drawn and a key turning in a lock: the next moment a door opened and laid a path of light across the lawn. A large figure appeared silhouetted against the light and a typical parade-ground voice demanded, with menaces, to know exactly what the hell was happening in his garden, and if it was a runaway steamroller they would hear about it on the County Council. A torch was then switched on and the speaker advanced.

"This is the goods," said Tommy. "Come on."

Followed by Cobden, he went forward to meet the large figure, removed his hat, and said: "Sir, I owe you a thousand apologies, but before I begin, tell me, is this England?"

"England? Of course it's England—"

Tommy uttered a yell of triumph and flung his hat in the air.

"We've won! We must have won. At least, it's been a damn good trip."

"What is all this—"

Tommy laughed apologetically.

"Sorry to appear so excited, sir. This is a balloon race, though why they call it a race when it's a question merely of who goes furthest has always been a mystery to me. A duration test would be a better title."

"Balloon race? Good God, I didn't think anybody went in for that sort of thing nowadays."

"They've only just started them again," said Tommy, blinking in the light of a torch directed steadily upon his face. "In fact, I believe this is the first since some time before the war."

"Indeed. And where's the balloon?"

"Here, sir", said Tommy, and led the way to the collapsed balloon which sprawled limply across the cabbages or bulged weakly in places where rockets of gas were still retained in the folds. The basket lay on its side with loose ropes wreathed about, the newcomer directed his torch upon it and remarked that it looked very small.

"Cramped," said Hambledon with feeling, "very cramped. But lightness is the primary object."

"How many of you in it?"

"Two. May I introduce my friend and accomplice, Mr. Cookson—"

"How d'you do?" said Cobden.

"And my name's Harrington."

"How d'you do? My name's Waterbury, Colonel Waterbury. I should think it was damned cold floating about in that thing, what? Better come in and get warm."

"I am nearly frozen," said Tommy, allowing his teeth to chatter, "and Cookson's about as bad."

"Come in and we'll blow up the fire," said Colonel. "What d'you want to do with that balloon?"

"If we might leave it for a short time to allow the gas to dissipate, we'll pack it up later. Valuable things, balloons."

"Certainly, certainly. Come along to the house," said the Colonel, leading the way. "What's it made of?"

"Silk," said Tommy, who had not the faintest idea.

"Nylon," said Cobden. "Doped nylon."

"Well, it looked like silk—it's not my balloon, I borrowed it," said Hambledon truthfully. "I believe the latest models are made of nylon."

"So that's where the stockings go," said the Colonel, chuckling. "Next time my nieces moan at me about nylon stocking I'll tell them to apply to you."

"Delighted," murmured Hambledon.

"And what's the gas inside it?"

"Hydrogen."

"Oh. Very inflammable. Have to be careful with that stuff."

"That's why I proposed leaving it for a time," said Tommy. "It'll soon disperse."

"Quite right. Quite right. Well, here we are, come in."

The Colonel was now visible in detail as a big man with a bald head and a white moustache, and dressed in pajamas and a Paisley-patterned dressing-gown. He urged them down a passage and into a lounge with the dying embers of a fire still glowing in the grate. Hambledon and Cobden went straight towards it and crouched down, rubbing their hands.

"You look perfectly blue with cold, let me put some more logs on. It will soon burn up. Tell you what, I'll get a firelighter. Splendid things, firelighters." He left the room.

"What do we do now?" whispered Cobden

"Get warm," answered Hambledon. "Gosh, I didn't realize how cold I was."

Colonel Waterbury returned, thrust a firelighter among the logs, lit it, and was rewarded by leaping flames. Hambledon said "Ah!" in a comforted voice and relaxed into a heap on the hearthrug.

"Spot of whisky?" said Waterbury.

"You ought to have been a doctor," said Cobden. "You'd have been a world-famous Harley Street consultant."

The Colonel laughed and took a decanter and glasses from a corner cupboard. "Soda? Or, I say, wouldn't a drop of hot water do you more good? Yes, I shall prescribe it, that's the word, isn't it? Won't take a minute, a kettle on that fire." He hurried away.

"I'd rather have something to eat," murmured Cobden.

"Consider the poor man's rations."

"Think he's got any bread and dripping?"

Waterbury came back with a kettle in his hand, thrust it among the blazing logs, and said it wouldn't take long, he'd filled it from the hot tap. "I gather you started from the Continent since you asked if you were in England. Where have you come from, Paris?"

"No," said Hambledon. "Monte Carlo."

"Monte? Monte Carlo? Not really? That's a hell of a long way. How long did it take you?"

"Fifty-seven hours," said Tommy, yawning. "I beg your pardon, so much fresh air. Very fresh. Yes, fifty-seven hours and eleven minutes to the moment when we touched down on your lawn. We left Monte at three in the afternoon two days ago, went up to three thousand two hundred and found a nice steady breeze, so we carried on at that level. As no doubt you know, Colonel, in ballooning the idea is to rise to a level where there's—"

"I don't know anything about ballooning," said Colonel, "but I should think you must be damned hungry." Hambledon smiled. "I suppose you carried rations? Of course, and ate them up far too soon, I'll bet. I'll go and raid the larder—"

"No, Colonel, certainly not," said Hambledon firmly. "We're not going to eat your rations, we shouldn't think of it. If you'd be so good as to direct us to the nearest hotel—incidentally, where are we?"

"At Agersfield, near Swaffham, in Norfolk. Rations my foot, there's some cold partridge, nice plump birds though I shot them myself. You won't get anything like that at the local pub, believe me, and anyway they're all in bed hours ago. Look here, let me give you a shakedown here for tonight and I'll drive you into Swaffham in the morning. You're going to London, I suppose? Yes, I can drop you at the railway station. I've got to go in before ten, anyway, I'm on the Bench. The kettle's boiling."

They were refreshed, fed and warmed, and the Colonel's kindly but open curiosity about them only added interest to a cheerful hour. He asked about ballooning and said it seemed very risky to him, suppose the wind changed and they were blown out into the Atlantic? He then abandoned a topic which he was plainly only pursuing out of politeness, and asked Cobden if he were any relation of the Cooksons of Malvern, particularly old George Cookson who had been a subaltern with him—Waterbury—in the Middlesex Regiment in ninety-seven and eight. Good fellow, old George, would have done well in the Army only, of course, his father died and he had to sell out and go home to look after the property. After which he turned upon Hambledon and asked if he were any connection of Bill Harrington who was killed in the South African War, his sister married that extraordinary Dago fellow who played the 'cello, they went to live in New York and had been lost sight of years ago. Hambledon said that he'd heard his father speak of a cousin Bill who was killed in South Africa, and added modestly that his late father, Erasmus Harrington, had been Professor of Archaeology at the Sorbonne. The Colonel nodded thoughtfully and said he believed he'd met the man once at a party in one of those big Kensington Palace Gardens houses in Bayswater Road. "Damned dull party, I remember. I only went there to meet a girl and then the hussy went off and married a Major in the Guards. Let's have some port."

After which the party became practically a family affair, and it was as in a dream that they went into the garden, folded up the now flaccid balloon into its basket and stowed it in a disused stable. Hambledon said that he would arrange to have it taken away in two or three days, and the Colonel told him to come and fetch it himself and stay longer next time. "Well, I hate to break up a jolly evening, but d'you know it's past two? Haven't been up so late since the last Reunion Dinner when some of us fellows went round to Fortescue's rooms in Albany and yarned till the milkman came. I'll put you in the spare room together, if you'll forgive me, there are two beds in it and I know they're aired. Not made up, or whatever they call it, though. You can manage with blankets, can't you? You'll be called at seven-thirty, breakfast eight-fifteen. Well, good night."

Hambledon, his eyelids dropping with sleep, warmth and port, sat down at once and pulled his shoes off. Cobden watched him with surprise.

"Are you going to bed?"

"Of course I am. What else d'you suppose I'd do at this hour?"

"Get away. We'll have five hours' start before we're missed."

"Look here, Cobden, don't be an ass, there's a good fellow. We're going to be seen off at the station in the morning by a pillar of the local magistracy who's known our families for five generations and will tell everyone so. If the station platform's crowded with police two-deep waiting for us they'll only stand at attention and open the carriage door. Take the gifts the good gods send and sleep on a spring mattress for a change. We shall have to borrow razors in the morning. Turn out the light when you're ready. G'night."

"You know," said Cobden in an almost awestruck tone, "you ought to be the con man, not me." But Hambledon did not hear him, for he was asleep.

At Swaffham station next morning the Colonel insisted upon coming on the platform to see them off. Hambledon and Cobden bought first-class tickets for London, and passed the barrier in company with their escort who was kept busy exchanging greetings with practically everyone he met, including two police-constables in uniform. They were standing inside the barrier watching the people come and go; when they saw Colonel Waterbury they came to attention and saluted.

"Oh, hullo! Morning, Griggs. Morning, Simpson. What are you doing here?"

"On duty, sir."

"So I see, but why?"

"Two convicts escaped last night, sir, we've had orders to look out for them."

"What, those two from Northern Moor? Saw it in the paper. They won't come here, man, why should they? They're hiding in a haystack five miles from the jail, that's where they are. Wasting your time."

"We often do, sir."

The Colonel laughed. "Used to it, eh? Well, I expect you have to be. Here's your train, Harrington, dead on time for once. Look here, I haven't got your address, or yours, Cookson."

"The Royal Aero Club will find us," said Tommy libellously. "Good-bye, and a thousand thanks——"

The Colonel waved his hat in farewell as the train pulled out, his pink bald head shining in the morning sun. Hambledon and Cobden settled down in the compartment they were lucky enough to have to themselves and laughed.

"Nice old boy," said Cobden, "but what an obvious victim! The con man's dream."

"Now then, where's this address I've got to find? Sixty-seven North End Road, Neasden, N.W. Doesn't sound very aristocratic, does it?"

"What did you expect? A number in Park Lane?"

"You never know," said Tommy. "You aren't coming with me, are you?"

"I think not. There seems no point in our both going, and I might be more useful if they don't know me. You can say I ran away, can't you?"

"I shall say you baled out of the balloon half an your before she grounded and I haven't seen you since. In fact, I think we'd better not be together too long now, the next time this train stops one of us had better find another compartment. Where can I get in touch with you in Town?"

"I must find somewhere to live," said Cobden. "We'd better not live at the same address, either, had we? No, I was afraid not. Then you'll have to find somewhere to live, too. We'd better meet for dinner tonight, I think. There's a restaurant called The Kobold at the top of Edgware Road—the Marble Arch end—about a hundred yards up on the west side. Lots of small tables. Meet you there at a quarter to seven?"

"I'll be there, tide permitting," said Hambledon. The train slowed down at a station, Cobden left the compartment and disappeared along the corridor, nor did Tommy catch even a glimpse of him at Liverpool Street.

Sixty-seven North End Road, Neasden, was a small newspaper and to-bacco shop. The window was crowded with cigarette packets which were certainly dummies, a number of women's weeklies of the cheaper sort and some children's comic papers printed in two colors. On either side of the windowpane were a number of cards stuck inside the glass with bits of stamp paper; they were written in various hands and advertised Pram for Sale, Good Cheap; also Lodgings for Single Man; Lost, a Fur Tippet; Lost, A Tortoiseshell Kitten with white paws' Found, a Fur Lady's Glove; Wanted, Cleaning Work Mornings Only; Wanted, a Baby's Bath. Hambledon pushed open the door and in so doing rang a bell, he waited at the overcrowded counter till a harassed woman bustled in from a back room.

"Good afternoon," said Hambledon. "I was told to call here and show you this." He gave her the envelope with the pencilled address written across the back; she took it from him and looked at it carefully.

"Oh, yes," she said, in a tone of elaborate unconcern, "I do b'lieve I've got a letter for you somewhere." She dropped Hambledon's envelope in her pocket, took from a drawer behind the counter another envelope, pale pink and flimsy, and gave it to him without looking at him. Hambledon took it, there was something stiff inside.

"Thank you," he said.

"Thanking you," she answered, still keeping her eyes down, nor did she look up until he had left the shop and shut the door behind him.

"Odd," said Tommy to himself. "Now why?" Then it occurred to him that if she did not look at him attentively she could neither describe him nor, probably, recognize him again. A woman of experience, evidently. Safety first, and all that.

He waited until he was some distance away before he tore open the envelope and looked at its contents. There were two numbered tickets for stalls at the *matinée* showing of *Gas and Gaiters* at the Vavasour Cinema in Marjorie Street, Soho, and the date was the following day.

He showed the tickets to Cobden that evening. "I shall go," said Tommy, "if only to see what they look like. I should probably get more æsthetic satisfaction in the monkey-house at the Zoo, but I may be wrong. Some golden-hearted film star, as beautiful as good, may be behind all this, though I doubt it."

"So do I," said Cobden. "They want their money back, that's what they want."

"They'll be unlucky."

"I'm coming too. No, not inside, I'll leave that to you. I shall lurk in the offing for the satisfaction of seeing you come out again. Remember what I told you about my friend who was found shot? These animals are dangerous."

"Not gentle folk, no," said Hambledon.

V

AT THE VAVASOUR

The Vavasour Cinema had a modest lobby adorned with a magnificent commissionaire; Tommy Hambledon strolled casually in and showed his presentation tickets. The General-Admiral inspected them, bowed with, as it were, a trace of foreign accent, and led the way down a long passage. Evidently the Vavasour was not, in any real sense, in Marjorie Street at all but behind it; Hambledon considered uneasily that there was not likely to be any other exit. No, there must be others or the place would never have been licensed; he stepped out more confidently. At the end of the passage were swing doors and a staircase going up; the commissionaire led him up them, past more swing doors from which cheerful music oozed, and down another passage to a small door labelled "Private." He knocked, opened the door and said, "The gentleman, sir."

Tommy walked in and the commissionaire shut the door behind him. There was a large rolltop desk in the middle of the room, and behind it a neat man in a grey-striped suit and gold-rimmed spectacles. He rose as Tommy entered, bowed and asked him to sit down. "Mr.—er—Hawkley, is it? My name is Robinson."

"How d'you do?" said Hambledon, and sat down.

"I am well, I thank you, and I hope you are."

"I have to thank someone," said Tommy, "is it you? For the gift of two presentation tickets for your show this afternoon. I am sorry I can only make use of one of them, I could not find a friend to come with me at such short notice."

The neat man fiddled with his glasses. "We were hoping you would have brought your friend Mr. Cobden with you."

"Cobden, yes. Unfortunately I have lost touch with Cobden. We were travelling together, but he left me somewhat abruptly and I have not seen him since."

"Left you? Where?"

"I really couldn't say," said Tommy blandly. "It was dark."

"I think we are wasting time," said Robinson precisely. "Under what circumstances did you part from Mr. Cobden?"

"We were travelling by air and he became apprehensive lest we might be heading out over the North Sea. He accordingly adjusted his parachute harness, wished me luck and—er—abandoned the ship."

"I see. You, however, carried on as arranged?"

Tommy nodded. "I was advised to go to a certain address and I did so. That's where I got these tickets I'm still trying to thank you for, but I expect you know all about that."

"It must have dawned upon a man of your intelligence," said Robinson, "that considerable trouble and expense must have been incurred in arranging your escape."

"*My* escape?"

"You have put your finger upon the spot, the arrangements were not intended for you. May I ask how you found the lorry?"

"Purely by accident," said Hambledon. "The fog came down when we were in the fields, Cobden and I were a little apart from our friends. Our guardians had just summoned us to return to our dwellings when there was some sort of disturbance among the company. Cobden and I decided to make a change, so we left. Perhaps it was unwise, the fog was so thick that in five minutes we were completely lost. However, we kept on walking and presently we bumped our noses against a grey lorry. Do I bore you with all this?"

"Not at all. Please go on."

"Two men appeared from the lorry; we were about to turn and flee when they uttered words of welcome and we gathered they were willing to help us. I will be frank with you, Mr. Robinson," said Tommy earnestly, "and admit that I've never been so surprised in all my life. Words failed me. They urged us into the lorry and pressed a change of clothing upon us. Not to embarrass you with sordid details, we needed a change of clothing and we accepted. It was as men in a dream that we dressed ourselves in the garments provided, and when we were invited to ascend a rope ladder into the ambient fog it only seemed to make the dream more real, if you understand me. A few last hurried words and we were off before any suitable expression of our sentiments had occurred to us. I am happy, therefore, to have this opportunity of expressing, to one who is doubtless in touch with our benefactors, my deep sense of gratitude for the helping hand so timely and ingeniously extended. I beg you will do me the favor of conveying the sense of these few inadequate words to those whose kindness I can never repay."

Tommy sat back in his chair and beamed upon Mr. Robinson.

"I wouldn't say that," said Robinson. "I mean, that you can never repay. I have been instructed to suggest that you could."

"In what way?"

"Rumor said that when you ceased your financial operations you had a certain sum put by. Some fifteen thousand pounds was, if I remember correctly, the amount mentioned. The police are said to have entirely failed to locate it."

"How people do exaggerate," said Hambledon sadly. "Fifteen thousand—you did say fifteen thousand, did you not? I only wish I had one-tenth of that sum."

Mr. Robinson smiled. "There is a pleasant story," he said, "of a Quaker of old time who witnessed a street accident. A crowd gathered, commiserating loudly. The Quaker took off his broad-brimmed hat and went round the crowd with it saying, 'I am sorry half a crown, how much is thee sorry?' You said just now that you were grateful and I am sure it is true. Shall we say, then, that you are grateful five thousand pounds?"

"Oh dear, no," said Tommy.

"No?"

"Definitely, no. Listen. You did not make these expensive and ingenious arrangements for my benefit, you admitted as much yourself." Mr. Robinson nodded. "Neither I nor Cobden ever approached you or suggested that you should help us. Capricious Fortune alone sent your plans agley, if I may quote the poets. Whoever your friend was he did not arrive, and I would point out that your work had already been done even to filling the balloon. I should suppose that putting the hydrogen from the balloon back into its native cylinders was even more impossible than the classic replacement of the toothpaste in the tube. No, Mr. Robinson, no. We did not urge you to risk your money, and I am sure Cobden, if he were here, would agree with me in saying that I must regretfully but firmly decline to indemnify you. A small sum to some worthy charity to be selected by your good selves, certainly, but five thousand pounds! Really, Mr. Robinson!"

Robinson raised his eyebrows and sighed. "I am sorry you should have taken the suggestion like that. If, however, your mind is made up there is no more to be said." He pressed a bell-push on his desk and added: "I must apologize for keeping you talking so long that you have even missed the picture, it is now only twenty minutes from its close and will not be repeated until seven-fifteen tonight." The door opened and the commissionaire stood waiting for orders. "Show this gentleman out, Morgan, will you, please? Good afternoon, Mr. Hawkley."

The moment Tommy was out of the room Robinson snatched up the telephone, dialled a number and spoke almost at once. "That you, Parker? He won't play. Go to it." He replaced the receiver.

Hambledon followed the magnificent Morgan down the corridor, expecting some concealed door to open and a strong hand to pluck him inside, but nothing happened. No one tripped him on the stairs or molested him in the long passage to the entrance door. He gave Morgan half a crown, remembering the Quaker, and was graciously thanked; he lit a cigarette, settled his hat firmly on his head and walked out into the street.

"If that's really all," he said to himself, "it's a very odd affair. Very queer. I shouldn't think it is all, for a moment, but here I am, aren't I? And quite a lot of useful dope for the Home Secretary." He walked on along the street; twenty yards ahead of him was a telephone call-box with the dimly-seen figure of a man inside it and another man outside, waiting for him with his back towards Hambledon. As Tommy came level with the call-box the man outside crossed the pavement, the man inside came out and they fell in on either side of him.

"Keep walking, brother," said Parker, who had been telephoning. "Keep walking, and if you make the slightest fuss I'll blow a hole in you." Something hard prodded Hambledon in the waist. "And look pleasant about it, too. See?"

Hambledon looked from one to the other and recognized them at once—they were the two men from the alleged Industrial Gas Association's lorry from which balloon had ascended on the hills above Northern Moor Prison.

"Oh, good afternoon," said Hambledon. "What a pleasure. Can I keep my boots on this time? Except that they're not boots, they're shoes; the same, in fact, with which you kindly provided me the other night. I say, your Mr. Robinson must have some sort of pull with the telephone company, he got that call through much more quickly than I ever manage to do. I take it he rang you at that call-box and told you I was feeling lonely and needed cheerful company. What do we do this time, go down in a submarine or merely travel by Underground, it's quicker?"

"Be quiet," said Parker.

"Why? You told me to look pleasant, didn't you, and they tell me my face is much more attractive when animated than when in repose. Besides, I like talking, it helps to pass the time."

"You can talk later," said Parker.

Hambledon was anxious lest Cobden should make an incautious appearance, since the escort would naturally recognize him also. He need not have worried, Cobden was never incautious and in any case had recognized the two men by the call-box ten minutes earlier. He went to ground in a second-hand book shop and waited upon the outcome.

"Later," said Hambledon, continuing the conversation, "the mood may have passed."

Parker did not answer, but the other man who had not yet spoken laughed shortly and Hambledon thought it a most unpleasant sound.

"Left, here," said Parker.

They turned into a narrow street between warehouses; fifty yards ahead of them there was a space which had been cleared up after the Luftwaffe and levelled for a car park. At the corner stood a policeman. Hambledon hesitated; he had no wish to return to Northern Moor, but it might be a good deal more agreeable than being encouraged by these horribly capable men to talk about money he did not possess However, Parker helped him to make up his mind.

"See that cop?" he said. "Well, if you make one sound or sign, or so much as look at him in passing I'll blow your insides out."

"Then you'll hang," said Hambledon.

"That won't help you."

Hambledon gave up that idea for the present. Some other scheme would probably present itself in due course. They passed the policeman and turned into the car park: there were a good many cars there and the attendant came ambling from among them to show them theirs and receive his tip. The next moment Cobden, with his collar turned up and his hat over his eyes, slipped round the corner and took the policeman eagerly by the arm.

"See that man! The middle one of those three? That's Hawkley, the escaped convict from Northern Moor."

"What?"

"You look at him and see. I know it's him, I was at his trial. I like trials," added Cobden untruthfully.

"I thought when I saw him there was something," said the constable, and pursued the party with long strides. Cobden followed behind.

The car park attendant led the way towards an unusually well-preserved Ford V8, and held the door open; Parker continued to control Hambledon while the silent half of the escort produced a tip. At this moment the police constable rounded the stern of a Daimler saloon, placed his hand upon Tommy's shoulder and said: "Here. I want you."

The result of this simple and even habitual action surprised him considerably. The ex-convict practically fell into his arms while the other two, against whom he had no unfriendly intentions, leapt into the car, pressed a responsive starter, backed out and were away before P.C. Grierson had time to do more than say "Hi!" and observe their number. He turned to Tommy.

"You are Edwin Vincent Hawkley," he said.

"Office," said Hambledon with emotion, "you are a credit and an ornament to the Force which is ennobled by your allegiance."

"That'll do," said Grierson.

"But I mean it," protested Hambledon.

The car park attendant appealed to Cobden. "What is all this 'ere?"

"Only done a bunk from his wife and she's after him," said Cobden. "Look, there's another car going off without you."

"Pore beggar," said the attendant, referring to Hambledon, and went away to attend to a Hillman Minx.

"Will you come along quiet?" asked Grierson. "Only make more trouble if you don't, you know."

"Nothing so lamb-like as me," began Tommy "has been seen in the streets of London since—"

Cobden, who had watched the attendant out of sight, turned in a flash and hit the unsuspecting Grierson hard under the jaw. His eyes closed, his knees gave way and Cobden lowered him gently to the ground.

"Run!" said Cobden to Hambledon. "See you later—run!"

"You are terrible sudden," said Hambledon, and ran one way while Cobden disappeared in another.

When it was discovered that two convicts had escaped from Northern Moor, the great bell on the roof of the main block was tolled to warn the countryside. In every house within earshot doors were locked and barred, windows shuttered and bolted, outhouses padlocked, washing snatched from lines and indignant children shepherded within doors. In the jail itself excitement mounted, since hysteria is never far from men unnaturally confined. The normally quiet corridors rang with shouting, jeers and song while the harassed warders banged on the iron doors with threats of "no supper" unless the uproar ceased. In the Prison Governor's office a clerk at a telephone rang up the County Police, Police Headquarters rang up the Divisions and Divisions notified the rural Constabulary; within a ten-mile radius round the prison men buttoned up uniform jackets, threw on oilskin capes, snatched up helmets, lamps and truncheons, and left their well-earned tea to patrol in the fog and the gathering darkness. There was an Escape Plan laid down ready for such emergencies; the district was cordoned off, all roads blocked and all traffic stopped for investigation. The Plan was put into immediate operation.

One such roadblock was on a bridge which carries a lane from the moors over the river Faraday which here runs deep and swift among boulders, a barrier to discourage the most daring. This was a likely spot; a sergeant and two constables waited beside a pole crossing the road with a red lamp hung in the middle of it. As soon as the arrangements had been completed the sergeant sent one of his constables forward each way to slow down any vehicle which came along.

"If they're driving," said the sergeant, "they may be here any minute, if they're walking they may not be here for hours."

"If they come this way at all," said one of his constables, preparing to take up his post.

"Tell yourself he certainly will," said the sergeant sternly, "then perhaps he won't" he added, as soon as the constable was out of earshot. A pole on trestles wouldn't stop determined men in a car unless they were very un-lucky.

The lane from the moor came down a steep hill to the bridge, a narrow lane with high banks and several sharp bends. The fog here was not so dense, it followed the river down, running like blown smoke through the light from the red lantern. Before five minutes had passed the sergeant cocked his head to listen, there was another sound besides the steady rush of the river. Lights appeared on the hill, something big coming, a lorry of some sort. The sergeant heart his constable shout but the lorry came on, accelerating in the clearer air. The sergeant also shouted and waved his torch, but he had to jump for the bank as the lorry thundered past—it swept the pole away like a twig and the red lantern sailed through the air like a discarded cigar-butt.

The third policeman, thirty yards further on, was a man of initiative and a cricketer. He also shouted, but at the moment when it became plain that the lorry would not stop he hurled a lump of rock straight at the windscreen. There was a resounding crash. In the light of his torch he saw the glass star and splinter right in front of the driver's face, but still the lorry went on. Not so fast now, and with the driver's head craning out of the side window, but without hesitation. They heard him change gear for the next hill, then he disappeared in the fog. The sergeant ran to his motorcycle parked at the side of the road, dragged it off its stand, kicked the starter and was off in pursuit.

At the top of the hill the road forked and the sergeant had to slow down and look for wheel-tracks. He saw them and started again, two miles further on he found the lorry canted over on its side in the ditch. It had not been a serious crash and there was no sign that anyone had been hurt. In fact, there was no sign of anyone at all; the driver and passenger or passengers had gone.

The County Police rang up the Industrial Gas Association as early next morning as they could reasonably expect a reply, and reported that one of their lorries, registration number so-and-so, had been found at a certain spot ditched and deserted. It contained a number of empty hydrogen cylinders. The Company replied, after looking into the matter, that they had no lorry bearing that number and furthermore that none of their lorries was, so far as they knew, in that district the night before. Details of the markings on the hydrogen cylinders would be informative, also the engine number of the lorry, and confirmation that the registration number, as quoted, was correct. The police supplied these details and the Company replied that, unless the markings had been tampered with, the cylinders would appear to be theirs, but not the lorry. Definitely not, and they hereby disclaimed responsibility for any acts or the consequences of any acts which had etc., etc.

Since Chief-Inspector Bagshott of Scotland Yard had been put in charge of the inquiry into the series of prison-breaks, the evidence at this point was laid before him. He sent for Detective-Inspector Ennis.

"If the Company are telling the truth," said Bagshott, "the lorry was faked to look like one of theirs, but they ought to be able to tell us who had the cylinders."

"Yes, sir," said Ennis. "Hydrogen cylinders," he added thoughtfully.

"If you were going to ask me what hydrogen is used for in industry, I believe the answer is in some types of welding, but you can find out. Of course, there's much more familiar use for hydrogen."

"They used it to fill barrage balloons, didn't they?"

"Yes. It would fill any balloon, Ennis. If you had a balloon you didn't want, Ennis, what would you do with it?"

"If the wind was right, sir, you could bail out, let it go and hope it would drift out to sea."

"Somebody might spot it," said Bagshott.

"If you could deflate it—"

"There's still the basket."

"Yes," said Ennis. "I suppose the basket could be chopped up and burnt? And the envelope would burn, or—"

"If you're an escaping convict you don't light bonfires. And you can't direct a balloon to land in a friend's garden. You come down where the wind takes you—I think this discussion is unprofitable, we don't' even know there was a balloon. We are not even sure that that lorry was concerned with the escapes, but the driver had something on his conscience. Find out what it was."

"Yes, sir."

"Helpful things consciences," said Bagshott. "What would the police to without them?"

"A good bit better, sir if you ask me," said Ennis.

VI

CRIME IS A BUSINESS

Detective-Inspector Ennis called upon the Industrial Gas Association and was politely if not enthusiastically received. He was given the impression that if more care and attention had been used by those in charge of convict, a busy firm wouldn't have to waste their time answering tiresome questions. It was, of course, true that their cylinders were involved, but need they have been? However, they turned up the serial numbers of these cylinders in their records and told him that they had been delivered to the Coolar Radiator Company.

"You have dealt with them before, have you?"

Never before and particularly never again: the I.G.A. were very definite on that point. The Coolar Radiator Company were a new concern making radiators for the trade. They had taken over a small factory built for Ministry of Supply contracts during the war and thereafter closed. It was on the Great North Road between Hatfield and Stevenage, "our driver will tell you exactly where it is."

"I should like to see the driver presently, if it is quite convenient," said Ennis politely. "Tell me, is it usual to be asked to supply hydrogen? I am anything but an expert, but I thought oxygen and acetylene were the gases most commonly used in welding."

The I.G.A. agreed. "But hydrogen is used for soldering whenever a particularly hot flame is required. You see, to use untechnical language, if you are soldering a number of small parts together, as in the case of radiators, you want a tiny concentrated flame or you will melt the adjacent joints you have just made. The smaller the flame the hotter it must be, naturally. No, we were not surprised at being asked for hydrogen, we were a little surprised at being asked for so much at once."

"A larger order than usual?"

"These people explained that they were full up with orders and it would be a convenience to have a good stock. We looked into their bank references and they were quite satisfactory, so we agreed. There's no difficulty about hydrogen cylinders because vast numbers were made during the war to supply the balloon barrages. Far more than are ever likely to be required now. I will be frank with you. We have a large stock of hydrogen cylinders already filled for which there seemed no immediate demand—surplus war stock— we were not sorry to find an outlet."

"So you naturally agreed. I see. Now, if you would kindly give me their bank references and then let me have a word with the driver concerned—"

The driver said that the factory wasn't much of a place. On the road there was only a high wall and big double-doors with "Coolar Radiator Company" on a brand-new board above. "Brand-new, I said, there was men on ladders just finishing putting it up. We 'ad the doors opened for us and drove in; there was a sort of yard with workshops round and we backed up to a ramp and unloaded the stuff. Made quite a fuss of us, they did. Said it was their first load to come in and now they could really start in and make their fortunes. Offered us drinks, but me and my mate don't drink when we're driving so we 'ad coffee in the office. Then they took our photos—"

"What?"

"Took our photos. Me and Tom standin' against the lorry with the ramp and the cylinders be'ind, for a memento. Several, they took. Said they'd send us some, but they've never come yet. Then we shook 'ands all round, wished 'em luck and come away. That's all."

"I see. This was"—Ennis referred to his notes—"on Wednesday, October the first?"

"That's right. Three weeks ago Wednesday, 'bout three in the afternoon."

"Thank you very much. Now, where exactly is this place?"

"Well, it isn't near anything much as you might say, stands out in the country, like. Going north from Hatfield," said the driver, and gave expert directions for finding it.

Ennis found it without difficulty, though there was no longer any name-board over the big gates. The Hertfordshire County Police told him that men arrived quite openly and went in and out there, the notice-board was erected and hammering noises heard from within. Nobody interfered, why should they? The place had been empty and had now presumably been let.

The agents whose names had appeared on the TO LET board when there was one said they had not let it. Property like that was a little difficult now. They had had a few inquiries—four, perhaps, in six months—but none of their inquirers had gone further into the matter. Keys, certainly. Mr. Simpkins, the keys of the factory property for this gentleman.

Ennis returned to the factory. There was the yard which the driver had described and the ramp upon which he had delivered the cylinders. There were three large sheds of corrugated iron with concrete floors stained with oil and bearing marks of machinery having been set down on them and subsequently removed when the factory was dismantled. Only in one of them was there any sign of recent use; tire tracks on the floor, marks where lengths of something had been laid down and later dragged away. The floor had been hastily swept but small pieces of new wood-shavings had been overlooked. A small curl of stiff paper had rolled into a corner; Ennis picked it up—it was a photograph of the driver and his mate smiling broadly beside the grey lorry with I.G.A. in a monogram on the side "Very useful for faking a copy," said Ennis to himself. "No chance of forgetting details. Bright idea, taking photos."

No further evidence offered itself about the men who had worked there. They had not bought bread or milk or cigarettes anywhere in the immediate neighborhood, or even dropped in for a glass of beer at the local. They arrived by car or on bicycles, not by the passing bus. They came and went openly, grinned at the local girls and spoke to nobody, until one day they did not come and were not seen again. They were not there long, only a week or so. Less, maybe.

Ennis took some photographs of the tire tracks for comparison with the tires on the ditched lorry, though if they did not coincide it did not mean anything as tires can be changed. A collection of fingerprints from various places about the factory was added to his bag and might prove helpful when the fingerprint people had gone through them. Ennis returned to Bagshott and reported.

"They received the cylinders on Wednesday, October the first," said Bagshott, "and took about a week to fake up that lorry. The jailbreak was two days ago, October the twenty-fourth, so that lorry was sitting somewhere, all ready, for about a fortnight waiting for a fog. Somewhere handy for Northern Moor. That, thank goodness, is a matter for the local police. I'll turn 'em on to it."

"Where does one buy balloons?" said Ennis.

"We'll go into that when we know there was a balloon, at present I'm merely guessing. Or when we run completely dry of other ideas. I have given instructions for the lorry to be very thoroughly fingerprinted indeed; we'll start with that."

There were numerous fingerprints on the lorry, most of them naturally coinciding with those Ennis collected at the factory. The most recent in the cab, on the driving-wheel, on the bonnet and on a small transmitter-receiver inside the bonnet, were those of Harold Parker and Jonas Tetlow, already known to the police as smash-and-grab raiders. This helpful news reached Bagshott on the same afternoon as that on which Hambledon went to the Vavasour Cinema to meet Mr. Robinson.

"Parker and Tetlow," said Bagshott. "According to the records it's nearly two years since they came out of jug and, so far as we know, they've behaved themselves till now. Parker is noted as being a particularly good driver. They are Londoners, I notice. Let them be brought to me. They were in Yorkshire two days ago so that's one place where you won't have to look for them."

He returned to the Fingerprint Department's report on the lorry. Another set of prints found inside the van were those of Alexander John Cobden, one of the missing prisoners from Northern Moor.

"Cobden," said Bagshott. "We are on the right track, here's the proof. The faked lorry did help in the escape, I knew it did, of course, but it's always a help to know you're right. Hawkley's fingerprints there too? No? That's a little unexpected, I wonder where he went to."

The fact was that not even the Home Secretary's influence extended to falsifying the records of the C.I.D., even if a Home Secretary would ever wish to, which is quite inconceivable, and the prints in the Records were still the original Hawkley's. There were some more prints inside the lorry, sometimes superimposed on Cobden's but they were not known to the Records.

"We shall find out one of these days," said Bagshott. "Perhaps Parker and Tetlow can be induced to tell us."

But Parker and Tetlow were not to be found, nor were the convicts Edwin Vincent Hawkley and Alexander John Cobden. They kept quiet in their respective lodgings and were very careful when they met; Hambledon was bored to extinction and said so.

"I'm doing no good," he said. "I can now tell the police where to look and I think that'll have to do. I'm tired of dodging the police, I'm sick of wearing this suit, my mattress has got lumps in it and my landlady can't cook."

"I met a man today," said Cobden. "He's been inside, too, he was working for a syndicate which faked-up stolen cars. I used to know him when I was on my job. He looked very happy and I'm going to meet him again tonight. I want to know why he's looking happy."

"Perhaps he's won a prize in a football pool," said Tommy grumpily.

"Come along and meet him," said Cobden.

Cobden's friend was a small dark man named Lewis who still retained in his speech the dim shadow of a Welsh accent. He was indeed unaffectedly cheerful, he joked about the weather which was vile, the food which was worse than indifferent, and even the Government which, said Tommy, was not a subject for jest. Guy Fawkes, Tommy added, was the only man who had ever thought of a good joke about Parliament and even that didn't come off. The couple at the next table got up and went away; there was no one else with earshot and the talk became more confidential.

"How are you getting on these days?" asked Lewis.

"Not very well," admitted Cobden. "Actually, we're still resting after a rather trying journey we had last week, I dare say you read all about it in the papers."

Lewis laughed. "I read something about it, certainly, but by no means all, I am sure. They left out the most interesting part. So this gentleman was with you on that occasion—I thought I recognized the name. A very stout effort indeed, I congratulate you."

"Thank you," said Hambledon. "We have left off being squirrels in a cage and become rabbits in a cabbage-patch. They don't know exactly where we are but they know we're somewhere about."

"There is that, of course," said Lewis. "What you want is some intelligent backing: in my opinion the day of the lone hand is over. Surely your friends can help you?"

"Our friends?"

"Don't imagine I'm asking questions, but you didn't work that escape all by yourselves, surely."

"Oh, that," said Tommy, and laughed. "That was all a mistake, the arrangements were made for somebody else and we availed ourselves, that's all. The—the arrangers are not at all pleased with us, in fact, two of them tried to abduct me the other day only a policeman rescued me."

"A policeman?"

"He arrested me and I don't mind telling you I was quite pleased to see him."

"As bad as that," said Lewis. "I think I know the people you're talking about and I should prefer the cops myself. But, excuse me, you appear to be still at liberty?"

"I didn't stay arrested, thanks to Cobden. Did you say you knew the people?"

"Not personally, no. I meant that I knew which set of people you're talking about. My firm doesn't like 'em, either."

"Your firm?" said Cobden.

Lewis laughed. "I've got a good job with a good form. Regular pay with prospects on a salary-plus-commission basis. Well, I must admit the prospects are a bit mixed, but if misfortunes befall any of us the firm does its best at the trial and looks after the wife and family during absence."

"What is all this?" said Tommy. "If I'm not being inquisitive?"

"Crime," said Lewis, "is a business like any other, with different ethics. What happens when the small man does a burglary? He takes the stuff to a fence who gives him a tenth of what it's worth. The small man has probably been hard up for months and got into debt, or merely gone short on everything. He gets some money and pays up what he owes, or gets the wife a new carpet or a couple of frocks, or just goes on the binge. The police get to hear about this and they pick him up, nine times out of ten he's for it. You know. Alibis don't work out in real life as they do in books. Well now, suppose he isn't working on his own, suppose he's got a job in a firm as I said just now. He's paid a decent living wage so, unless he's a fool, he can keep a nice home going without getting into debt. When there's a job in prospect all the spadework is done by somebody else, you know, all the inquiries. Which room do they keep the safe in, what sort of a safe, how many in family, when do they go out, what staff do they keep—oh, you know."

"I don't," said Tommy. "If anybody asked me to burgle a house I should faint."

"Not your line, of course, but when you're used to it it's just a job like plumbing. As I was saying, no one at the house has seen him so there's none of this 'That's the man who's been hanging round lately.' Makes identification much less likely. Then we pay in the whole proceeds and get a commission on it; if it's really big it's invested for us. So you don't get the police saying, 'Bill Jones is throwing money about, go and ask him where he got it.' Then the firm itself disposes of the goods and gets a correspondingly good price for it."

"It must take a really first-class organizer," said Cobden.

"It's got one," said Lewis simply.

"You'll probably think me extremely simple," said Hambledon, "but I had no idea that there was any organized crime like that in England. I believe they do it a lot in the United States."

"Quite different," said Lewis. "They're a lot tougher in the States. Our fellows have got to behave themselves or out they go. No rough stuff. Our firm won't have violence at any price, and quite right too. Once you got a murder the chances are the whole thing would come out. Can't have that."

"I quite see your point," said Tommy solemnly. "But the crowd we fell into have no such finer feelings, believe me."

"They've done one murder to my knowledge," said Cobden in a low tone.

"Can you prove it?" asked Lewis eagerly.

"No."

"Pity. However, they'll go too far one of these days."

"Provided I'm not the body in the case," said Tommy, "the sooner the better. Life's quite difficult enough dodging the police without having to watch out for this gang as well. Besides, I only know four of 'em, they might be anybody." He sighed. "You know, I should like to meet your—your Chairman. We might be of use to each other."

Lewis hesitated. "I don't know whether that would be possible. You won't take offence, I'm sure, but you'll understand how careful we all have to be."

"Oh, quite," said Hambledon. "Absolutely. Only simple prudence. It's merely that I do know a little about my lot and you said he didn't like them either—"

"He's absolutely sizzling at the moment," said Lewis. "There was a job all arranged, a nice job, safe full of Treasury notes, no trouble about realizing as there is with jewelry. We took no end of trouble over details and got it all worked out to the final click. Then what happened? Two of our fellows went in and found the safe door ajar and everything gone. Instead of beating it then and there they stood there gaping like owls till the police walked in and collected 'em both. They did manage to prove they hadn't had the stuff, but they went inside for three years all the same. Burglary with intent, and all that."

"Not a first offence," murmured Hambledon.

"No. Oh, no, they were quite experienced. What had happened was that information had leaked out somewhere. Of course, you can't have a firm the size of ours and every man honest."

"Too much to expect," agreed Hambledon. "Even crooks are but human," and Cobden kicked his ankle under the table.

"Exactly," said Lewis. "Well, your friends in the other gang heard all about it and just went in half an hour earlier."

"Too bad," said Cobden. "The idea of a leakage is rather upsetting, isn't it?"

"I expect there was a pretty big bribe," said Lewis. "We shall find out. Like the police, we shall watch to see who's got too much money. About your suggestion, Mr. Hawkley, I'll put it through and let you know, if I may, but you'll understand I'm not in a position to make promises, won't you?"

After Lewis had gone Hambledon and Cobden strolled together towards Tommy's despised lodgings. "What did you say Lewis's line used to be?" he asked. "Faking stolen car? I think he's a burglar now, don't you?"

"I think he's in the burglary department," said Cobden, "but he may not do any actual burgling. He may drive a car—"

"Or count the takings or go round with a duster wiping off fingerprints, or make a noise like handcuffs clicking when he sees a constable heading their way."

"Suppose the constable heard it too?"

"He'd think it was wishful thinking. Can one think a thing is a think? Wonder what his Old Man is like?"

"He's probably Chairman of a Bench of Magistrates somewhere," said Cobden, "with a face like a barrage balloon and strong views on Sunday observance."

"Or a tall thin comedian with a Lancashire accent."

Two days later Lewis met them by appointment at the Kobold restaurant and said: "You're in luck. He'll see you tomorrow morning at eleven-thirty."

"Tomorrow, Sunday," said Tommy.

"That's right. The address is Kuminboys, Parson's Close, Wimbledon Common."

"What?"

Lewis laughed. "Kuminboys. It used to be called Manor View but Savory changed it when he bought the house. It's a very respectable neighborhood indeed, all the houses have names like Lansdowne and Glendalough an Court Lodge, with inhabitants to match. You should see 'em look over the hedge at Sal Savory and his friends at church time on Sundays. Sal says their looks save him the expense of a refrigerator. He like entertaining his friends on Sundays, on the front lawn if fine. It's a nice lawn."

"Savory? Is that his name? And who's Sal?"

"He is. Salvation Savory. Called after somebody in a book his mother was reading at the time, or so he says. I'm not a reader myself."

"I seem to have met the name before," said Tommy. "It's nice and easy to remember, anyway."

"So is he," said Lewis. "Well, there you are. Have a nice time."

Parson's Close on a Sunday morning even in November was all that Lewis had implied, in the summer it must have been quite remarkable. It was a rather narrow road lined with plane trees severely cut; on either side substantial family mansion stood back form the road, each in its own garden divided from its neighbor by hedges topped with either trellis or sheep-hurdles, trellis predominating. The same type of screening defended the houses from the intrusion of passing eyes, only over their white or green gates was it possible to see the tidy polite houses in their orderly gardens.

"Even Nature," said Tommy, "has to behave herself here. Even last year's birds-nests are tidy."

They came to one house which was different. The front hedge was not tall nor topped with trellis, it was as it were scalloped between points only three feet high at their tallest; between them the clipped privet curved down to little more than a foot from the ground. No impediment was therefore offered to observation and the house invited it. It had probably been originally a pleasant square house of Georgian type and still had good proportions, but instead of the traditional white paint and green shutters the walls were a deep buff, the color of a brown egg, and the woodwork all a clear scarlet. Not the door, however, that did not need painting, for it was of polished copper. The one redeeming feature was the lawn in front, smooth and unworried by flower-beds; only two magnificent beeches grew close together to adorn and shade it on a summer's day.

"Well," said Hambledon at last. "Lewis was right. It is a nice lawn."

There was no knocker on the copper door, there was a chain with a knob on the end for a bellpull. Hambledon took hold of the knob and saw that it was a miniature skull in ivory with ruby eyes' he pulled it and heard the Westminster Chimes answering within.

"Who's going to open the door?" murmured Tommy. "Bluebeard or Nell Gwynne?"

"Or a trained gorilla," suggested Cobden, but when the door did open they saw a very small man, thin to emaciation everywhere except beneath his waistcoat where he was globular. He had bow legs in tight black trousers and wore a striped cotton jacket, he stood without a word staring up at them with bright brown eyes in a wrinkled face.

"Is Mr. Savory at home?" said Tommy. "He is expecting us, I believe. Mr. Hawkley and Mr. Cobden."

The man opened the door widely and stood back for them to enter.

"Come this way," he said, and opened a door on the left. "Sit down and make yourshelves at 'ome. I'll shee if I can find Mishter Shavory. Excushe me shushing at you, I've losht me teeth." He grinned at them and the fact was obvious.

"Very tiresome," said Tommy. "I hope you'll soon find them again."

"I think I know where they are. I exshpect I left them up the apple-tree."

"Been picking apples?" asked Cobden.

"What, in November? Naow, I wash tryin' to cash the cockatoo. Blashted bird," said the man bitterly, and left the room.

"He had a bandage on his finger," said Tommy, and looked about him. The room was furnished as a drawing-room, with yellow silk draping the windows and covering the chairs and sofas. There were numerous plants in majolica pots on stands, a blue Chinese carpet on the floor with a tiger-skin rug before the fireplace, ormolu brass fire-irons inside the cut-steel fender and a gas-fire bubbling from cast-irons logs. Between the windows there was a cabinet which might have been beautiful in another setting, it was of polished ebony set with agate, lapis lazuli and sardonyx. It contained a display of red glass decorated with enamels. Another cabinet opposite was of Dutch inlay with gilded brass mouldings, this one contained a Crown Derby dinner-service and a peacock-feather fan, displayed. On the walls were flower-pieces in watercolor, mainly of azaleas.

"Colorful, isn't it?" said Cobden, in a rather awed voice.

"By Full Purse out of Auction Room," said Tommy, and at that moment the door opened.

VII

SALVATION SAVORY

Hambledon went forward to meet the big man who came in. "Mr. Savory? My name's Hawkley and this is my friend Cobden."

"Yes," said Savory, shaking hands. "Yes, I am Salvation Savory at your service, gentlemen. It is a pleasure to me to meet you. Mine is a humble establishment, gentlemen, but there is always room in it for another friend or tow. You'll have a whisky, won't you—Dick! Where has that old fool gone? Dick!"

"If you mean your butler," said Cobden, "he said he was going up an apple-tree to find his teeth."

"Oh Lord, has he lost 'em again? I wish somebody'd invent a kind you could screw down. Most embarrassing sometimes. However, he does his best, I hope and believe. Excuse me." Savory walked to the door, put his head out and bellowed for his servant, who came trotting. "Bring the whisky, Dick, you can climb trees later. Sit down, gentlemen, please. Mr. Hawkley, cigar or cigarettes? Mr. Cobden, what's your choice? You'll find those chairs reasonably comfortable. You know, I take it very kindly of you to come out here to see me, I do love having friends who like me well enough to drop in. When I called this house Kuminboys I really meant it, I didn't do it just to annoy the neighbors though none of 'em will ever believe it. They do not drop in, they don't even come near enough for us to fall out. Never mind, I can manage nicely without 'em. Ah, here's Dick. Irish or Scotch? Splendid. As I was saying, now you've found your way here I hope you'll often come again, I'm always here on Sundays and most other days as well. Well, chin chin. That'll do, Dick, thank you. Give Mr. Hawkley an ashtray and then you can go and gather nuts in May."

Hambledon watched his host with interest, no replies being required from him. Savory was a tall man with a round red face, a wide mouth and shrewd blue eyes, he wore green checked tweeds of extreme hairiness with a plain cloth waistcoat, rugged stockings and enormous suède shoes. There was a diamond ring on his left hand. Tommy said, "Bookmaker," to himself and

56

"Ex-jockey," to Dick's retreating back. There was a short pause after the door closed, Savory sipped his whisky and looked from one of his visitors to the other.

"It is extremely kind of you to receive us like this," began Tommy. "I take it Lewis has given you a few details about us, am I right?"

Savory nodded and his eyes crinkled pleasantly at the corners. "Lewis has told me all he knows, but don't let it embarrass you. We all have our misfortunes and I've heard a lot of sad stories in my time."

Hambledon laughed. "I didn't come here to inflict my own sorrows on you but, frankly, in the hope of bringing sorrow upon somebody else. The trouble is that we don't know who that somebody is—we were hoping you did."

"Will you start," said Savory, "by telling me the whole story of your dealings with these people? Lewis gave me a general idea, but firsthand accounts are much more useful."

Hambledon did so with complete frankness: when he had finished Cobden added his story about the man who was murdered near Southampton.

"Thank you," said Savory. "I am sorry to disappoint you, but the fact is that you really know more about these people than I do—at the moment. I haven't come into such personal contact with them as you have. What happened in my case was this. I have a brother who was unlucky enough to receive a four-year sentence for forgery. You see, I am returning frankness for frankness. He has been inside for eighteen months now. Well, of course we've all heard of an organization specializing in jailbreaks so I naturally took steps to get into touch with them, and that wasn't easy. Eventually a man in my employment brought along a skinny little weasel of a fellow who said he could take a message to them. To cut a long story short, I asked what their terms would be for getting my brother out and they quoted fifteen thousand pounds paid in advance. Well, I'm not a poor man, Hawkley, but I'm not a millionaire, nor is my brother, besides which that wouldn't be the end of the expense by any means. I should have had to get him abroad and keep him going, probably start him in some business or other, and so on. To put it bluntly, my brother had only about three years to run by then and he wouldn't earn anything like fifteen thousand in three years, especially being hunted about by the police and having to live in hiding and so on—I beg both your pardons! I let my tongue run away with me."

"Don't apologize, please," said Tommy. "All you say is perfectly true, please go on."

"So I told them the price was too high and there was nothing doing. Apparently that annoyed them because I've had quite a lot of trouble from them ever since. Lewis told you I've got a little business of my own. They keep on sticking their oar in and I'm getting very tired of it. But my weak point is that the only man of theirs I've ever met to my knowledge was the fellow who came about my brother, and he's dead. Not my brother, the go-between. He died quite respectably of pneumonia in Charing Cross Hospital, and I don't know of anybody else who knows them. I imagine they take darn good care I don't! Now you come along with some good hard facts and you'll understand why I was so delighted to see you."

"Yes," said Tommy. "Yes. It is in a way a disappointment. I was hoping you'd be able to say, 'Oh yes, that's Ivan Skivinsky and he's got a flat in Maida Vale.' However, I'm still hoping something can be done. You see, my point is that I'm no longer in my ardent boyhood shall we say; I want to go somewhere quiet and settle down. I've had my lesson, and I object with all the violence of which I'm capable," said Tommy, with furious energy, "to being chased about by a gang of crooks trying to skin me out of practically all I possess. Either I pay up and live on a pittance which 'ud hardly leave me enough for half a pint on a Saturday night, or they'll kidnap me and burn my toes off or cut my throat, or simply give me away to the police and back I go to prison again. I don't like prison, I don't like torture, I don't want my throat cut and I hate the idea of being reduced to penury. Something's got to be done about it." He banged the arm of his chair with his fist and Savory watched him with sympathetic amusement.

"I feel for you," he said, "I do indeed. I think that between us something might be done. Mr. Cobden, you hold similar views on account of your friend but not personally, if I have got your story right. They are not after you?"

"Not to my knowledge," said Cobden, "unless they have been watching Hawkley pretty closely and have seen us meet. Even if they have, the only ones who know me by sight are the two men with the balloon lorry, the same two who tried to abduct Hawkley the other day. I took care they didn't see me on that occasion, but there may been other times when I didn't see them."

"There's one point in that kidnapping business which interests me," said Savory, "and that is their immediate flight when the policeman accosted you. I realize of course that they wouldn't want to be questioned by the police as to why they were in the company of an escaped convict, but you'd think they would have made a rather more ingenious exit. I should have expressed horror, produced several plausible excuses and faded quietly away, not fled at once like that. Can it be that they didn't want the constable even to look at them attentively? That may mean that they're men with a criminal record, and if they are—"

"The police will know a lot more about them than we do," said Hambledon, and his soul yearned towards Chief-Inspector Bagshott.

"What I could really do with in my business," said Savory thoughtfully, "is one or two reliable men at Scotland Yard."

"Haven't you got them?" asked Tommy innocently, and Savory laughed.

"As a matter of fact, I haven't, but I think the other gang has. Shall we call them the Vavasour gang? It sounds nice and romantic."

"What makes you think they have?"

"Their tame weasel whom I interviewed distinctly implied it, and he was borne out by their telling me my brother was going to be moved—and when and where to—about a month before I had the official notice."

"It does look like it," said Tommy. "There must be an awful lot of money behind that gang."

"Blackmail does just as well if you can use it," said Savory, "and it's a lot cheaper. Well, look here, let's get down to brass tacks. You know four of these men, the two on the lorry—"

"But not their names," said Hambledon.

"No. And the manager of the Vavasour, Mr. Robinson, and the commissionaire, one Morgan. Is that all?"

"There's the woman at the newspaper shop in North End Road, Neasden. Number sixty-seven. She might not know anything at all, of course, it's only an accommodation address, but she behaved as though she smelt a rat. Of course that may be her natural manner, in which case I should think her neighbors simply love her."

"I'll send somebody along to look at her," said Savory. "Any other suggestions?"

Hambledon laughed. "If you've got a friend who looks sufficiently like Boris Karloff to terrify Robinson into opening his safe, there might be something interesting inside it."

"There might, but I think I'd rather send somebody along to look inside when Robinson wasn't there. I go to almost any length, Hawkley, to avoid violence."

"So Lewis told me, and how right you are. But if Robinson wasn't there the stuff might not be, either."

"Have some more whisky," said Savory. "When you speak of 'stuff' what exactly do you mean?"

"The Vavasour gang is a crime organization, isn't it? I was thinking that a cinema would be a useful depot for the receipt of proceeds. I was wondering whether the loot is taken there, in broad daylight, in suitcases. Much safer than slinking about at night and trying to reach some particular house without being noticed. Gives a house a bad name locally to have what are ambiguously called suspicious characters visiting it at odd hours. Besides, the said characters would then know where somebody important lived, and that might be a mistake. If they merely carry their little suitcases to a cinema and put them in some appointed spot from which they automatically disappear, it's much easier all round, isn't it?"

"You know," said Savory, with a laugh, "for a quiet company-promoter in the City you have a refreshingly ingenious mind."

"I have had a good deal of time lately," said Tommy sadly, "to sit and think."

"So you think Robinson collects the goods, puts them in his safe and carries them away after the show with the takings?"

"I just wondered," said Hambledon.

"I shouldn't think he'd do that," said Cobden. "Carry them home himself after dark, I mean. Not very wise, really."

"Then who would take them away?" said Savory, "and where to?"

"It's all rather vague at present," said Tommy. "Some light might somehow be acquired. I can't do much, I'm afraid, they know me."

"How big is the staff at that cinema?" asked Savory. "Come to that, how big is the cinema?"

"I don't know," said Tommy. "I didn't really go into it, only straight up to the manager's office and straight out again. There's a gallery upstairs as well as the ground floor, that's all I know."

"I was only thinking how useful it would be if there was a friend of ours on the staff and in these days all sizeable concerns are shorthanded. But probably he selects hi staff rather carefully. Look here, I'll send a man along to have a look round and, believe me, if there's anything interesting to see he'll see it. Come and dine with me here on Wednesday night, will you? Both of you? I've got a brace of pheasants a friend sent me from Scotland. I'm only sorry I can't ask you to have lunch with me today, but I'm meeting a friend at the golf club in half an hour. Wednesday night at seven-thirty? Splendid, and I hope I shall have some news for you."

Hambledon decided to go out of town until Wednesday evening. It is true that the country in November is not everybody's choice but he was very sick of streets limy with damp fog, frowsty lodgings and evading the police He bought an ash-plant and went into Hampshire, where he stayed at a country inn and ate home-cured bacon, walked on the Downs in dry cold weather and encouraged the wind from the sea to blow his cobwebs away. There was one item of news in the papers which he found mildly interesting, some most important visitors staying in a London hotel were ingeniously deprived of their very valuable jewelry. Tommy wondered idly whether the robbery were some of Savory's work or the Vavasour gang's, but it all seemed unreal and far away. If it wasn't either of them it was somebody else' to be allowed to help the shepherd put up the hurdles for the lambing pens was much more interesting and useful. He returned to London feeling several years younger and went to Wimbledon to keep his dinner engagement with Savory; Cobden had arranged to meet him there. As it happened Hambledon was the first of the party to arrive, even his host was not yet at home. The manservant Dick, complete with a set of dentures which reminded Hambledon of an overcrowded cemetery, greeted him warmly.

"Come right inside, Mr. 'Awkley, out of this 'orrid fog. Mr. Savory ain't in yet but 'e'll be 'ere any minute. Lemme take your coat. Damp, ain't it? Best 'ang it in the 'ot-cupboard for a while, dry it off."

"Thank you," said Tommy. "Good idea, if you would be so kind. I hope I haven't arrived too early."

"Not a bit, no. It's 'im that's late. 'Sides, wouldn't matter if you was early, this is Liberty 'All, this is. You go and set down by the fire an' I'll bring you a drop of somethink, what's your fancy? Cocktail or sherry?"

Tommy turned in the drawing-room doorway to prefer sherry just as a latchkey rattled in the lock of the front door. Savory entered in haste, threw his hat to Dick and grinned cheerfully at Tommy. "Hawkley, that's right. Glad to see you. Sorry I'm late, been delayed. Sit down and have a drink, I won't be a moment." He dashed up the stairs two at a time and a door slammed overhead. Tommy sat by the fire warming his hands, sipping an excellent dry sherry and wondering idly why Savory had gone upstairs still wearing his raincoat over what looked like an extremely nice suit from what he could see of it. One doesn't usually take a damp raincoat up to one's bedroom when there is a manservant, however unconventional, to bear it away to a hot-cupboard. Nice suit, to judge by the trouser-legs, a good dark grey with a faint stripe of some kind and a particularly neat tie. Very unlike the flamboy-ant Savory who also, by the way, looked much more discreet than usual. Perhaps he'd been spending the day in the City. What was more important was that Cobden was late, Tommy left off considering Savory to fidget a little about Cobden.

Savory came in; if he had been restraining himself all day in the matter of dress he made up for it now. He was wearing dark green corduroy trousers, a Fair-Isle pullover and a pale green tie with brown spots.

"Well, well, got everything you want? That's right. Where's Cobden, do you know? Bit late, isn't he?"

"I was just beginning to think so myself," said Hambledon in a rather anxious voice.

"No need to worry yet, he may have just missed a Wimbledon train. We'll wait another five minutes, shall we? Dick! Dinner in five minutes. It's barely a quarter to eight now. Let me give you a little more sherry, come on. Oh, there's the telephone, blast it, how I hate telephones. Excuse me, I'd better go myself: if there is a mistake to be made about a message Dick'll make it." He went out of the room and Hambledon thought how unexpected was his remark about hating the telephone; Savory was the sort of man you would expect to have silver-plated telephone receivers in every sitting-room and a pink or blue enamelled one in every bedroom. But that all depended upon whether Savory really was the sort of man you'd expect from the look of him and his house.

Savory returned. "No need to worry, that was Cobden. He says he'll be another half an hour at least, he rang up from Charing Cross, and we are on no account to wait form him, so we'll begin, shall we? We'll take the sherry along with us."

The dining-room was Tottenham Court Road Tudor with brass whims, also large oil-paintings in gilt frames. There was one opposite to Hambledon where he sat at table and it drew his eyes as with a magnet. Against a background of purple-headed mountain it showed a large stag with wonderful antlers; he was looking down with an expression of fatherly concern upon a small calf—a deer-calf, naturally—at his feet in the heather. Away to the left and artistically obscure lay the form of a hind relaxed in death. A label upon the wide gilt frame said simply: "The Orphan." Tommy tore his attention from it with an effort.

"I've been down in the country since I saw you last," he said. "I am not a Londoner and I can't take it in too large doses at a time. I went into Hampshire and stayed at a pub. I do, really, prefer air that hasn't been breathed by a couple of thousand people before it reaches me."

"I am a Londoner born and bred," said Savory, "and I shouldn't be happy for long away from it, but even I feel overstimulated at times. London rather reminds me of those brilliant women of the eighteenth century who had salons. Their minds glittered, their wit was like a rapier and their knowledge encyclopedic. Everybody who was anybody came to call and sat round the room sparkling their brightest. Very stimulating, very inspiring. But what did their husbands do? They took a little flat in a quiet street and installed a placid wench with just enough brains to sit and smile, hold her tongue and cook an omelette. What a relief!"

"I'm sure you're right. My 'placid wench' is the Hampshire downs, where's yours? Or haven't you found her yet?"

"I think so. There's village in Somerset I've been to several times and I've got my eye on a small house there. I hope it may be coming into the market shortly and then we'll see. My brother, I think, will like to go somewhere quiet for a time when he comes out—he tells me he is getting quite keen on gardening."

Hambledon turned his attention to the pheasant and thought that Savory was certainly quite different tonight. "I hope you get your small house," he said. "How will Dick like it?" The manservant was not in the room at the moment.

"Believe it or not I think he'd love it, but I don't know that I shall take him there. In the meantime," said Savory, with a return to his loud and cheerful tones, "there's Maidenhead in the season and that's good enough for yours truly Sal Savory. Had a houseboat there last summer, used to run down weekends. Nice cheery parties and all that."

"I'm sure it was most enjoyable," said Hambledon.

"It was, it was. Hope to get it again next summer, you must come down."

"Thank you," said Tommy, "I shall look forward to it. I can't help admiring that picture of yours," he added, indicating "The Orphan." "The expression on that stag's face is really wonderful. One would think he knew."

The expression on Savory's face was also rather wonderful, momentary horror immediately changed to complacency.

"Nice bit of color and it suits the room," he said. Hambledon agreed with him, undoubtedly it did, but that flash of aversion was revealing.

"By the way," said Savory, "when you were at Northern Moor did you meet that fellow Gosling?"

"Gosling?"

"The Rhodesian Retirement Company."

Hambledon remembered the case and the man. Gosling was a tall handsome man with graying hair and the manners of a benevolent butler. He had a wonderful scheme by which elderly clergymen paid a lump sum down and small regular payments thereafter to ensure for themselves a happy inexpensive old age in Rhodesia when the time came for them to retire. Wonderful climate, low taxation, no servant troubles, comfortable small houses, and the passage money paid in advance all the way from door to door. Hambledon recalled the details very clearly now that he was reminded of them; an elderly and regrettably unworldly relation of his own had been one of the bitten ones. He had lost all his savings and nothing could be done to recover them.

"That swine," said Hambledon. "Yes, he was there and I never saw him without wanting to kick him. Plausible oily brute. I never spoke to him; even in jail one must draw the line somewhere."

"Oh, quite," said Savory, and went on to draw out Tommy about conditions of prison life at Northern Moor compared with those at Maidstone where his brother was serving his sentence. Hambledon answered him willingly until the door opened and Cobden was shown in.

"I do apologist," he said, "for being so infernally late, but I've had rather an interesting time and, what is more, I've got something to show you."

"Splendid," said Savory. "Dick, bring the pheasant back for Mr. Cobden, and then you can put the cheese on the table and we'll manage."

As soon as Dick was out of the room Cobden pulled a flat cardboard box from his pocket, laid it on the table and opened it. Inside, the green fire of emeralds blazed up at them, the rainbow flash of diamonds and the unholy splendor of opals.

"Well," said Cobden, "what d'you know about that?"

VIII

FIVE MINUTES MORE

Savory looked carefully at the jewels and Hambledon rose in his place to get a better view, the sight was breathtaking. "I've never seen such gems," he said.

"You won't often see such gems as these," said Savory. "In fact, I don't think I ever have. There's no doubt about what they are, this is the proceeds of that robbery at the Capitol Hotel two days ago, there was a list in today's *Times*. Better shut the box up again, Dick will be back in a minute."

Cobden put the box back in his pocket.

"Where on earth did you manage to acquire those?" asked Hambledon.

"At the Vavasour Cinema," said Cobden.

When the manservant had finally retired Savory said, "I sent a man to the Vavasour this week but he wasn't very lucky. He merely reported that the low wall at the back of the rear seats was unusually thick and might, in his opinion, contain cavities, so he sat there and looked for something of the kind but didn't find it. It was a little difficult for him, because if you go several times to see the same film an observant management might wonder why. He did his best to awaken romance in one of the young ladies who usher but he only got the frozen raspberry. Very 'aughty they all are. He is going again tonight and taking a girl with him to disarm suspicion and, of course, he can go again tomorrow when there is a fresh picture to see, but I gather you have rather wiped his eye."

"He was quite right, though," said Cobden between mouthfuls. "Marvellous pheasant this is, I am enjoying myself. Well, I went there first on Sunday evening, after we left here, I thought it pretty safe as even those fellows with the lorry hadn't had a really good look at me. The cinema entrance is merely a passage with the box-office like a sentry-box standing in it. You couldn't pass anything bigger than a letter through the grille to the girl in the box and if you put it through the door she gets in by, anyone passing in the street could see you. The passage is quite bare of concealment and the walls must belong to the shops on either side. So I went upstairs, again only a bare

passage with the swing doors leading to the gallery—my mistake, the circle—
and one door further along."

"The manager's office," said Hambledon.

"I guessed so. I went in and sat at the back merely because that's the only
place where you can watch everything and everybody without turning round.
Not very luxurious, the Vavasour dress-circle, merely a passage behind the
banked seats with three little flights of stairs between the blocks, and only a
brass rail behind the seats to keep you from falling on to the heads of pa-
trons. So after a bit I went downstairs and told the Ruritanian Admiral that
I'd changed my mind and wanted to sit in the stalls. The place was pretty
full, I couldn't do much but have a general look round, and sat in the back
row, it was then that I noticed the curiously thick wall. Not much to go on but
there seemed to be nothing else—no Grecian urns or banks of pot plants or
even sumptuous velvet curtains. Nothing happened so eventually I left, only
stopping to tell the Admiral in impassioned terms my very high opinion of
Judy Garland. She was in the big film. Her ankles, I said, her eyes, her deli-
cious curly hair, her dimpled wrists—when I got round to her ankles for the
third time he edged away. Next morning I read in the paper about the robbery
at the Capitol, so I saw the big film twice through and the Admiral merely
looked at me pityingly. This evening I went again."

"Let me cut you a little more pheasant," said Savory. "My heavens, you
deserve all I've got to offer and then some. I can recommend the claret, let
me—please go on."

"I sat in the back row again," said Cobden, "near one end, the place was
rather empty. There were three or four people in that row besides myself.
Presently a man came in and sat down about eight seats along from me, an
ordinary looking man with sandy hair and a turned-up nose. He sat quiet for
some time and then took a parcel from a pocket inside his raincoat and held
it on his knees, not obviously if you hadn't been watching him, but I was.
Presently he took out his handkerchief, fussed with it a bit and then dropped
it. He leaned down to pick it up and took longer than he should, I thought.
When he sat up again he hadn't got his parcel. I memorized the exact seat
and went on adoring Judy Garland. Apparently he didn't go much on her
because he went out before the end of the picture. I waited till a few people
got up to go and moved along the row, the seat is number twenty-nine. Well,
I've got long arms, if I slumped down in the seat I could touch the floor. I sat
there feeling about under the seat and came across a little knob. At that precise moment two schoolgirls came in and sat only two seats away." Cobden
paused for refreshment. "You were right about this claret, where on earth do
you get it?"

"Here's the decanter," said Savory, "let me—what did you do about the
girls?"

"Looked straight in front of me and made faces. Awful faces. They stood it for ten minutes and then moved two rows forward. I then dealt with the knob, which slides sideways, and a little door opened. I put my hand in and there we were. I then waited for Judy's last smile and came away. End of story, except that I retired to a secluded spot and looked to see what I'd got. Then I rang you up and came along. May I open the box again now?"

"Of course," said Savory. "Just a moment, I'll get *The Times* and we'll go through the list, but I'm sure those are the Capitol jewels." He fetched the paper from another room and locked the dining-room door when he came back. "Now then, let's have them out on the table. Here we are: Stolen from the Capitol Hotel and so on, one diamond six-pointed star three and one-quarter inches across, yes, that's it. One *rivière* necklace of emeralds with bracelets, earrings and brooch *en suite*; my aunt, what a display. Emerald and diamond corsage ornament in form of a spray of leaves five and one-quarter inches long. Necklace of opals and diamonds in rosettes of gradu-ated sizes—"

"I say," said Cobden, "was our distinguished foreign visitor wanting to pay off his national debt or buy a couple of battleships?"

Savory went through the remaining items on the list. "Yes, they're all here except one platinum wristwatch set with diamonds. You've very quiet, Hawkley?"

"I am struck speechless," said Tommy, who was really wondering what he ought to do about the stolen jewels. "Do you mean to tell me one woman owned all those? She must be a very expensive lady."

"Yes," said Savory thoughtfully. He hesitated for a moment, looking from Hambledon to Cobden, and then appeared to make up his mind. "You know," he said bluntly, "I'm sorry, but these have got to go back."

Hambledon nodded but Cobden stared in surprise.

"Why," he said, "can't you deal with this stuff?"

"It's not quite that," said Savory, almost apologetically. "I hardly know to put it, but the fact is that I don't do jobs like this. The only pathetic part about it is that I don't for the moment see how Cobden is going to apply for the reward."

"I can't," said Cobden, "that's obvious. Sad, but true. But why can't you?"

"Because they'd want to know where I found them and how and when and why. Frankly, I can't afford to have the police nosing round me, they might think I'd stolen them myself and then got frightened when I saw what they were. I'm sorry, but I daren't do it."

"Oh, well," said Cobden.

"I'm sure you're right," said Hambledon. "If you said you'd found the packet in a Tube train they'd want to know which, and then produce a dozen witnesses to prove you weren't on it."

"But they must go back," said Savory again. "Anonymously."

"Pack them up and post them in Shoreditch," suggested Tommy.

"No, leave it to me," said Cobden. "You can't post a packet this size without being seen by the girl behind the wire-netting and they aren't all stupid. If you'll wrap them up for me I'll deliver them all right. You needn't be afraid," he added awkwardly, as Savory hesitated, "jewel robberies aren't in my line either. I'd like the reward, but I don't want the goods."

"My dear chap," said Savory, "it wasn't that. I was wondering what risk you were going to take."

"None at all, honestly."

The parcel was repacked with gloved hands, Cobden dropped it in the pocket of his raincoat and then put the coat on. "If you'll forgive my cutting short a pleasant evening," he said, "I think I'll go and get rid of it now. It'll be nearly ten by the time I get back to Piccadilly Circus and the crowds will be thinning out. I want a crowd for this job. Thank you very much for a delightful dinner, the best meal I've had for over a year. See you tomorrow evening at the Kobold, Hawkley? I'd better hurry, I think. Good night."

"I hope he'll be all right," said Savory, when Cobden had gone.

"All right in what way?" asked Hambledon, and Savory smiled.

"I really meant that if he were caught with that packet on him—"

"He knows that perfectly well and he's very capable. Besides, if he chooses to take the risk it's his affair, we can't interfere. He won't make away with them, you know."

"No," said Savory, "I didn't think he would. Confidence men are fairly honest in their private lives, as a rule. One of them explained to me once that his victims were all people who wanted something for nothing or they wouldn't play. He would have thought robbery far beneath him."

"So would Cobden," said Tommy.

"Funny the things we draw the line at, isn't it?" said Savory. "Robbing parsons in your case, apparently."

"Yes. My father was a parson," said Hambledon thoughtfully, "perhaps that's why."

"Nothing, and I've no doubt that it's perfectly true. Actually I was just wondering who the devil you were."

"You know perfectly well. I'm Edwin Vincent Hawkley, ex-company-promoter—"

"Who made nearly as much money out of the guileless clergy as he did out of guileless widows."

"At one time I'm ashamed to say that was true," said Tommy, averting his face. "I changed my mind about that and, believe it or not, I paid quite a lot of them—"

"And who was not only a bosom friend of Gosling's but actually put some money into the Rhodesian Retirement Company—"

"Yes, but we had a frightful row. That business was really what influenced me—"

"Into laying off parsons?"

"Well, yes."

"You know," said Savory, "you really ought to get up your facts a lot more thoroughly. Hawkley's last raids on his fellowmen showed no such scruples, and that was after Rhodesian Retirement Company was wound up. No, it won't do. You're not Hawkley; I don't think you were ever a company pro-moter, you don't think like one; and finally I don't believe you're a crook. I'm a pretty fair judge of men and if you're a crook. I'm a pretty fair judge of men and if you're a criminal I'm an Archbishop." He went on after a pause: "I did at one time think you were police, but there's no doubt you've been in jail, you know so much about it, and policemen don't go to jail. At least, they aren't policemen afterwards if they do. You aren't the prison warder type so what are you? No business of mine, you may say, but I think it is." He added with great emphasis: "The point is, I don't want you after me."

"I am not," said Tommy instantly. "I am not after you and I've no such intention. I am after the Vavasour gang as you called them, not you. I hope you believe me."

"Oddly enough," said Savory with a laugh, "I do."

"Thank you. If we come down to brass tacks," said Tommy in a lighter tone, "you're rather a queer crook yourself, aren't you? Here's Cobden of-fering you enough emeralds and what-have-you to keep a reasonable man in comfort for the rest of his life and you won't look at them. Lewis implied that you ran a sort of Universal Criminals Incorporated, some of everything like the Army and Navy Stores. Well, now it's my turn to say I don't believe it. You don't like oil paintings by the yard either, and I doubt if you really enjoy rowdy Sunday parties or houseboats at Molesey or wher-ever it was—"

"Maidenhead—"

"Maidenhead, then. In short, Salvation Savory, it's all very well to sit there and laugh, but what's your game? Not organized crime—"

"Oh, yes it is," said Savory. "If you will stay here with me for"—he glanced at his watch—"another three-quarters of an hour, I'll prove it to you. I just didn't want those particular jewels. And don't laugh at my name; it's a nice name, Salvation Savory, I made it up myself. Let me give you a little more port, I hope you approve of it. No more? Then let's go and sit in my beautiful drawing-room of which I am so proud and Dick shall bring in the coffee."

It was rather less than three-quarters of an hour before a noisy sports car drove up with laughter and song from its occupants. They were three young men in evening dress. When Savory switched on the porch light and opened the front door they greeted him with joyful sounds. One of them had a bugle.

"Come in," said Savory, beaming at them in the doorway. "Come in. This is a real pleasure, this is."

"Not too late, Uncle Sal, are we? Been to a show in Town and everything shuts up so beastly early we thought we'd drop in if you didn't mind."

"Uncle Sal, I've bought a bugle, listen." The boy blew a long blast. "I'm going to take music lessons," he added proudly, and released another even longer and more wavering. It appeared to remind the driver of something for he stood up on the running-board, stuck one finger in his ear and bellowed "Gone Awa-a-ay," to the unappreciative give shades of Parson's Close.

"You'll get this house a bad name, so you will," said their host, laughing loudly. "Come inside, blowing bugles is thirsty work, or so they tell me, never tried myself. Meet a friend of mine, Mr. Hawkley. Hawkley, three young friends of mine, this is Peter, that's Bob with the bugle, and Johnny— where's Johnny? Here he is. Johnny, this is Mr. Hawkley."

Johnny was a red-faced young man carrying a suitcase. When he saw a stranger in the room he paused, glanced down at the case and said: "Look at me, bringing the luggage in here! Mind if I dump it in the hall? Didn't like to leave it in the car, too many robberies—"

"No, bring it in here, Johnny boy. Hawkley won't mind, I'm sure. He understands," said Savory deliberately.

Hambledon was in the act of shaking hands with Peter, a tall lanky boy with a vacant expression and a lock of black hair falling into his eyes. The vacant expression vanished suddenly and Hambledon saw himself being very shrewdly sized up.

"One of those understanding sort of blokes, is he? Well, most of you friends are, Uncle Sal, I'll say that for them." He dropped Hambledon's hand and Bob came forward to take his place, a short fat youth with a round merry face, clasping his bugle as though it were a bunch of lilies.

"How d'you do, Mr. Hawkley? I like understanding blokes myself. We met a policeman tonight who wasn't Uncle Sal. I was trying to play 'Five Minutes More' and he came and moved us on. No appreciation of the arts."

"Where was this?" asked Savory.

"Outside a block of flats, forget its name. Granville, Grantham, Grenville, Greenfield, Greenwood, something like that."

"Greyville?" said Savory.

"Greyville, how did you guess? There was rather a pretty girl going in there so I stopped her and said: 'Excuse me, but do you know whether my aunt lives there?' She said she didn't know my aunt and I said no, of course not, but she might one of these days and her name was Bickersley-Throgmorton. Eulalia. But still she said no and I said couldn't I come with her and look. Then she said 'No, certainly not,' and simply cantered indoors, so I played 'Five Minutes More' hoping she'd come back. She didn't, but the policeman did. While we were talking to him I thought I saw Peter come out of the Greyville but I couldn't be sure. So we waved the cop goodbye and sort of oozed after the man I thought was Peter and it was. So we picked him up round the corner and came on here."

"Bright bunch of lads, aren't they?" said Savory.

"I think your nephews do you credit," said Tommy.

"Oh, they're not really my nephews, they just call me Uncle Sal. Lots of 'em do. What sort of an evening have you had, Peter?"

"Very dull. I went to the Greyville to say goodbye to a man who's going abroad tomorrow, but he wasn't there. I hung about in his flat for a bit, got fed up and came away." He yawned. "All packed up, he was, nothing but locked suitcases to look at, not even a copy of *Razzle*. And no beer."

"Talking about beer," said Savory, "I told Dick he could go to bed but you know where it's kept, don't you, Bob?"

"Oh, rather. Here, you hold this," said Bob, thrusting his bugle into Hambledon's arms. He left the room with an elaborate slow dancing step to the tune of "Five Minutes More."

"I wish Bob wouldn't keep on with that damned tune," said Peter. "I shall have it on my alleged brain for days."

Hambledon was examining the bugle with the careful interest of one who suspects a booby trap and Johnny laughed at him.

"To look at you, anyone would think you expected a rabbit to jump out at you," he said.

"Not a rabbit, no," said Tommy.

Bob returned with a large tray and Savory told him to deal out its contents. "In the meantime I'm going to have a look inside Peter's suitcase." He brought it across the room to a table at Hambledon's elbow and threw the lid back. It was packed with bundles of notes, mainly of the £1 and 10s. values, though Peter indicated with a long thin forefinger one larger packet and said that that one was fivers. Hambledon made no attempt to disguise his enthralled interest and the other two young men abandoned their beer to come and look also.

"Naughty old man," said Bob. "Very naughty," and Johnny bubbled suddenly with laughter. "I was—was just imagining his face when he opens his little suitcase tomorrow and finds he's only got back numbers of the *Telegraph*," he spluttered.

"But," said Hambledon, and stopped. "Sorry," he apologized. "No business of mine. Indeed, I was only going to say that there'll be a frightful uproar over this, won't there?"

"None at all," said Savory. "You heard Peter say that the man he went to see—but he was out, naturally—was going abroad tomorrow. By air, private charter. This was part of his luggage. He is going to the Riviera."

"I've got it now," said Tommy. "Smuggling currency abroad. Why, he can't even complain about it if he does find out in time."

"He won't," said Peter. "A farewell party is in progress. He didn't arrange it and nobody is farewelling him, it just sort of happened."

"You know how these parties sort of arise, don't you, sir?" said Bob. "All spontaneous-like." He returned to his beer.

"There's a little bag in the corner, Uncle Sal," said Peter. "Didn't wait to look inside, just brought it. It was in with the rest. Well, I think we'd better blow along now or my mother will be getting the needle. She's always afraid I shall get into bad company." He shook hands with Hambledon. "We'll be meeting again, I dare say. Good night, Uncle Sal. Come on, you two."

"Good night, Mr. Hawkley," said Bob. "Next time we meet I'll give you a lesson on the bugle. 'Night, Uncle Sal, and thanks for the beer an' all."

Johnny shook hands in silence and Savory went to the door to see them off. There were shouted farewells as the sports car roared into life, one last toot on the bugle, and the sounds of departure died away. The door shut and Savory came back into the room.

"Well?" he said. "Do you believe now that I organize crime?"

"On this occasion," said Tommy tactfully, "you seem to me to be preventing it."

"The gentleman who thought he owned this property wasn't only dealing in currency, he was a blackmailer. I don't like blackmailers, Hawkley. That, of course, was where the money came from, that's why they're mostly old notes. I know that people should go to the police when they're blackmailed, but it's rather an ordeal and such a long-drawn-out business after that. Giving evidence, and so on. My methods are highly illegal but they save a lot of trouble."

"Lewis . . ." began Hambledon.

"Lewis doesn't know. He is a criminal and I don't trust him any further than I need. He's well paid, does what he's told and is useful, that's all. London is full of Lewises. These lads tonight are quite another matter. By the way, I didn't give you their surnames on purpose."

"Don't apologize," said Tommy with a laugh. "I haven't given you mine. I will one day soon, but there's rather a lot in this business."

"We all seem a little shy on surnames tonight, don't we? Let's look at the little bag Peter mentioned." Savory took a small washleather bag from the suitcase and felt it between his fingers. "Feels like small pebbles," he said. "Well there's pebbles and pebbles."

"Not more jewels, surely," said Tommy. "Tell me, are all your days as begemmed as this?"

IX

GENTLEMEN IN TROUBLE

Savory untied the string round the neck of the bag and poured out the contents upon the table.

"Oh, not more diamonds," said Hambledon.

Savory picked up several of them, examined them carefully, and began to laugh.

"Not really," he said. "These are imitations, but they're quite good, aren't they? My own little chickens come home to roost. I had thought this might happen."

"Are they yours, then?"

"They were. It's rather a comic story. I told you this fellow was a blackmailer, didn't I? Well, like black marketeers and others with sources of income they can't afford to reveal, he found it difficult to know what to do with his money. The Inland Revenue is a bit nosey if you buy securities, so he bought diamonds instead. Lots of 'em do, really good diamonds. I had some. So I sent another young friend of mine to see him and offer them for sale. He said he would buy them provided they were passed by a competent valuer, he himself was no judge of diamonds. I agreed and a meeting was arranged. My young friend brought out the diamonds and the assessor valued them. He was then shown out and my agent argued the price with the buyer. They sat on opposite sides of a table, my man had his hands round the diamonds as they lay, he didn't trust the buyer, and rightly. At last they agreed, the blackmailer counted out notes—lots of notes—and my young friend pushed the diamonds across the table. I forgot to say that he's a sleight-of-hand expert, he does it for a living on the halls. You can guess the rest."

"He gave him these instead, of course," said Tommy.

"Just so. He returned to me with the real diamonds and the money, and now I've got these back too. Very nice. I am pleased. They may come in useful again some day," said Savory calmly.

"If that man knew even half of this," said Hambledon, "I wouldn't insure your life."

"I also had his safe opened, but he doesn't know that. We only took some photographs."

"Didn't he miss them?"

"I mean, we made some photographs, not abstracted them. They came out very well though they weren't artistic, the subjects were the pages of a book. An address-book, with a few notes against each name. What with the money I got for the diamonds and the contents of that case, there's enough to give each of his correspondents a very pleasant surprise and leave some over for my expenses. They won't get all their money back, of course, but they deserve to pay something for being silly. Don't you agree?"

"I do, absolutely," said Tommy sincerely. "They wouldn't have got much of it back if they'd gone to the police. But what's to stop him starting all over again when he comes back from abroad?"

"Me," said Savory simply. "I'll stop him."

Hambledon believed him.

"I liked those boys tonight," he said. "Especially the clown with the bugle."

Savory nodded. "But Peter's is the best brain of the outfit, and he does look so helpfully silly. Of course the idea behind tonight's show was simple, but they carried it out very well. Another squad took the victim out almost by force and amused him all round London, they won't leave him alone till he goes off at 5 a.m. to catch his plane. Peter went to the flat—they're service flats, it was quite empty—and changed over the contents of the suitcases, old newspapers for that." Savory tilted his head towards the money. "Then he hung about till he heard 'Five Minutes More' on the bugle, came out and just walked on till they overtook him. The only thing that puzzles me is how he recognized the tune, for heaven knows Bob can't play."

Piccadilly Circus at ten at night is busy with people going home from their various diversions, for London still retires early. Among them was a Detective-Sergeant who was loitering about in the hope that something or somebody interesting would come along. He was dressed in what is practically the uniform of plainclothes police, a soft felt hat and a raincoat, but most Detective-Sergeants are known at least by sight to the criminal is their district and Cobden, lurking modestly in the background, recognized him at once. The crowds drifted into the Circus from all the six streets which meet there, and a steady stream of people passed down the stairs to the Underground station. Presently the detective saw a pickpocket of his acquaintance drifting towards a point where the press was thickest; the Sergeant followed after the pickpocket and Cobden after the Sergeant. The pickpocket, warned by instinct, looked round straight into the detective's face and at once as-

sumed an expression of innocence which would have done credit to any of
the Children of the Chapel Royal. He disengaged himself from his neighbors
and took a twopenny ticket from an automatic machine. The detective reminded himself that the first duty of the police is the prevention of crime, in
which he had just scored a boundary, and turned away; as he did so several
people bumped into him. He raised his hat to apologize to a lady ("a policeman is always polite") and, as he did so, felt his coat pull at his arm as though
there were something heavy in the pocket. He put in his hand; there was a
flat packet which had not been there the moment before. He looked round
quickly but without result, Cobden was on his way elsewhere.

A quarter of an hour later an excited Inspector was telephoning to Scotland Yard.

"We've got the Capitol jewels, sir."

"Oh, have you? Good. Where were they? What? In the pocket of one of
your Sergeants? At Piccadilly Circus, I see. Pocket-picking in reverse. Very
odd. Very odd indeed. He didn't see who did it—no, I understand. I only
wish I understood why it was done. Are they all there? All except one watch,
perhaps that's following by post. No, sorry, Inspector, that was meant for a
joke. Well, the Insurance Company'll be pleased, anyway, and in the meantime we can go on looking for the watch. Yes, go over the parcel for prints,
naturally, and I wish you luck. Right. Good-bye."

Hambledon rang up Savory the following morning. "I have a message for
you," he said. "You remember our discussing last night the return of a missing consignment of nuts?"

"Clearly," said Savory. "Those Cob-nuts, you mean."

"That's right. They are safely in the hands of the agents who were inquir-
ing about them."

"Glad to hear it. I should have thought there might have been a small
paragraph in the papers but apparently there isn't."

"No," said Hambledon, "they're not advertising it, evidently, but I know
it's true. I had a firsthand account of the affair. Refined but funny."

"I should like to hear about it too, also I have had another idea I'd like to
discuss with you. Could you both come out here about five this evening?"

"Can do," said Tommy. "That's a date."

"Good," said Savory, and rang off.

The other idea to which Savory referred was about the man who had taken
the Capitol jewels to the Vavasour Cinema and put them in the cubbyhole
from whence Cobden had taken them. "I don't know in detail how the gang
is organized," said Savory, "but I imagine some innocent-seeming signal is
passed, probably to the Commissionaire, whenever one of the boys has
brought the boss a present. Your friend with the turn-up nose just put the

parcel in and went away again; it would stay there until the show closed for the night unless there is an interval—"

"No," said Cobden. "Continuous performance."

"After the show, then, somebody—the cinema manager, probably—would go to the cubby hole to take out the parcel. It isn't there. What happens next?"

"He shoots himself," said Tommy.

"He shoots the Commissionaire," said Cobden.

"I wish he'd done both," said Savory, "but I doubt it. I don't think it would occur to him that he'd been robbed. Either, he would say, the Commissionaire mistook the signal or the man who brought it made some mistake or is double-crossing them. He—the cinema manager—would ask the Commissionaire first, wouldn't he?"

"Certainly," said Tommy. "This signal, what is it? Something furtive, stealthy and feline. No hopping three times upon the left foot, holding the right foot in the hand while whistling the Marseillaise. Most likely, I think, to be some prearranged phrase like 'Has my mister come yet?' or 'How's your granny tonight?' What I am trying to suggest is that it must be something ordinary enough to arouse no surprise if overheard and therefore the sort of thing some one else might happen to say, or do, and so a mistake is possible if improbable. Yes, I think our Mr. Robinson, the manager, might naturally conclude a mistake had been made but I think he'd make certain at once. If the Commissionaire Morgan had been sent home before the pie was opened, a conscientious manager would follow him there and make sure. And Morgan is quite sure there was no mistake. So the manager goes on the look for Snub-Nose. Now you carry on."

"Snub-nose has no idea there's anything wrong," said Savory, "so he hasn't bolted. Why should he? He doesn't even bolt when he sees Robinson coming towards him. Robinson says, 'Did you give Morgan the signal when you came in this afternoon?' and when he says he did Robinson asks him, 'Where's the packet, then?' What happens next?"

"He protests his innocence," said Cobden. "He says he did put it in the cubby-hole, and since he really did it's possible that the accents of truth would make Robinson hesitate."

"So that it's just possible he may be still alive," said Hambledon. "But there'd be a court of inquiry, wouldn't there?"

"Of course there would," said Savory, "with the very good chance of an execution at the end if he didn't satisfy the judges. Which brings me to what I was going to say. If Snub-nose is still alive he's a very frightened man if he's got any sense, and frightened men will sometimes talk. If we could find him I wondered whether he would talk to us in exchange for a passage to South America or something helpful like that."

"If we knew where to find him," said Hambledon doubtfully, and Cobden smiled.

"I didn't have time to tell you this morning," he said to Hambledon, "but last night after I'd got rid of the loot I went on a little round of visits to some men I used to know. I wanted to find out if anybody knew a fair-haired young man with a snub-nose—it isn't snub really, it just turns up—who takes an interest in hotel robberies. Eventually I found out quite a lot about him. His name is Arnott, David Arnott. He has been operating quite a lot for nearly a year, they told me, specializing in hotel robberies. He is 'quite the gent,' I was told, nice way of talking and all that. He just strolls about hotel corridors as though he were one of the guests, and the bigger the hotel the safer he is. Never been pinched. Gets good information beforehand but they didn't tell me where from, and one doesn't ask too much. He lives in a rather queer boardinghouse in Camden Town, I've got the address."

"You don't know whether he's still there, do you?" asked Savory. "Today, I mean?"

"No. I didn't take any steps. I hadn't, actually, thought it all out as you have and I hadn't had time to talk it over with Hawkley." Cobden paused for thought. "I could go there and ask for a room; I dare say I should get it. The landlord—man named Bates—has a reputation for kindness to poor gentlemen in trouble. I should whisper that I was Cobden, the escaped convict, and all would be well. Or so they tell me, it might be worth trying."

"Let's both try it," said Hambledon, "perhaps someone there can cook, which is more than can be said for the haunt of vice I inhabit at the moment. But how does Landlord Bates get away with it if he makes a habit of storing wanted criminals? Haven't the police ever heard of him?"

"I believe they did raid the place once," answered Cobden, "but the house has been carefully adapted. Built-in wardrobes conduct you to the next bedroom and there are means of arriving on the roof. The police didn't find what they were looking for."

"Doesn't sound as though there's much real privacy there," said Tommy. "I mean, if people can emerge from your wardrobe without even knocking—"

"It is now twenty hours since they missed their parcel," said Savory. "I shouldn't think Arnott is still there. Either the gang has got him or he's fled."

"I think it's worth going there to see if any trace can be picked up," said Hambledon. "Some screwed-up envelop with a barely decipherable address left lying in the neglected grate, or even some brokenhearted damsel wailing for her demon lover. One never knows."

"You think she might be persuaded to wail to you?" said Savory, with lines of laughter deepening round his eyes.

"Not me necessarily," said Tommy. "Cobden has more the physical attributes of a consoler of female misery though I also have not been without my successes, believe it or not. We move in tonight, Cobden, do we?"

"After dark," said Cobden, "well after."

Hambledon paid off his unloved landlady, packed up his cheap suitcase and met Cobden by appointment in Camden Town. Cobden led the way to a maze of small streets which had been originally laid out by someone who loved a garden, Anchusa Road led into Lobelia Avenue from which both Primula and Petunia Streets branched off. The first turning to the left down Petunia Street was Clematis Lane, the second was Verbena Street.

"Down here," said Cobden, turning the corner. "Number five."

"It doesn't look much like the picture on the packet to me," said Tommy, looking at the smoke-darkened houses with their deep narrow areas in which small bits of dirty paper blew about and empty tins overflowed from dented dustbins. "Yet these were nice houses once, if you like the type, which I don't."

They were tall houses with three floors of bedrooms above the ground-floor. Originally they had been designed in one continuous line the whole length of the street; a repeated pattern of flat-pillared porticos over fanlights with two sizeable windows between each doorway gave the street an air of faded gentility. But there were gaps in the row with traces of fireplaces and staircases on the end walls, the gaps had been levelled and cleared and Portal houses crouched between their tall neighbors. Alternate streetlamps only were lighted and the whole neighborhood carried an air of disrepute. There were plenty of people about who glanced quickly at Hambledon and Cobden; a group of men under a lamppost impeded the path and did not seem inclined to let them pass. Cobden said "Sorry, mate," and slid between them, Hambledon followed with a pricking sensation down his back and nothing happened after all.

"Only wanted to have a look at us," murmured Cobden. "We might have been police, you know. There's number five, over there."

They crossed the road and rang the bell of number five. The door opened very promptly if not very far, only about six inches, and an eye peered at them through the gap.

"What d'you want?"

Cobden moved close to the gap. "Want to see Mr. Bates. Urgent. Quick, let us in, we don't want to stand out here." He pressed against the doorpost with his head down as though even that degree of cover was a refuge. Presumably the woman had seen men on the run before for the opened the door suddenly and they both slipped in. She shut the door again behind them without a sound and Hambledon remembered that it had opened without a sound also, a curiously quiet front door, this. They stood in a long hall lit only by an electric light on the curving staircase which wound upwards at the back. The woman was middle-aged and stout but her black eyes were sharply upon them.

"What's your name?" she said, addressing Cobden, but he only answered with another question. "Who are you?"

"I'm his wife, Mrs. Bates." She hesitated and added: "You can talk to me."

"Oh. Well, I don't know—I want to see Mr. Bates."

She looked from one to the other, nodded as though she were satisfied, and opened the door of a small room next to the front door. "Wait in there," she said, "I'll call him."

Cobden nodded. "Police photographs, front and side view. 'Wanted, the following two men.'"

Hambledon glanced round the room which contained only a table, two or three basket chairs and a sideboard. Over the fireplace was a framed colored supplement from a Christmas Double Number of the *Illustrated London News*—it showed a party of children capering before a Christmas tree, and it was crooked on the wall. Hambledon had what is oddly called a "straight eye" and crooked pictures worried him, his hand instinctively went out to straighten it.

"Don't touch it," snapped Cobden. "They'll think you've been looking behind it."

"Dear me," said Tommy mildly, and turned his back so that he need not see it. The door opened and a man came into the room, a large untidy man with red hair thin on the top and no collar on. He closed the door behind him and looked at them, again Hambledon noticed how quietly the door shut.

"Mr. Bates?" said Cobden.

"That's my name. I don't think I know you two gentlemen?"

"You know of us, I'm Cobden and this is Mr. Hawkley."

"I seem to have heard the names somewhere," said Bates, and smiled slowly.

"You know what we want," said Cobden urgently. "Somewhere to lie close for a bit. Not long, we're getting fixed up to go abroad."

"Who told you to come here?"

"Nobody. I heard of you—oh, a couple of years ago, then when we were a bit pushed I thought of this place. Lallia told me last night you were still here."

"Lallia. Mario or Benedetto?"

"Mario. Benny's inside, isn't he?"

"So they tell me," said Bates, "but folk don't always stay there, do they? Well now, I'm sorry but really I haven't got a room."

Cobden's face fell so abruptly that Tommy would have sworn he heard a small thud. He thought it was time that he took a hand.

"Any room," he said, in a tone husky with emotion. "The box-room, the loft, the coal-hole. Man alive, to go back to the place will kill me!" His lower jaw quivered, a very useful accomplishment in time of trouble. "Just one night to sleep in peace—"

Bates looked at him with sympathy. "Ah, it's hard on men of your age, being on the run." Tommy was so indignant that his jaw quivered in earnest, but Cobden leapt at the opportunity.

"Look," he said, "we don't care where you put us but for Pete's sake do something!"

"Well, there is a room but strictly speaking it's let," said Bates. "My tenant is away—"

"The moment he comes back," said Hambledon, as one who makes the final sacrifice, "we go, if the Governor of Northern Moor himself is standing on the doorstep. Just a few hours of peace while I rebuild my soul."

"Talks like Henry Irving, don't he?" said Bates, and Cobden admitted, in a voice impeded with emotion of some sort, that he often did.

"I can't think it can hurt much if you have my tenant's room for a few days," said Bates, "seeing the case is as it is. He's a good-hearted boy, so he is, and never know when we shall be in trouble ourselves, do we? Tell you what, you stay here and have a bit of something on a tray while my missus and I tidy up the room. You'll find my missus can cook, I'll say that for her."

Hambledon sank into one of the basket chairs as though his legs had failed him. "Not only shelter," he murmured, "but also cooker. 'Seeking the food he eats and pleased with what he gets.'" He relapsed into silence as one beholding visions.

"Been living rough, has he?" said Bates to Cobden. "Poor old buffer." He left the room and Cobden turned to Hambledon.

"What on earth induced you to put on that act?"

"Pure whimsy," said Tommy. "Or perhaps in order that a description of me should be as misleading as possible. What I want is an overcoat with an astrakhan collar. When I played Hamlet at Newcastle, laddie—"

"What I want to find out," said Cobden, "is whether Arnott is here."

"What I want to know," said Hambledon in a low tone, "is whether there is a microphone behind that sideboard. In a house where one walks through wardrobes one can't be too careful." He raised his voice. "If I hadn't been engaged in business from my youth I should have been an actor. I know it. When I was quite a lad I took the part of Joseph Surface in an amateur production of *School for Scandal*, and Tree—the great Tree—who chanced to be present, said that I had given him an entirely new reading of the character, one which he had never seen before and never expected to see again. I have treasured those noble words all my life," said Tommy with simple dignity.

"I remember being Sir Walter Raleigh in Mrs. Jarley's Waxworks once when I was a kid," said Cobden. "Spreading my cloak for Queen Elizabeth, you know. Rather fun."

"Indeed, yes. Simple and even childlike, but you also have known the touch and smell of greasepaint and the glare of the footlights. You also understand."

The door opened and Bates came in with a large tin tray bearing two plates of extremely fragrant stew and two glasses. He set the tray down on the table, added a couple of bottles of Guinness from his pockets and told them to draw up their chairs. "I hope I've brought what you like," he said. "I've made inquiries and I don't think my tenant will be back for a while. I'll come back as soon as your room's ready, you'll be well advised to stay in here till then."

He returned a quarter of an hour later and said that everything was ready. He led them up three flights of the graceful curving stairs to the top floor and along a passage which seemed to Hambledon surprisingly long. He said so in a tone of innocent inquiry and Bates explained that he had three houses together which communicated on the top floors. They came at last to the open door of a lighted room where Mrs. Bates was performing final tidings. It was an attic room with a ceiling which sloped above the window, there was an elaborate brass bedstead which had come down in the world, a table and a couple of chairs, a washstand and one large wardrobe.

"I couldn't take his thinks away," she said, "so I've locked up the wardrobe and you'll just have to manage. There's some hooks behind the door."

"Perfect," said Hambledon, "quite perfect. All I asked was the humblest pallet and a rough blanket to wrap round me, and I see a bed fit for royalty. Sleep is all I ask, 'the innocent sleep, Sleep that knits up the ravelled sleeve of care'—forgive me. I am overtired and I become perhaps platitudinous."

"Good night." said Bates and his wife as one person, and hastily left the room.

X

GORILLA MAN

"The first thing to do," said Cobden, locking the door, "is to find out whether Arnott is still here."

"If I were he I wouldn't be," said Hambledon. "Not with the Vavasour gang asking me to explain what I'd done with fifty thousand pounds' worth of jewels. Of course, he may have thought up a convincing explanation, in which case I cannot but admire him."

"I think I'll go down and see if Bates has got any cigarettes he can let me have," said Cobden. "The name of Arnott might crop up in conversation."

"You'd better be careful. This place strikes me as one where questions about fellow-guests are the height of bad manners. How unlike Bayswater. There is one thing we might do first." Tommy looked thoughtfully at the wardrobe. "If he has fled this might be his room and perhaps there is evidence of identity among the things in there, if there are any things in it." He got up and looked closely at the lock. "What a good thing you've got black hair like the landlady, if I'd been alone I couldn't have done anything."

"Why not?"

"Come and look. Our landlady has a suspicious mind. She has wound a single hair across the opening from one knob to the other: one glance tomorrow morning and she thinks she'll know whether the door's been opened or not. An old dodge." He felt in the bottom of his waistcoat pocket and brought out a piece of wire. "I am not expert at locks, but these are usually fairly simple. Now watch Uncle and see if you can spot the conjuring trick." He bent his wire at the end, inserted it in the lock and felt about. "Open, barley! Open, wheat! Oh come on, do." Cobden leaned forward the better to watch the intent face with a little frown between the brows and a quarter of an inch of tongue moving in sympathy with the bent wire, and he laughed suddenly.

"What is it?" asked Tommy.

"Sorry. I was only thinking that whatever you've been in the past it wasn't a safecracker."

"Well, no. Are you any good at this? No? What a pity. When you consider what a useful accomplishment this is it should be taught in all schools. So useful when Mamma mislays her keys. Or even when she doesn't. Perhaps that's why they don't teach it. Open, maize; open, rice—ah! Open sesame. Now what have—oh, good heart alive!"

The door opened at first slowly, then swung abruptly wide as though pushed from within and a man came out, he rolled out limply, slumped the few inches to the floor and lay motionless face downwards. Cobden recoiled with an exclamation of horror.

Hambledon bent over the man, lifted his arm and felt for his pulse in vain since there was no pulse there. He was quite dead and Tommy, after a few simple tests dictated by experience, said so. "He hasn't been dead long," he added, "he's still quite warm."

"It's—it's Arnott," said Cobden in a shaking voice. "Who killed him?"

Hambledon examined the body more carefully. "Might have been natural death, he looks quite peaceful and I see no wound of any kind. He wasn't strangled or suffocated. Died in his sleep, I should say. May have been an overdose of something, can't tell without a p.m."

"You—you aren't going to—"

"Conduct one here and now?" said Tommy with a laugh. "Heavens, no, what do you take me for?"

"I don't know," said Cobden. "But you're—you don't seem to mind."

"Frankly, so long as nobody accuses me of bumping him off, I don't. I wonder, by the way, whether that was the idea of putting us in here? I mean, guests are not usually offered rooms with corpse-filled wardrobes, it isn't done. Not without a motive. There's no doubt the Bates couple knew he was there, however he came to die. If the next move is to call the police and he's in there, and 'you're here and I'm here so what do we care'—"

"For God's sake, stop," said Cobden, and his voice ran up the scale.

"Pull yourself together," said Tommy sharply. "Hysterics won't help us. What's the fuss about? He wasn't a friend of yours."

"No, but if the Vavasour gang killed him because the jewels were gone it's my fault because I took them."

"Nonsense. He had no business with the jewels in the first place, and you aren't responsible for the Vavasour gang's nasty habits. Beside, we don't know they did it, he may have died of suppressed measles."

"Why suppressed measles?"

"He hasn't got spots," said Tommy simply, and Cobden uttered a strangled laugh that was more like a snort. "That's better," went on Hambledon. "These matters must be encountered without fuss, you know. All men die and we shall look like that one of these days. Let that inspiring thought cheer you up, though I can't imagine why it should. I'm just going to have a look in the wardrobe."

He pulled open the second door and looked inside. There were a couple of suits and an overcoat on hangers, two pairs of shoes, a locked suitcase, three or four books and a small heap of the miscellaneous oddments a man keeps on his dressing-table. "Put there my Mrs. Bates when tidying up," said Tommy. "I'd like to see inside that suitcase and I only hope the keys of it are in his pocket." He picked up the shoes to move them out of his way and something fell out of one of them, a small narrow leather case. Cobden opened it—inside was a platinum wristwatch with a ring of diamonds round the face the more diamonds studding the links of the flexible bracelet.

"The missing watch from the Capitol loot, surely," said Tommy.

"But why did he keep it?"

"Present for the girlfriend, of course. Bates said he'd got a young lady, don't you remember?" Hambledon closed the case and dropped it in his pocket. "Now for the—listen!"

"Somebody coming," whispered Cobden.

"Help me," said Hambledon, and between them they bundled the body of Arnott back into the wardrobe and shut it up before the footsteps they had heard reached the door of their bedroom. Hambledon made one leap into bed and pulled the bedclothes up to his chin as the door-handle rattled. Next moment there was a tap at the door ad Cobden said: "Who's there?"

"It's us, you fool, open the door."

"Go away," said Cobden indignantly. "I'm in bed."

There was no answer from outside except a small sliding noise followed next moment by a sharp crack, the door swung open and three men walked in. They pushed the door shut and stood together; one was a tall man in a heavy overcoat with a scarf over his mouth, he wore wide army-pattern goggles which crossed his face like a mask, and a leather helmet. Another was a broad-shouldered man with immensely long arms and an oafish, sullen face; the third both Tommy and Cobden recognized at once, the neat businesslike figure of Robinson, the manager of the Vavasour Cinema. Tommy stirred beneath the bedclothes like a heavy sleeper half aroused, groaned sleepily, apparently decided that the visitors weren't really there and settled off again. Cobden stood with his back to the wardrobe, his face as white as ivory and his hands opening and shutting. The light over the washstand flashed on the glass in the tall man's goggles as he looked from one to the other. Robinson stood on tiptoe and whispered in his ear.

"Oh, really," said the motorist. "Messrs. Hawkley and Cobden. What a pleasant surprise. But where is our young friend Arnott?"

He had a pleasant cultured voice and Cobden, after a moment's pause, seemed to be reassured. The color returned to his face, his strained attitude relaxed. In point of fact he had just realized the implications of the question

about Arnott, therefore they had not killed him and Cobden was not even
remotely responsible.

"No idea," he said shortly.

Hambledon woke up, lifted his head from the pillow and stared at them
owlishly over the top sheet.

"Who are these people?" he asked, blinking. "Want to read the gas-meter?"

Robinson stepped forward. "You know me, Hawkley."

Hambledon looked again. "You know me, Hawkley." You're the cloak-
room attendant at Madame Tussaud's."

Robinson snarled and the motorist laughed.

"I am sorry to disturb your rest," he said, "but I am sure this interview is
going to be a pleasure. Where is Arnott?"

Hambledon sighed. "I don't keep Arnotts," he said, "whatever they are.
Sounds like a new breed of rabbits. But if by any chance you're referring to
the previous tenant of this room, he's gone away. That's why we're here
instead. Try Bates, perhaps he knows his present address."

"He gave this one," said the motorist

"Gave what?"

"This address. This room. Here."

"Bates told you Arnott was here," said Hambledon thoughtfully.

"Eventually the penny dropped and the mechanism emitted a faint creaking sound," said the motorist. "Having succeeded so far, perhaps you will
now tell us where Arnott is, or would you rather I looked under the bed?"

"I told you before," said Hambledon patiently. "Arnott has gone and I
know nothing about his destination."

"Get up," said the motorist.

"Certainly not," said Tommy, tucking the bedclothes more firmly round
his neck.

"Do you always sleep in your clothes? If not, where are they? Sammy!"

The oafish man shambled forward and Hambledon noticed that his enormous hands hung level with his knees.

"I knew another man once who had a pet gorilla," said Tommy, "but he
kept the creature in a cage."

Sammy seized the bedclothes and ripped them off the bed, Tommy came
up with them, threw his legs over the edge and sprang at him at the same
moment that Cobden hit him with a chair which disintegrated. Sammy did
not even grunt; he drove his elbow into Cobden who doubled up, winded.
Hambledon he picked up by wrist and ankle, threw him violently to the floor
and held him there with one hairy hand on his chest. The man in the goggles
laughed easily, he had not even taken his hands out of his pockets.

"Tame gorillas have their uses," he said. "I wouldn't struggle, he can break
your ribs if he feels like it. Now, where's Arnott?"

Tommy could not answer because he could not breathe, he drew up his feet with a sudden convulsive movement and let drive with both heels against Sammy's left knee. It gave way and the man fell heavily. Tommy kicked him on the head which had no effect at all, the motorist joined in and the battle became general with assistance from Cobden. Robinson, by the door, merely dusted his hat and waited till the conflict was over. It ended with Cobden nursing his jaw in the corner by the window, and Tommy on his face having his arms tied behind him with the cord from Arnott's dressing-gown which Mrs. Bates had left on its peg behind the door.

"Now. Once more, where's Arnott?"

"In the wardrobe," said Tommy sulkily.

The motorist threw the wardrobe door wide, Tommy wriggled round to see the body fall out once more and Cobden shrank further back into his corner.

There was nothing in the wardrobe but the clothes and the suitcase and two pairs of shoes.

"You know," began the motorist, and stopped abruptly. "That's odd," he went on. "I could have sworn that for a moment you registered surprise. Did you notice it too, Robinson?"

Robinson was polishing his glasses with a corner of his handkerchief. "I noticed it, yes," he said. "In my opinion the surprised expression was factitious. Bogus, if you prefer it." He replaced his glasses and looked at Tommy as if he were some kind of specimen.

"I dare say you're right," said the tall man. "Sammy! See if either of these two gentlemen are armed."

"Eh?"

"Frisk 'em for guns."

Neither Hambledon nor Cobden were armed, but Hambledon's coat pocket contained a narrow leather case which the tall man opened. He stood for a moment looking at the wristwatch, then showed it to Robinson who nodded.

"After this," said the man in goggles, "I suppose even you will see the folly of pretending you don't know Arnott. However, it seems as though we might manage quite well without him. I only wanted to ask him a question and I think you will do instead. Where are the rest of the jewels?"

"What's the use of my telling you?" said Hambledon. "You won't believe me."

"Your statement will be proved, naturally. Where are the jewels?"

"I'd love to see you proving it naturally. I wonder how you'd set about it?"

The motorist nodded at Sammy who kicked Hambledon in the ribs.

"Where are the jewels?"

"I don't really know with any degree of accuracy. I should think they are probably at the assessor's, being tested for substitutions. The last news I had of them was that a policeman was seen carrying them to Scotland Yard."

"You—"

"In a cardboard box," finished Hambledon.

The motorist sighed. "I see there is a gas-fire here," he said. "Robinson, oblige me by lighting it. Sammy, remove Mr. Hawkley's shoes and socks, his feet may be cold. If we warm them for him he may be more inclined to talk."

"He won't be able to kick so good, neither," said Sammy, and the shoes and socks flew off.

"You can't do that!" shrieked Cobden.

"Oh, can't we? Why not?" said the motorist. "Sammy. See to him."

Sammy took Cobden by the throat, threw him against the wall and held him there with a large revolver within an inch of his nose.

"Now," said the tall man. He took hold of one of Hambledon's ankles while Robinson took the other and they dragged him towards the fire. Hambledon fought and struggled so violently that, even hampered as he was, a notable battle ensued, in the course of which Robinson fell over the victim and was savagely bitten in the arm. At last they got Hambledon into position and held his bare feet close to the flame.

"Where are the jewels?"

There was a feminine squeal from behind them and both men started up, Hambledon shot backwards on elbows and heels and tried to get under the bed. There was a girl in the room, a fair girl with fluffy hair and blue eyes round with astonishment.

"What are you doing? Where's my boy?"

"Who is this?" asked the tall man in an exasperated tone, and Robinson answered in a voice muffled by the fact that he was holding the corner of his handkerchief between his teeth and winding the rest of it tightly round the wound on his arm.

"Her name is Miss Mary Gregory," he said. "She is the fiancée of David Arnott."

"Where is David? I want him."

"I don't know," said the motorist. "I understand he has gone away, and now will you please go too? We are busy." He crossed to Hambledon and stood looking down at him.

"And I am sure you know better, Miss Gregory," said Robinson, "than to talk about anything you see here. The consequences might be disastrous— for David," but she was plainly not listening, she was looking at Hambledon.

"Who is that man? What are you doing?"

"Will you get to hell out of here?" snarled the motorist.

"No, I won't. What have you done with David?"

"Stay, then, and see what happens to people who don't do what they're told."

"Why hasn't he got any shoes or socks on?"

"Get over there and shut up," said the motorist, and gave her a push which sent her staggering against the wardrobe. When he and Robinson once more began the tumultuous business of conveying Hambledon towards the fire-place, the relation between the bare feet and the lighted gas-fire dawned upon Mary Gregory.

"Oh, you beasts! Beasts! If you do that I shall scream the place down!"

"Please don't trouble, Miss Gregory," said Tommy, between gasps, "I shall be doing all the screaming that's wanted, believe me." He swung himself up suddenly and crashed the top of his head into Robinson's face, the manager uttered a yelp and abandoned Tommy's foot to attend to his own nose, which was bleeding, and Hambledon seized the opportunity to give the motorist a lot more trouble.

"Sammy," he said, panting. "Here."

Sammy, obedient as always, came to help and threw down his big revolver on the bed in passing. Before Cobden could move, the girl had snatched up the gun and fired off all five chambers without the slightest attempt at aiming it. Two shots went through the window with a crash of breaking glass and the other three were distributed about the room. The three men of the Vavasour gang went down flat. Hambledon's survey of the matter was blurred by the heavy form of Sammy laid across his face. In the silence which followed the last shattering bang, cries could be heard in the street below made the blowing of police whistles. The tall motorist made up his mind at once.

"Police," he said softly. "Come on. Scram, Sammy."

Hambledon's face was disburdened, there was a rush to the door and a click; the electric light went out and left the room lit only by the warm glow of the gas-fire. Rapid steps retreated along the passage as the Vavasour party retired.

"Cobden," said Tommy sharply.

"Are—are you all right?"

"Yes, don't worry. Get out and keep going, the police'll be here in a minute. There they are." The sound of someone hammering with the knocker on the front door below came clearly in through the broken window. "There are three front doors, use one of the others if there isn't a way out at the back but I'll bet there is. Get away, Cobden, at once."

"But you—"

"Get out, damn you!"

When the police entered the room a few minutes later they found a gentle-man lying on the floor with his head propped against the bed and bare feet extended towards the glowing fire. One of the constables sniffed and said: "It was here all right." Indeed, the air was heavy with the stink of cordite.

The other constable switched on the light and looked sternly at Tommy.

"What are you doing?"

"Warming my feet," said Tommy mildly. "I always do this before I go to bed. Cold night, isn't it?"

"Turn over," said the policeman sharply, noticing that Hambledon's hands were behind him, "and if you've got a gun you'll have some awkward questions to answer."

Tommy laughed and the constable rolled him over.

"Why his hands are tied behind him."

"Just untie them, will you, Constable, please?"

"Doesn't look as though it was this one as fired the shots," said the constable, and cut the cord because the knots had been pulled too tight to undo.

"Thank you very much," said Tommy gratefully, and rubbed the red weals on his wrists.

"Who fired that gun?"

"I really am not sure," said Hambledon with perfect truth. "There were a number of people here and there was a certain amount of horseplay going on. Then somebody loosed off that cannon and everybody went down flat, one of 'em across my face. When you blew your whistles they all got up and ran away."

"Oh," said the constable doubtfully, and took out his notebook. "What is your name, please?"

"James Kekener," said Hambledon, and was beginning to spell it for him when the other constable intervened.

"I don't think so," he said. "I recognize you. You are Edwin Vincent Hawkley and I am taking you into custody on a charge of being an escaped convict. You will put your socks and shoes on and I shall take you along to the station."

"Oh, very well," said Hambledon. "I never obstruct the police in the execution of their duty." He got up carefully, for he was badly bruised and his side hurt him where Sammy had kicked him. "I think I ought to tell you," he added, collecting his footwear from about the carpet, "that when I first arrived here this evening there was a dead man in that wardrobe. He isn't there now, I suppose somebody removed him—I was here all the time, too." He sat down on the edge of the bed and began putting on his socks. "I hardly expect you to believe me, but it really is perfectly true."

"Oh," said the elder constable blankly. "Can you prove your statement?"

"Not at the moment, but I expect he'll turn up. Corpses generally do. I thought you might like to look for him, I know who he was, if that's any help. A man named David Arnott."

There was a heartbreaking wail which startled them all, the bedclothes trailing over the foot of the bed heaved up and Mary Gregory crawled out, still clutching the heavy revolver which the nearest constable immediately removed.

"Great heavens," said Tommy, "I didn't know—I thought you'd gone. You poor kid—"

"David," she said, "David—"

From the street below came the sound of two cars being driven away, on was apparently an ordinary private car but the other sounded like a racing car with a powerful engine and a sharp cracking exhaust.

XI

THE CHIEF-INSPECTOR'S FRIEND

The elder constable sent his junior to telephone to the police station and report. "We will wait here till the Sergeant comes," he added to Hambledon; "he won't be long." Tommy nodded resignedly and went on tying up his shoes, Mary Gregory sat on the floor and cried and the constable stood by the door looking embarrassed. The silence became oppressive and Hambledon broke it by asking the constable how long he had been in the Force.

"Why do you want to know?"

"Oh, just for something to say."

The constable grinned sympathetically and said that he had not, in point of fact, been in the Force more than a few months and the other constable was doing his first patrol.

"I think you did extremely well to recognize me," said Tommy handsomely. "Smart work."

"Well, we're trained in recognition work," said the policeman. "You learn what to look for."

Mary Gregory blew her nose violently, threw here hair back and said: "Who killed him?"

"I don't know that anybody did," said Hambledon. "He hadn't been shot or anything so far as I could see. He may have died of heart failure or something like that."

"Then why didn't they send for the doctor?"

"Who do you mean by 'they'?"

"The Bateses. Or whoever put him in there. Why couldn't they even lay him out proper?"

"I expect that'll all come out in the inquiry, miss," said the constable.

"You must be simply bursting with questions," said Tommy, but the constable merely said they'd best wait. A few minutes later a heavy official tread approached along the passage and a Police-Sergeant entered. The constable gave a brief summary of events as he knew them and the Sergeant opened the wardrobe door and looked inside. There was certainly no corpse there. The Sergeant turned to Hambledon.

"Are you Edwin Vincent Hawkley?"

"I am," said Tommy.

"You say that earlier this evening you opened that wardrobe door and saw inside the dead body of a man whom you believe to be David Arnott?"

"That is so."

"How long have you been in this room?"

Hambledon thought for a moment. "I came to the house soon after seven and had a meal downstairs while this room was being tidied up for me. I suppose I came up here at about eight or a little before."

"And you found the body at once?"

"Soon after."

"There is no doubt in your mind that he was dead?"

"None at all," said Tommy, and added a few details. "I saw no marks of violence on him but I didn't examine him very closely."

"He might have died a natural death," said the Sergeant, and Tommy nodded.

"But who put him in there?" asked the girl

"What is your name?"

"Mary Gregory. I live here, in number nine on the second floor. David lived here, in this room."

"And when did you last see him?"

"'Bout half-past six when I come in to tea after work. We had tea together."

"Did he seem to you then to be in his usual health?"

"Yes. We was going out to dance at the Palais."

"I see. What happened next?"

"I said I'd get poshed up and he said he'd call in for me soon after eight, he'd got things to do. But he didn't come and the time went on. 'Bout a quarter to nine I come up here and found—"

"All right, we'll go into that presently. You did not see anything of Arnott?"

"No, I didn't."

"He could have left the house without your seeing him?"

"Oh yes, easy. What, d'you mean p'raps he isn't dead after all?"

"I couldn't say one way or the other at this stage of the inquiry. Hawkley, I am taking you to the station where you will be charged with escaping from prison, and I will take from you there a statement as to the events which occurred here tonight. Mary Gregory, I am taking you also to the station for the purpose of obtaining from you a statement as to what occurred here tonight, though you are not at present charged with anything." The Sergeant addressed his constables. "Take the prisoner Hawkley down to the police car, and, Benson, he will be in your charge. I see the lock on this door has been broken. Parson, you will come back here and remain on duty in this room till you are relieved." They went out of the room taking Hambledon with them. "If you wish to go to your own room for a coat and hat you are at liberty to do so, I will come down with you."

"'Ave I got go to the police-station?"

"Yes, I'm afraid so."

"Well, I don't think my people 'ud like it. 'Sides, suppose David comes back and me not here."

"Then the constable I'm leaving here can tell him. Come along."

He waited outside number nine on the second floor till Mary came out with a coat and a gaudy silk triangle tied over her hair. The police car was waiting with a crowd round it.

"Take them to the station and then come back for me," said the Sergeant, and returned indoors. As the car drove away the crowd closed in round the door and gaped at the empty hall until the Sergeant shut the door in their faces. Constable Parsons was already on duty in Arnott's room at the top of the house—on the ground floor there seemed to be no one about and the place was curiously quiet.

"Odd," said the Sergeant to himself. "Why aren't there heads poking out of every door? There ought to be heads. Where there isn't curiosity there's something worse."

He heard movements behind the door nearest to him and tapped upon it; the door opened and a man looked out.

"Can you tell me where I can find the manager of this place?"

"Two doors further back, sir, two doors further back. Number five, Mr. Bates lives." The Sergeant thanked him and went along the street to number five where Mrs. Bates opened the door with a promptitude which suggested that she had been waiting inside it.

"Yes, sir, Mr. Bates is in. Come this way."

Bates said that he had but that moment come in, he had spent the evening watching a darts tournament at the Bunch of Grapes in Lobelia Avenue. In fact, he would have been there still if his wife hadn't sent boy for him when the trouble broke out upstairs. The boy went to the wrong place first and Bates had only just started hearing about it from his wife. Most unpleasant and unusual this business was, his house being always quiet and well-conducted as the police knew perfectly well. Must have been some rowdies come in from outside, probably under the influence of drink, and fired off a gun lighthearted like. Happily it appeared that no one was hurt and one of his lodgers had seen some men run away out of the back of the house when the police knocked on the door.

The Sergeant waited patiently for the story to come to an end and then asked who was the tenant of the room where the shooting took place.

"A young man named Arnott," said Bates. "David Arnott. Very respectable. Been here a long time, hasn't he, my dear? Over a year."

Mrs. Bates said it was more like eighteen months but she could look it up if the Sergeant wished.

"And where is he now?"

"Isn't he up there? In his room, I mean?"

"No," said the Sergeant.

"Then he must be out," said Bates, with the air of one who has solved a problem.

"How do you account for the fact that the room was in fact occupied by an escaped convict named Hawkley?"

Bates was thunderstruck and so was his wife. An escaped convict! Surely not. Improbable as it must seem, the Sergeant must be mistaken.

"Your story is that you know nothing about his being there, either of you?"

They agreed.

"You would deny that Hawkley came here soon after seven and was given a meal while the room was being prepared for him—"

"He said that?" exploded Bates. "The—liar!"

Mrs. Bates said she'd often thought convicts must be a bit wrong in the head and this, to her mind, proved it.

"My dear," said Bates, "did you give a meal tonight to any stranger? Did any fresh lodger come to the house tonight after I went out?"

"No," she said. "No. We don't serve food to any but residents, and we haven't had a new one since old George Morris came in last Tuesday week."

"Thank you," said the Sergeant. "That will be all for the present, though I may have further inquires to make."

"Anything we can do," said Bates. "Either of us—can't have this kind of thing going on. Not in my house, anyway."

"Escaped convicts," said Mrs. Bates, "and gunmen. What next, I should like to know?"

The Sergeant shut up his notebook and was driven back to the police-station, where he found his Superintendent having trouble with the prisoner Hawkley who was flatly refusing to tell him anything. What is more, he had the effrontery to demand to see Chief-Inspector Bagshott of the C.I.D., Scotland Yard, at once.

"Says he's got something he'll tell him and no one else," said the Superintendent to his Inspector.

"Damned nerve, if you ask me, sir," said the Inspector.

"Yes, but there's this about it. Chief-Inspector Bagshott is in charge of the inquiry into all those jailbreaks we've had this last couple of years, and Hawkley is one of the prisoners concerned. If he wants to talk—"

"Exactly, sir," said the Inspector.

So the prisoner Hawkley was returned to his cell while permission was sought through all the various grades of higher authority right up to the Commissioner of the Metropolitan Police to call in the C.I.D.—that is to say, Chief-Inspector Bagshott—in the case of the recaptured convict Edwin Vincent Hawkley. In the meantime the local police proceeded with the questioning of Mary Gregory. She was brought into the charge-room by a policewoman who seemed faintly embarrassed because Mary was clinging tightly to her hand. There were tear-marks on the girl's face and she looked thoroughly frightened, which surprised the Sergeant. She had been anxious and unhappy about Arnott when the Sergeant last saw her, but not frightened. However, the Superintendent had a kindly manner.

"Now, Miss Gregory, come and sit down in this chair. I won't keep you any longer than I can help, but I want you to tell me all you know about what happened tonight. First of all, your name—"

Her age, her address, her occupation, had she parents living, where did they live, and so on until the steady quiet voice produced its effect. She relaxed her strained attitude and even smiled when he said: "Hampshire? So you come from Hampshire, do you? So do I. Hampshire Hogs they call us, don't they? Well, now then. You were expecting Arnott to take you to a dance tonight, weren't you? Yes, and when the time went on and he didn't come you went up to his room, is that right? Now tell me what happened next."

"The door wasn't quite shut and I could hear there was people inside so I just pushed it open a bit and looked in. David wasn't there."

"Who was?"

"Five men."

"Five? Who were they?"

She hesitated. "The man who came along in the car with me and four others."

"Did you know any of them?"

She shook her head. "No. No, I didn't. Not any of them. Never seen them before." She looked down at the floor as she spoke, and when she raised her eyes again the look of fright had come back to them. The Superintendent did not believe her, but he let it pass for the present.

"When you came to the door, were the men talking?"

"I—I don't remember."

"Try to remember. Imagine yourself just coming to the door and putting out your hand to push it open—I think you remember something now, don't you? Oh, surely. You look as though you did, you know. What was it?"

"Somebody said something, I don't know what. I didn't take that notice."

"Oh. Well, we'll leave that for the moment, perhaps it'll come back to you presently. What were the five men doing?"

This, apparently, was easier to answer. Two of the men were over by the window and one was holding up the other with a gun, "the gun the policeman took away." Two more men had "the gentleman who came along in the car with me" down on the floor with his feet bare and they were pulling him towards the fire. "I said I'd scream the house down."

She described how the man with the gun had put it down, she admitted she had snatched it up and fired it till it wouldn't fire any more. They all fell down and then got up and ran away and somebody switched out the light. Then the gentleman with the bare feet had called to the man by the window, and told him to get away quick because the police were coming. So he went too.

"When the prisoner Hawkley—the man with the bare feet—spoke to the man by the window, how did he address him?"

"Eh?"

"Did he call him by name? Did he say, 'Here, Jim!' or anything like that?"

"He called him some name," she said, frowning. "Colman, or Cobham, something like that. I can't be sure."

The Superintendent nodded as though something had pleased him.

"What did Colman or Cobham say?"

"He didn't want to go but the other gentleman made him, so he ran away."

"Let me make sure I've got this right. Five men in the room till you fired the gun and then three ran away. Right? Then one more ran away, Colman or Cobham, leaving you and Hawkley. Right again? You know, I wonder you didn't run away too after all that."

"Well, to tell you the truth my knees was wobbling so I sat down on the floor and couldn't get up again. Then when I heard the police coming I got behind the bedclothes, like, and kept quiet till the gentleman said that about—about David—"

"He said he saw Arnott's body in the wardrobe but that when the door was opened later it wasn't there?"

"That's right."

"Did you believe that?"

"Oh yes, you see—" She stopped suddenly.

"What?"

"Oh, I don't know, I just thought he—he wasn't lying. He didn't sound that way, if you get me."

"Which is more than can be said for you at the moment," thought the Superintendent, but he did not say it aloud. "If I've got the story right, Hawkley told Constable Benson that he had been in the room all the time, is that right? You heard him say that, did you? Yes, and yet the body disappeared out of the wardrobe without his seeing it go. How did that happen?"

"Does sound a bit silly when you put it like that, don't it?" she said brightly.

"And yet you believed him."

"I—I expect it was silly of me," she said, and wound her handkerchief round her fingers.

"Can you suggest any way the body could have been got out of the wardrobe?"

"No, I can't! And I think it's horrid of you to make me talk about it if—f it was David—" She began to cry.

"Well, we'll let that go for the present. Don't cry like that, it may not be true after all, you know. Cheer up. Let's go back to something else for a moment. When you first came into the room, did anybody speak to you?" She did not answer. "Oh, come on. You don't mean to tell me you walked into a room where one man was holding up another with a great big revolver, and two more men were trying to roast another chap's feet at a gas-fire, and nobody even said 'Hullo!'"

"Somebody said who was I," she answered unwillingly.

"Which of them was that?"

"I don't know."

"Go on. Who answered him?"

"I said I was David's fiancée and where was David."

"Go on."

"They didn't answer."

"Why didn't you run away then?"

"'Cause they—'cause I wanted to see what was going to 'appen."

"And they just let you stand there looking on and didn't say a word?"

"More or less," she said sulkily.

"What d'you mean, more or less? Did they speak to you or didn't they?"

"Said I could stay," she mumbled.

"Who said that? Try and speak up."

"One of 'em."

"Which one?"

"Don't know. Didn't know any of them."

"Listen," said the Superintendent. "The light was on in the room then. I know it was, because you told us they switched it out when they left, these three men. You must have seen them quite plainly. What did they look like?"

"Nothing much. Just ordinary."

"All exactly alike?"

"No, of course not. But all just ordinary."

The Superintendent gave it up, it was plainly no use trying to get a description of the three men from her.

"Now, when the two men were pulling Hawkley towards the fire, what did they say?"

"Eh?"

"You heard me. What did they say?"

"Say?"

"Listen. If a man is being tortured, ninety-nine times out of a hundred it's to make him answer some question. What was the question?"

"I didn't hear no question."

"Listen, Mary Gregory. When these three men attempted to burn Hawkley's feet they were committing a felony. Do you know what a felony is? It is a very serious offence indeed. Do you understand that?"

"'Course I knew it was wrong. That's why I fired the gun, to stop them doing it."

"Yes, I know. But it is your duty to help the police by telling them all you know, and I am quite sure you are not doing that. You must answer my questions—if not, you are obstructing the police in the execution of their duty, and that is a very serious matter indeed. Do you understand that? Answer me, please. Do you understand what I have just said?"

"Y—yes."

"And that isn't all. When these men are caught—and they will be—they will be tried on a charge of felony. If you refuse to help the police you will be committing what is called misprision of felony yourself, and will get into very serious trouble."

"T'isn't fair, then," she flashed. "I didn't do nothing wrong, it was them, and I stopped them. T'ain't right I should be spoke to like this, I haven't done nothing."

"You are doing something wrong now, you are refusing to tell me what I want to know. What question did these men ask Hawkley?"

Before she could answer a constable came in with a whispered message and the Superintendent rose to his feet.

"I have to go away for a short time to attend to something else," he said. "In the meantime, please think over what I've said. When I come back I will see you again."

It will be remembered that none of the police were in the secret of Hambledon's impersonation of Hawkley. Since it was possible that some members of the police force were involved with the people who organized the escapes from prison, and it was impossible even to guess who was implicated, the Home Secretary agreed with Hambledon that complete secrecy was necessary and had made arrangements which rendered it possible. Even Chief-Inspector Bagshott thought that Tommy Hambledon was in Germany interviewing Nazis of varying degrees of blood-guiltiness. When Bagshott was told that the convict Hawkley had been caught and wanted to see him, he fully expected to see Hawkley and hoped for some light on the jailbreak problem. He came at once to the police-station and was given a room to himself in which to interview the prisoner. Bagshott sat down behind a desk, opened his attaché-case and had hardly arranged his papers to his liking when the door opened and the prisoner walked in, followed by a constable.

Bagshott looked up and his mouth slowly opened, but the prisoner made such a truly horrible grimace at him that he shut it again. As soon as his voice was under control he told the constable to leave the room he thought he could manage this prisoner. The moment the door was shut his astonishment broke loose.

"Hambledon! What the devil are you doing here?"

"Chasing jail-breakers. I'm supposed to be Hawkley, I'll tell you all about it presently but at the moment there's something more immediately urgent. There's a dead man somewhere in that awful lodging-house, David Arnott by name, and he was concerned in the Capitol jewel robbery."

"Murdered?"

"I should imagine so, though the cause of death wasn't obvious." Hambledon gave a brief sketch of his evening.

"Oh. What a party you have had. I think the first thing to do is to get the Superintendent in and tell him about it." Bagshott summoned the constable and sent the Superintendent the message which gave Mary Gregory a respite from questioning. "Are you going on being Hawkley—I say, were you really in jail?"

"Certainly I was, I'll tell you later."

The Superintendent came in and Bagshott said: "I have got a disappointment for you, Superintendent, I'm afraid. This man is not Hawkley."

"Not Hawkley? But he admitted to my men that he was. And he corresponds to the description of the escaped convict in every respect—excuse me, but are you certain—"

"I am, but I'll prove it to you. I have got Hawkley's fingerprints here in his dossier, look. This is the official card from the Records and these are the prints which were taken when he was first convicted in 1945. Yes, well, now take this man's dabs and compare them. You'll have to destroy them afterwards, but—"

The Superintendent, moving as one who disbelieves a bad dream, opened a drawer and took out the familiar ink-roller, pad and official sheets of squared paper. Hambledon submitted without a word to having his prints taken and sat disdainfully watching while Superintendent looked from one set of prints to the other.

"There's no resemblance at all," he said. "They are not even of the same basic type."

"I was at pains to prove it to you, Superintendent," said Bagshott, "because I wanted no shadow of doubt to remain in your mind that this was a case of mistaken identity."

"Thank you, Chief-Inspector," said the Superintendent in a choked voice. "I appreciate that." He paused, turned on Hambledon and demanded: "But why did you admit it when my constable charged you with being Hawkley?"

"I owe you an apology, and your constable too," said Hambledon. "I do apologize most sincerely and I beg you to accept it. The fact is that I was in a damned tight corner in that boardinghouse and was very glad indeed to be arrested out of it. If he'd said I was Jack the Ripper I should have agreed with him."

"I see," said the Superintendent in a slightly less furious tone.

"And believe me," said Bagshott, "I sympathize very deeply in your disappointment and your constable's It would have been a satisfaction to us all to have recaptured Hawkley. I will add, also, that there is undoubtedly a strong resemblance between this man and the published photographs of Hawkley, and had it not been for the fact that I have known this man for years I might have been deceived myself. I hope you won't feel too bad about it, Superintendent, and if you manage to catch the real Hawkley nobody will be more delighted than I shall. Even in this disappointment there are compensations, because this man is a completely reliable witness and will help us a lot. There's a dead man somewhere in that house, Superintendent."

"The girl Gregory told me that this witness had said so. I was interrogating her when your message reached me."

"Get much out of her?"

"She spoke freely about this witness and a man who was apparently on friendly terms with him, but she won't give anything away about the three men who attacked them."

"She won't, won't she? Well, it doesn't matter much, Superintendent, because my friend here can tell you all about in much better than she can."

"Then if you'll excuse me a moment, sir, I'll send her home if you don't want her."

The Superintendent left the room.

"Sergeant!"

"Sir?"

"That fellow you brought in isn't Hawkley."

The Sergeant turned slowly purple.

"Did I hear you say, sir, that that prisoner is not Hawkley?"

"You did. And it's quite true, I took his dabs and they're nothing like Hawkley's."

"Who the devil is he, then?"

"I haven't been given his name, but he's a friend of the Chief-Inspector's."

"A friend—" said the Sergeant faintly.

"Of the Chief-Inspector's," said the Superintendent, nodding. Regardless of discipline the Sergeant reached for a chair, put it carefully behind himself and sank slowly into it.

XII

THE FIDDLER DISAPPEARS

Hambledon gave Bagshott and the Superintendent a detailed account of everything that happened at five Verbena Street from the time they first arrived there until the moment when the body of Arnott rolled out of the wardrobe.

"Did you know Arnott personally?" asked Bagshott.

"No, but the man who was with me knew him. Arnott was mixed up in the jewel robbery at the Capitol."

"We'll go into that later," said Bagshott. "One crime at a time—if it is a crime. We don't know that Arnott was murdered, he may just have died."

"People do," agreed Hambledon. "But why push him in the wardrobe? One point is quite clear, the Bates pair knew all about it. For one thing, his shaving-tackle, hair brushes and so forth were in there with him, they must have been put in when she cleared up the room. Unless of course he felt his last moment approaching, packed all his things neatly away in the wardrobe, climbed in on top of them and quietly passed away."

"But," said the Superintendent, "with a corpse in the wardrobe why the heck did they put you and your friend in that room?"

"That's the principal reason why it may be murder," said Tommy. "I think this. If we hadn't found him, and if the other three men hadn't turned up, I think Mrs. Bates would have found the corpse herself in the morning, let out a series of piercing screams and sent for the police. Hawkley and friend might have found it difficult to clear themselves. Again, when those three men came in, their leader asked for Arnott because, he said, Bates had told him Arnott was there. Arnott was one of their gang and though I don't think they were very pleased with him at the moment—that's a bit of the Capitol story—they would have been even less pleased with Bates for bumping off one of their pals. So we were to take the can back with them, too."

"But somebody removed the body," said Bagshott.

"Yes. I think Bates did, but of course it may have been someone else altogether. I mean, such odd things people do collect, don't they? If Bates could remove the body before the gang found it, so much the better. If not, they didn't kill him, we did. Quick thinkers, these Bates."

"I understood," said the Superintendent, "that the body was removed from the wardrobe without your knowledge although you were in the room the whole time."

"Yes," said Hambledon, "but from what I've heard about that house the problem is not so insoluble as you'd think. Certain structural alterations have been made which enable a man of retiring disposition to step into his wardrobe, shut the door after him and walk quietly out of the corresponding wardrobe in the room next door. There are also, I'm told, means of getting out on the roof which I didn't have time to investigate. Taken in conjunction with the fact that the place is really three adjoining houses complete with their original three staircases, three front doors and three back doors too, no doubt, it sounds an ideal place for a really jolly game of hide-and-seek. Have you ever sought anybody there, Superintendent?"

"Once," said the Superintendent. "The Mulligan forgers, two men and a woman. I didn't find them though they were arrested later at Woolwich. In future when I have occasion to search the place I will take a gang of furniture removers with me. When I think of those two smart alecs and their girl friend hopping lightly between wardrobes and laughing fit to burst—" His voice died away.

"Well, now you can have a thorough hunt for the body of David Arnott," said Bagshott cheerfully, "and no doubt you'll find a lot of other interesting things at the same time."

"My Sergeant left a constable on duty in that room," said the Superintendent. "We will start first thing in the morning. I am looking forward to it."

"I shall leave it to you with the most complete confidence," said Bagshott, rising.

"Just one thing more," said Hambledon. "The man and wife Bates. They also thought I was Hawkley, that's how I got in there. If I might suggest, it may perhaps be helpful if they go on thinking it."

"They certainly shall," began the Superintendent, but Bagshott broke in.

"Do you mean to imply that you were only admitted because he thought you were an escaped convict? What sort of a boardinghouse is this? A Felon's Repository?"

"Not entirely," said Hambledon. "Some or even many of his residents may be honest though I wouldn't tempt them with much. But there's no doubt the Bates have a soft corner for poor gentlemen in a little trouble, and if you can't get in anywhere else they'll do their best for you."

"Including saddling you with a nice warm corpse to explain away," said the Chief-Inspector.

"Oh, I don't suppose that often happens," said Hambledon tolerantly. "Embarrassing corpses don't occur every day, you know, even in Verbena Street,

This may even be the very first time it has ever happened, we don't know."

As the Superintendent appeared to be engaged in prayer, Hambledon and Bagshott took their leave and left him to it.

"We will now go back to my office," said Bagshott, "and then you can tell me all about it."

The telling occupied the time into the small hours and the only thing Hambledon suppressed was any reference to Salvation Savory's more illicit activities. He merely figured in the story as one who had made an abortive approach to what Tommy called "The Escapes Facilitation Company" on behalf of a brother who had sinned and was paying for it.

"This Cobden," began Bagshott.

"You let Cobden alone, he's very useful besides being a stout feller. He's my link with crime, I can't manage without him. Besides, he gave you back the Capitol jewels, remember."

"That doesn't alter the fact that he's an escaped—"

"Don't be so damned official. We're after murderers, not a harmless mug-bouncer."

Bagshott sighed and let it pass. "About your Escapes Facilitation gang," he said, "where have we got to? There's Robinson, the manager of the Vavasour Cinema and his commissionaire, Morgan."

"Also the two men who drove the balloon lorry and who tried to abduct me later," said Tommy. "I don't know their names, but—"

"We do. We got their dabs off the lorry. They are"—Bagshott referred to his file—"Harold Parker and Jonas Tetlow, convicted of smash-and-grab raiding in 1944. They haven't been out long and their tickets-of-leave have only recently expired."

"Oh. Well, you ought to be able to gather them in easily enough, or have you got 'em already?"

"No," said Bagshott.

"You can't have been trying. Then there's my tall motorist about whose appearance I can tell you nothing except that he is tall and slim, speaks in a charmingly cultured voice and has dark hair going silver at the temples. He probably drives an open sports car, though of course the goggles and so forth may have been put on just to cover his face. But I did hear what sounded like a big racing car drive away from Verbena Street after the police arrived. Then there is his friend the gorilla, Sam. That's all, unless the lady at the accommodation address in North End Road, Neasden, knows anything, but I rather doubt it. She's not worth bothering about."

"This lot at the Vavasour are a versatile crew, aren't they?" said Bagshott. "According to you there's no doubt that they are the people we're chasing for the prison breaks and very little doubt that they worked the Capitol robbery. Or do you think they are just receivers?"

"No. I think they are definitely running a crime racket and they don't even stop at murder. Do you remember the case of a man who escaped from prison and was later found murdered in a lane near Southampton?"

Bagshott nodded. "About eight months ago. His name was Edward Stone and he'd been shot."

"He was a friend of Cobden's. According to Cobden the gang wanted Stone to do some job for them and he refused. They threatened him, he threatened back and they shot him. That's why Cobden's after them."

The Chief-Inspector made a note. "I'll look into that case again at once. Of course it's still wide open as we didn't get anybody, but if Cobden's right we might get a fresh start. I should like to interrogate him about it."

"Without arresting him?" said Hambledon. "Do you think your conscience would let you? Of course you could exchange hostages and, both carrying white flags, meet in some neutral spot. I suggest the Whispering Gallery at St. Paul's because then you needn't see each other. You could each keep because then you needn't see each other. You could each keep to our own side of the dome, sit on the floor and whisper."

"In the meantime perhaps you could interrogate him for me."

"Oh, certainly. If you can clamp that on the Vavasour gang we needn't worry about their minor peccadilloes. It's my tall motorist you want though, not the small fry at the Vavasour. You weren't thinking of gathering that posy yet, were you?"

"That's for the Assistant Commissioner to decide," said Bagshott, "but I shall suggest leaving them along and watching them. He may not agree if it's really a murder case. There was the Heath case, you remember, where we held our hands for more proof and the fellow murdered another girl while we waited. A nasty business."

Hambledon nodded. "But the Vavasour gang don't kill without reason."

"You can never be sure when they may think they have a reason," objected Bagshott.

"No. That's for the Assistant-Commissioner, not us, as you remark. Well, I'm going home to bed in my own flat in my own pajamas, good night. If you want any more help from me you can have it the day after tomorrow, not before."

At seven o'clock the following morning the police moved in upon number five Verbena Street, and the burden of their song was: "Where is David Arnott?" Bates was voluble, pained, indignant and silent by turns, while such of the other residents as had not left in haste the night before didn't know anything and couldn't remember it if they did. The only exception was Mary Gregory who leaped out at the detective in charge as he was passing along her corridor, dragged him inside her room and shut the door all in one movement.

"Why are you asking everybody where David is?"

"Because we want to know, of course. Do you know where he is?"

"No, I don't. Honest I don't, I wish I did. But why are you worrying about him? You don't believe that silly story about him being in the wardrobe, do you?"

"Don't you?" asked the detective.

"No," she said, but her voice faltered.

"There was a body in that wardrobe," said the detective, and watched her turning white. "And Arnott has disappeared."

"I don't believe it," she cried, "I don't, I don't, and I hate the lot of you! Get out of my room."

He went at once and carried on with the search. At first it seemed that the wardrobe in Arnott's room was perfectly normal, no door opened in the back and no panel slid. When they came to examine the corresponding wardrobe in the next room they found fresh screws had been put in the back of it; when these were withdrawn there was a door which opened and showed no wall but the back of Arnott's wardrobe. What settled the matter beyond doubt was that there were no cobwebs such as wreathe the back of fixed furniture in even the cleanest houses, also there were more bright screws. Arnott's wardrobe gave up its mystery and Bates had some explaining before him.

"Who had the room next Arnott's?"

"We do. Me and my wife. Only this last three—no, four nights." He explained that they had moved up there out of the kindness of their hearts, having given up their bedroom on the ground floor of number five to a poor old couple who found the stairs a trial. As for any hole in the wall behind the wardrobes, he didn't know there was one. They had bought the house with the principal furniture in it and none of the wardrobes had ever been moved: "Why should they be? They was all right where they was and we used to paper round 'em, like." Asked about the indications that the doors had been recently screwed up, he said he didn't know anything about that, either. He blamed it on the previous tenant, a young man named Higginbottom who was, said Bates, a close friend of Arnott's. "Prob'ly they found out by accident due to a panel coming loose or some such, and thought it would be fun to make a way through between their rooms. You know what lads are, always up to somethink. Then he'd screw what lads are, always up to somethink. Then he'd screw them up again before he left, or Arnott did, not knowing who'd be living there next. Them screws would be fresh, it's only a week ago."

"Where is Higginbottom now?"

"On his way to Valparaiso. Got a job there. He's an electrician."

Shown similar arrangements for free passage in other rooms on other floors he said he didn't know and hadn't put them there. When you bought this old house-property you took what you found with it, good or bad. Fair sparks some of these old Regency gentry were, by all accounts, he'd read books about them. He was a great reader, they could ask Mrs. Bates. Asked about some ingenious means of access to the roof consisting of hand-grips and footholds from top-story windows he admitted to putting them there himself. "A.R.P. stuff. Fire-watching, like. When the raids was on." Told that the police were not impressed by his manner, and given the impression that they didn't believe a word he said, he shrugged his shoulders and remarked that if they held contrary opinions doubtless they could prove them.

The search continued for two days and though the police found several items which interested them—including tools of various shapes, a bunch of peculiar keys and even a couple of copper plates curiously engraved—no corpse came to light and no trace of destruction or dismembering were found. Throughout the search the detective in charge more than once looked up suddenly to see the blue eyes of Mary Gregory upon him from the end of a passage or over the banister rail of the stairs.

"She's got something to say," he remarked to the Superintendent.

"Bring her in, then," said the Superintendent, "if you think it'll be any good. Myself, I don't think she'll talk till she's convinced he's dead, you can bet she knew what he was up to and she's afraid of letting it out. If we'd found the body—"

"It isn't there," said the detective firmly. "We've found four skeletons of mice, two of rats, one of a bird, dozens of razor-blades and a ham-bone. If David Arnott, five foot eight and weighing eleven stone nine, had been there, don't you think we'd have noticed it by now?"

"They drop their razor-blades down between the floorboards, I suppose," said the superintendent thoughtfully. "I do myself when my wife isn't looking. Who's that playing a violin?"

From Verbena Street below came the sound of Dvorak's *Humoresque* rather charmingly played.

"Feller they call the Masked Fiddler," said the detective. "I've heard him several times while we've been searching here."

"Oh, him, I know him," said the Superintendent. "Supposed to have been Commander of a famous destroyer in the last war and fallen on evil days, so he wears a mask to preserve his anonymity and plays in the street for money. Very romantic, only nobody knows which destroyer he commanded and I never knew a Commander R.N. who talked with a Mile End accent. Well, do as you think best about the girl, I've got to get back to the office. How much longer will you be here?"

"Another two or three hours should see us through," said the detective.

He was walking down the stairs of the middle house soon after four that afternoon when he met Mary Gregory coming up.

"Just knocked off work?" said the detective pleasantly. "You'll be glad to hear you'll soon be rid of us, too. We're finishing here tonight."

"Have you found anything?" she whispered.

"Nothing to do with Arnott. Have you heard anything?"

She shook her head. "Not a word and I'm so worried." She looked up at him and her eyes were heavy with weariness and weeping. "I can't sleep. S'pose it was true what you said—what that man Hawkley said—about the wardrobe—"

"Well? Suppose it was, what then?"

"If I was sure it was true—"

"It was true. The man with Hawkley—the man he told to run away, re-member?—he knew Arnott though Hawkley didn't, and they both saw it. It is true, my dear, I'm sorry."

"Then I'll tell you something," she said. "Think they can kill my boy and get away with it—"

"Not here," said the detective quickly. "Come along to the station, you can talk there and not be overheard."

"I won't walk with you," she said. "If the gang saw me I'd be for it. I saw a girl once who'd talked, she'd had a broken bottle jabbed in her face. Look, I'll say I'm going to see my auntie in Fulham—I do sometimes—and go along to the station instead. Will you be there?"

"I'll follow you and then you'll be all right. Wear that bright thing you tie over your head and then I'll keep you in sight easily. When are you going?"

"I'll have my tea first, I think, my head aches. 'Bout half an hour?"

"Right. You go when it suits you, don't look round for me, I'll be there."

She nodded and ran on up the stairs while the detective went down. Hidden from him by the curve of the stairs a door below closed softly. He leaned over the balustrade but could see no one, he ran down and opened the door. It led into a sort of back hall and had a further door out into what was once the garden, but there was no one in sight. The detective shook his head anxiously but it was difficult to see what else he could have done; though the stairs were a dangerously public place for conversation the chance to speak to Mary Gregory had to be seized wherever it offered.

Half an hour later Mary slipped out of the house and walked wearily down the street; the detective in the hall of number five saw her pass. He gave a few final and clearly spoken directions to his subordinates, and added that personally he was going home to tea and thereafter to the pictures with the missis and if it was a gangster film he would walk out again. He then wished Bates a grumpy good night and went out. Mary Gregory's bright head-square was thirty yards ahead and he walked in the same direction. She reached the corner of Petunia Street and turned right, he lengthened his stride a little and followed. She was crossing the street when he saw her again and he kept to his own side of the road. Twenty yards ahead of her the Masked Fiddler was standing in the gutter playing "Silver Threads Amongst the Gold" and an elderly woman near the detective was humming it. A car which had been standing by the opposite curb moved off when the detective was level with it, a shabby saloon car but the engine ran quietly and steadily. Just as Mary Gregory reached the Masked Fiddler the car came up with them too and pulled suddenly into the curb. The tune stopped abruptly and somebody shouted.

"He's knocked the fellow down," said the detective, and started to run. Before he reached the spot a woman on the pavement screamed loudly, a grotesque sight with her mouth wide open' a door slammed and the car drove rapidly away. There was no pitiful heap in the gutter, the Masked Fiddler had gone, Mary Gregory had gone, and the only relic left was the fiddle thrown down on the pavement with the bow beside it, broken and muddy where someone had trodden on it.

"He pushed 'er in! Dropped 'is fiddle, grabbed 'er and pushed 'er and pushed 'er in! I see it meself."

"You are a witness, madam," said the detective. "May I have your name and address?"

Several other people saw it too, but most of them slipped away before he could hold them. He had automatically noticed the car's number and he wrote that down also, methodically but without hope. Cars which are used for such purposes as this have unhelpful number-plates as a matter of course.

He then picked up the violin by its strings and took it to the police station. Violins at least cannot be played with gloves on and a polished surface takes good prints. He walked straight into the Superintendent's room without knocking and said: "I've lost her," in a flat voice entirely without expression.

"Who?" said the Superintendent. "Mary Gregory?"

"I want a hurry call sent out to all patrol cars to look out for a Vauxhall saloon painted black, number RV 7053, girl kidnapped, stop and search," said the detective.

The Superintendent noted the number of his blotter with one hand, lifted his telephone receiver with the other hand and put matters in train. The detective put down the violin carefully on a side table, turned his back on the Superintendent and stood with hunched shoulders and hands in pockets looking out of the window. When the telephoning was finished he gave the Superintendent a brief and unemotional account of what had happened and the Divisional Inspector, coming in at that moment, heard it.

"The Masked Fiddler?" he said incredulously. "Are you sure? I've known the man for years."

"What d'you know about him?"

"Used to play in cinema orchestras up to about 1928 when the talkies froze him out. Plays quite well. Got odd jobs in restaurant orchestras and so on till he got too shabby and took to playing in the streets. Does pretty well out of it I believe, six or seven pounds a week unless the weather's too bad for his violin. Sound psychology, wearing that mask and saying he's come down in the world. Well, I suppose he has, but if he was ever a Commander R.N. I'm Admiral Benbow."

"Thank you," said the detective. "I'll take that fiddle with me, there may be fingerprints on it. I'll be getting along now." He picked up his hat.

"Cheer up," said the Superintendent kindly. "We'll find her."

The detective turned in the doorway. "She said she was afraid and I told her she'd be safe," he said, and went out shutting the door gently behind him.

XIII

FROZEN TERROR

Hambledon was with Bagshott in his office when the detective from Verbena Street came in, still carrying the fiddle, and told his story. He included the short account of the Masked Fiddler which the Inspector had given. At the reference to "playing in cinema orchestras" Bagshott turned to Hambledon.

"That may give us a lead," he said. "Some of the Vavasour crowd may have known the man before."

"May have," said Tommy. "There were hundreds of cinema orchestras."

Before the story was ended a message was brought in to say that a Vauxhall saloon car number RV 7053 had been noticed by a constable on point duty in Dean Street, Soho. He had not heard that the car was being looked for, his attention was attracted merely because it was being driven rather fast and a little recklessly; he automatically took its number. It was travelling south.

"That's the way you'd go to Marjorie Street if you came from Camden Town," said Hambledon. "The Vavasour Cinema?"

"Take that fiddle along to the fingerprints department to be tested," said Bagshott, "and then go along to Marjorie Street, Soho, yourself. There's a man on duty watching the place, ask him whether he saw anything of the Vauxhall or the girl. You can describe her and her scarf or whatever you call it. Telephone the result to me at once."

The detective went out and Hambledon asked what would be done if Mary Gregory had been seen going in. "Raid the place?"

"Not on this story," said Bagshott decidedly. "You must know I'd never get a search-warrant. What? She may walk out at any moment."

"I know," said Hambledon sardonically. "She may be sitting in the one-and-ninepennies enjoying Boris Karloff, or she may be having tea in the manager's office. Why interrupt?"

"But . . ." began the Chief-Inspector.

"What I really want to know," said Hambledon, "is why did the fiddler abandon his fiddle? It's his bread and butter."

"I don't pretend I like the situation," said Bagshott, "but you must know that search-warrants are not issued without clear evidence that—"

"Of course not, that's what's the matter with them in my opinion. Premises should be searched with a silent pounce if al all. Listen. If the girl was seen to go in and is not seen to come out again—"

"Well?"

"Will you withdraw your watchers tonight from midnight till five a.m. and also ensure that no flattie on his beat passes down Marjorie Street between those hours?"

Bagshott looked at him.

"Oh, they can stay at either end of the street with bent knees and truncheons drawn provided they don't interfere with the Invisible Window Cleaning Company."

"The what?"

"When windows are really clean they are invisible," said Tommy. "At least the glass is. Hence the name."

"Some of your devilments," said Bagshott. "Very well. If the girl was seen to go in and doesn't—"

The telephone rang and Bagshott lifted the receiver. After a short interval spent in saying "Yes" at intervals he added: "I agree. If nothing is seen of the girl when all the rest of the audience come out and the place shuts for the night, ring me again for further instructions. What time do they close down? Ten-thirty? Right." He replaced the receiver.

"So she did go in," said Hambledon softly.

Bagshott nodded. "Accompanied by a man in a dark overcoat such as was worn by the Masked Fiddler Our man didn't see his face. The Vauxhall dropped them and drove off again: I say 'The Vauxhall' but it wasn't RV 7053."

"It wouldn't be," said Tommy preparing to go "The driver winds a small handle on the roof and numbers change in their frames with the baffling fluidity of a bus destination panel at the end of its run. You've seen the conductors winding 'em round, haven't you? You've hardly grasped Epping before you're back at Ealing. I'll ring you at about ten to see it there's any news. Good-bye."

He went to a telephone kiosk at the nearest Underground station, and rang up Kuminboys, Parson's Close, Wimbledon Common, to ask if Mr. Salvation Savory was at home and could see him on urgent business. Mr. Savory would be delighted, and Hambledon made a rush for the first Wimbledon train.

On this occasion Savory opened the copper front door himself. Sounds of revelry coming from dining-room and drawing-room announced that a party was in progress and Hambledon hesitated on the threshold.

"Come in, come in," said Savory. "There are a few boys and girls enjoying themselves here, I am glad to say, but they can carry on quite well by themselves for a time. When you have told me what I can do to help you in any way, we can join them if you think it will amuse you. Come this way."

Hambledon followed his host upstairs to a room at the end of a passage, and was surprised to notice that Savory unlocked the door. Savory, who missed very little, saw his eyebrows go up.

"I am a great lover of cheerful company, as you know," he said, "but even the most gregarious of uncles must have a private corner to retire into occasionally. The blessings of peace, you know."

The room itself was an even greater surprise, a harmony of cream walls and brown furnishings. Three or four deep armchairs covered with hide and not too new, a big kneehole desk with drawers down both sides and a revolving office chair in front of it, a pair of bookcases filled with well-read books on either side of the fire, and half a dozen good etchings in narrow black frames on the walls; all this made a quite startling contrast to the rest of the flamboyant house. Hambledon naturally made no comment but he felt he was meeting another Savory.'

"Sit there," said his host. "I can recommend that chair. I keep whisky in this cupboard, the cigars are in this box and the cigarettes in that. Let us first be comfortable. Now, tell me all about it, or as much as you care to tell."

"When Cobden and I last saw you," began Hambledon, "we were going, if you remember, to a rather queer boarding establishment in Camden Town to look for David Arnott. It is a very queer establishment indeed." said Tommy with emphasis, and went on to tell Savory exactly what had happened there. "After the girl, Mary Gregory, had fired off that gun we heard police whistles and the Vavasour lot went away in haste. I told Cobden to depart likewise and he unwillingly obeyed, I stayed behind to be arrested, it seemed safer. The blessings of peace, as you said just now. I was identified as Hawkley and removed to the local police station where I remained until a Scotland Yard man came along and convinced them that it was a case of mistaken identity."

Savory burst out laughing.

"I was very apologetic to the police," said Tommy. "They must have been most painfully disappointed, but there was no getting away from the fact that my fingerprints and Hawkley's don't match. Besides, I'd known the C.I.D. man for years, and he kindly allowed me to follow what happened afterwards." Hambledon completed the story up to the kidnapping of Mary Gregory. "So now she is known to have gone into the Vavasour accompanied by a man who is almost certainly the fiddler who threw away his fiddle. Nobody likes the situation at all, but the police don't consider they've got enough evidence to justify a search-warrant, and the police," finished Tommy slowly, "can't and won't search places without a warrant."

There followed several minutes of silence while both men smoked and looked into the fire, until at last Savory moved forward in his chair and threw some more logs into the grate.

"Not a nice situation, as you say," he remarked "You have some further idea in mind, what is it?"

Hambledon looked at him, hesitated, and laughed. "Here is where I half expect you to throw me out," he said. "I was really wondering whether it would be possible to get into touch with half a dozen bright lads who knew a window-cleaner. A man who goes round with a small van which has extending ladders on the roof. They are usually carried on the roof, aren't they? If these bright lads could borrow such an outfit for tonight, an entry could conveniently be made through the skylight of the Vavasour Cinema any time between midnight and five a.m., and a thorough search of the premises made at leisure."

"But what will the police be doing? I take it they are watching the place?"

"Not between midnight and five a.m."

"Kind Heaven," said Savory in a hushed voice, "what an almighty pull you have got!"

"Of course," said Tommy, "all this is assuming she doesn't reappear before then. I have arranged to ring up shortly after the place closes down for the night, and if she hasn't come out before the commissionaire has gone home and the manager, Mr. Robinson, has turned the key in the big front door and walked away—"

"Yes," said Savory thoughtfully. "Quite. In the meantime I think some of the boys are here, if you will excuse me a moment I will go and bring them up here. As for the window-cleaner, there's a man who cleans the windows in this house."

At half-past one the night was clear and fine but bitterly cold. The sky was filled with brilliant stars and the light from the streetlamps sparkled in the frost which covered pavements and houses alike, for it had been foggy earlier in the day. At sunset the sky cleared, what little wind there was shifted to the northeast and the thermometer dropped sharply. One constable on his beat came to the end of Marjorie Street; normally he would have walked along it and met his opposite number at the other end, but tonight he stopped at the corner and looked down the street with natural curiosity. Nothing stirred; only a cat with its fur fluffed out to twice its normal size ran out into the road, paused, changed its mind and ran back again. Earlier in the day there had been a long narrow puddle of water in the gutter which had now frozen to hollow cat-ice; the constable pressed the edge of his boot on it for the pleasure of hearing the crisp crunching sound as the dry ice crystals broke.

He drew off one of his gloves and blew on his fingers to warm them, his breath drifted visibly away like steam. He shivered and had turned to retrace his steps when the sound of an approaching car became audible, he went back against the wall of the corner house and waited. A small van came along the road, slowed at the corner and turned into Marjorie Street: the constable saw that it had ladders neatly stacked on the top and a half-obliterated inscription on the side, "C.M.—" something illegible, and underneath "Window-Cleaners."

"That'll be it," said the constable to himself. "As though anybody'd clean windows in fifteen degrees of frost." the van went on down the empty street and round the curve in the middle, he heard it slow down and stop but it was out of sight. He listened a moment longer but there was no longer even anything to hear; he sighed and resumed his beat.

The van decanted its passengers outside the Vavasour Cinema, Tommy Hambledon rubbing his hands and hastily skipping out of the way as three young men lowered the extending ladders to the ground. The fourth young man was on the opposite pavement looking up at the façade of the Vavasour with Salvation Savory beside him pointing upwards and to one side. The tall young man came back to the van and spoke to Hambledon.

"Any idea whereabouts this skylight is, sir?"

"About in the middle so far as I could judge, and not far back."

Peter nodded. "We'll have the ladder up that end," he said, addressing his friends. "That triangular pediment across the top is probably sham and will be lower at the ends. Up with her."

They ran the ladder up the face of the building, which was not really very high, planted both feet on sacking and wedged them securely.

"I'll go first," said Peter. "Johnny, you come with me. Bill and Bob, you steady the ladder; if I whistle, Bill, you come up. Bob stays down here."

"I've got no more head for heights than an earwig," said Bob, with a comic grimace on his round face. "I was only brought to hold the steps and whisper encouragement."

"Go carefully," said Tommy anxiously. "Those roofs will be a slippery as glass tonight."

Peter, six feet up on the ladder, turned with a grin and waggled one foot at Hambledon who saw, in the light of a torch, that he was wearing thick woolen socks over his shoes. He went on steadily upwards; the silent Johnny waited till his leader was over the parapet and then followed. Hambledon stepped back into the road and watched the ladder closely.

"Shouldn't they tie it to something at the top?" he said.

"No need" said Bob, "It's got hooks, mister. They thought of that one when the ladder was made."

Hambledon retired abashed and they entered upon a period of waiting.

Ten minutes later a low entered upon a period of waiting. Ten minutes later a low whistles sounded from the roof and the redhaired Bill without a word mounted the ladder and disappeared.

The time dragged on. Bob remained leaning against the foot of the ladder with one arm hooked through the rungs. Savory and Hambledon lit cigars and strolled up and down in the road; twenty yards one way, turn, twenty yards back. The cold grew more intense till it seemed to press upon them. Hambledon shivered and Bob let go of the ladder to dance a sort of Cockney breakdown in the gutter, shoulders hunched and hands in pockets. Presently a man came along the road walking fast—all three men turned to watch him. When he came into the light of the nearest street-lamp Hambledon recognized him, it was the detective who had reported the kidnapping of Mary Gregory. He came straight up to Hambledon; Savory strolled away round the van.

"Chief-Inspector Bagshott sent me to report, sir, that we've found her."

"Alive?"

"No. She was found on the bank of the Serpentine dripping wet—that is, she had been wet but her clothes were frozen stiff. She had died of exposure, the doctor says."

Hambledon muttered something and the detective went on.

"It looks as though she'd tried to commit suicide by drowning and then got frightened, scrambled out again and collapsed."

"The cold tonight is intense," said Tommy thoughtfully.

"Yes," said the detective. "It is."

"You are not satisfied," said Hambledon sharply. "What is in your mind? Any marks of violence?"

"Nothing definite. It was only that there were two or three small things that didn't fit."

Hambledon looked at the man closely and saw that he was perspiring, which was remarkable in that temperature.

"Please go on," said Tommy gently. "I should like to hear about these small things."

The man looked down. "The Chief-Inspector noticed them, too. For one thing, she was wearing a cheap wristwatch and it was still going. Quite dry inside, it was. So the Chief took it off and dipped it in a bowl of water and it stopped at once. Full of water."

"If she waded in," said Hambledon, "she may have kept that arm above water—"

"Her head had been under water. Still, she might. Another thing, she wasn't wearing her raincoat she went out in, nor that handkerchief thing on her head. They were not found anywhere near the body."

"One doesn't naturally go out without a coat and with head uncovered in this cold," agreed Hambledon. "Still, if she ran away from somewhere—Anything else?"

"I've seen people who've died from exposure before, sir. They always look most peaceful, as if they'd just fallen asleep."

"Well?"

"She died terrified. I've never seen such a look, never. Frozen terror."

There was a movement on the edge of the pavement, and Hambledon turned to see Savory and Bob steadying the ladder while the three young men came down it, one after the other. Tommy, closely followed by the detective, went towards them.

"Well? Did you find anything?"

"She's not there, sir—"

"No. She's been found dead."

"Oh. Bad show. Down in the cellars we found this," said Peter, and pulled from his pocket a brightly-colored head-square.

"She was wearing that," said the detective.

"Oh. Bad show. It was dropped behind some junk as though somebody'd chucked it out of the way."

"I think I should like to see this cellar," said the detective politely, "if you would be so kind as to allow me."

"By all means," said Peter. "Better let me pilot you, the going's none too good on the roof." He took a step towards the ladder as the redhaired boy spoke in a slow drawling voice.

"Noticed one queer thing, water on the floor."

"What?"

"Looked like somebody'd been having a bath and upset the tub."

The detective made a leap at the ladder and was running up it before anyone could speak, and Peter followed him.

"Does the front door open readily from the inside?" asked Hambledon.

"No," said Johnny, "I tried. Key wanted."

"Oh," said Hambledon. "Tiresome." He threw away his cigar-butt, climbed steadily up the long ladder and stepped over the parapet on to the roof. The imposing front of the building was false, a mere wall, behind it the roof was flat concrete and desperately slippery with frost. Tommy made his way carefully to the skylight, now open and laid back, through which the figure of Peter could be dimly seen in the act of descending. He looked up as Hambledon came near, and said: "Good show. Mind the ice. There's flat ladder inside."

Tommy found Peter waiting for him at the foot of the ladder with his torch switched on. "You friend has gone on down," he said. "Can you see? I don't like to switch the lights on, the neighbors, you know."

"Carry on," said Hambledon. "I've got a torch myself I believe—here it is."

They went down a flight of mean stairs and came out in a carpeted corridor which Hambledon recognized. "I've been here before," he said. "That's the door of the manager's office."

"Is it now?" said Peter "Down the main splendid stairway and then—I'll show you."

When Hambledon arrived in the cellar the detective had the light switched on, not a very good light for it was one pearl bulb of low power and thick with dust. It was a large cellar and was used for storage; there were some rows of tip-up seats needing repair, several packing-cases, two or three rolls of linoleum, half a dozen buckets, some brooms and brushes and other oddments, and one very large steel cupboard with a heavy door. The floor was splashed and pooled with water and the detective was standing in the middle of the room with his hat in his hand. He looked as though he were paying respect to something Hambledon could not see. As Tommy came forward the man turned round, and the expression on his face shocked Hambledon to a halt.

"What is it?"

"She told me she was afraid," said the detective, "and she was in my charge." He cleared his throat and continued in the loud official voice of one delivering a lecture in class. "That large cupboard is, as you see, a refrigerator. In my opinion the method of murder was to bring the woman down here, remove her waterproof and throw buckets of water over her. She was then pushed into the refrigerator. There are smears of blood inside the door and the knuckles of the deceased woman are abraded. The regulator is, as you will notice, still set to freezing. That is my reconstruction of the method by which the crime was committed."

"Very original," said Hambledon evenly.

XIV

A LITTLE PETTY LARCENY

Bagshott was at his office early the following morning and spent some time reading the various reports upon the death of Mary Gregory, including an account of the cellar below the Vavasour Cinema and the deductions suggested by the evidence found there. He then had a rather uneven interview with the Assistant Commissioner who wanted to know what one of his detectives was doing on private property without a search-warrant. Bagshott said the he had only just perused the report which did indeed appear to contain elements of irregularity in procedure—

"Elements!"

Bagshott said that the operation had been organized by Hambledon of Foreign Office Intelligence, and it was more than possible that some form of authority had been issued from another source. He had not yet had any information from Hambledon himself on the subject, but no doubt—

"Look here, Bagshott, this won't do. If these infernal mystery-merchants want to break the law they can turn out the Guards or the Marines or the Beefeaters from the Tower, not suborn the police for the infringement of Regulations."

"No, sir."

"Hambledon's methods are not within my sphere of authority—thank goodness—but he must really be asked to employ other agents, not the police."

"Yes, sir."

"However, this case appears to be one in which a search-warrant can properly be issued and executed. The best thing to do now is for you to issue a search-warrant and send some of your men to discover this evidence all over again."

"Very good, sir," said Bagshott.

"And have a few words with that detective of yours."

Bagshott returned to his own room and rang up the Superintendent of the district which included Marjorie Street, Soho.

"There is reason to suspect that the death of the girl, Mary Gregory, may be due to foul play and not natural causes or attempted suicide as was thought, and there may be evidence of this at the Vavasour Cinema. I am sending Detective-Inspector Ennis there with a search-warrant within the next hour. Would you be so good as to make sure that the manager, Robinson, doesn't bolt? That is, unless he's bolted already."

"He doesn't live there, of course," said the Superintendent.

"He usually arrives at about ten, about now, in fact. I will send—excuse me one moment—"

Bagshott had several telephones on his desk for use on different lines: at that precise moment another one began to ring. He said: "All right, Superintendent, hold the line a moment, I've got another call coming through here."

He lifted the other receiver to hear a sleepy voice asking for him. "Hambledon here. I say, Bagshott—"

"Look here, Hambledon, what the devil were you up to last night? The Assistant Commissioner—"

"Has heard that one of his men was with me last night? Then why did you tell him? Of course he's annoyed, what did you expect?"

"Really—"

"Listen now, because this is important. If Robinson complains to the police about his safe having been robbed—"

"What?"

"His safe. Robbed. If he says it was, send your best man and tell him that when he's examined the said safe with even more than his usual care, he should look in the back of the second drawer down on the left-hand side of Robinson's rolltop desk. That's all. Having done my civic duty of assisting the police I shall now turn over and go to sleep again. See you later—much later. 'Bye, Bagshott."

"Hambledon" began Bagshott, but there was a click and the line went dead. Bagshott sighed and turned back to the police line to Soho.

"You there, Superintendent? Sorry to keep you waiting."

"Not at all, Chief-Inspector. You were asking just now about Robinson, the Vavasour manager. He's here, in the station."

"Indeed. Has he, by any chance, come to complain that his safe has been broken into?"

There was a sudden noise at the other end, a sound between a gulp and a hiccup, and Bagshott smiled. "Yes," said the Superintendent, having controlled his voice, "that is the object of his visit."

"Good. Keep him there, take all the particulars you can think of and all the rest of it. I'll send Ennis along as soon as possible. Right. Good-bye."

The Superintendent replaced the receiver and remarked to his Inspector that no doubt that was how one became a Chief-Inspector, C.I.D., by having second sight. "Send Robinson in," he added. "Without being clairvoyant I can at least see him."

Robinson entered, tidy, precise, with a tightly-rolled umbrella on his arm, a dark-grey felt hat in his hand and his gold-rimmed spectacles gleaming. He said in his prim vice than an outrage had been committed, the door of his room had been forced, his safe broken open and the sum of four hundred and eighty-seven pounds taken from it. One hundred pounds was in new notes from the bank and no doubt they could supply the numbers, the balance was in odd notes taken at the cinema pay-box and he could hold out no hope of being able to identify any of them.

The Superintendent expressed sympathy and said that a police officer would be ready in a few minutes to accompany Mr. Robinson to the cinema, in the meantime perhaps he would provide a few necessary particulars; his own name and address, how many staff he employed, their names and addresses, who had the keys to the building—the room—the safe, who finally locked them last night, who first opened them this morning and so forth, until there was a tap at the door ad Detective Inspector Ennis came in. The Superintendent introduced him as the officer in charge of the investigation, Robinson stood up and made him a jerky little bow. The Superintendent gave him a short account of the robbery and Ennis offered to drive the manager to the Vavasour in the police car.

"Very worrying, this kind of thing," said Ennis sympathetically.

"Very," said Robinson. "Very agitating. Very harassing. Particularly so as the money isn't mine. Being in charge of other people's assets—"

"Oh, quite. You are not the owner of the Vavasour, then?"

"No. No, I'm only the manager."

"Who is the actual owner? And have you notified him yet?"

"No, he's abroad. Travelling, on business. I don't even know where he is at the moment, I have only a *poste restante* address," said Robinson hastily.

"Then he'll have to wait for the bad news till he gets a letter, wont' he?" said Ennis cheerfully. "Well, here we are."

Outside the Vavasour there was another police vehicle already waiting, a long-bodied van painted black; in short, a "Black Maria." The manager seemed a little disconcerted and Ennis reassured him.

"Only my assistant," he said airily. "Fingerprint expert photographer and so forth. Shall we go in?"

Morgan, the commissionaire, arrived at this moment, oddly commonplace in civilian clothes instead of his gorgeous uniform. When he saw the forces of law upon the doorstep his plain disquiet almost mounted to panic and Robinson noticed it.

"Morgan!" he cried, in a prim but agitated voice. "Morgan, a most frightful thing has happened. We have been robbed!"

Ennis told Bagshott later that there was no doubt that the man's first emotion was relief. However, he responded at once with an excellent display of proper feeling.

"Robbed, sir? Good gracious, how dreadful! Who could have done such a wicked thing? Have we lost much, sir?"

"It is a very serious loss indeed," said Robinson, unlocking the door. "Come in, Inspector."

Ennis beckoned four men from the police van, one of them was a constable whom he left on guard at the door. He then shepherded Robinson and Morgan up the stairs and along the passage to the manager's office, followed by the other three policemen. No sooner was this party well out of sight when the constable at the front door opened it again to admit a Detective-Sergeant and two other men with cameras and other impedimenta who walked quickly and quietly across the hall and disappeared down the cellar stairs.

"I locked the door of my room last night as usual," said the manager, "now look at it. This was my first intimation that anything was wrong." The door was ajar and the tongue of the lock still projected from the jamb. There was the deep mark of a lever on the door itself and a corresponding mark on the side post of the door-frame. The moulding inside the frame was split and the socket into which the lock normally shot was wrenched away.

"Did you touch the door or its handle at all?" asked Ennis.

"I think not. I cannot be precise but I think not. My impression is that I rushed straight into the room. There is the safe, as you see."

The walls of the room were surrounded to a height of nearly four feet by steel filing cabinets, each drawer with its neat label in a little brass frame. One of these cabinets was evidently a dummy, for it stood wide open upon hinges like a door and revealed behind it the door of a safe, also wide open.

"There, officer," said Robinson. "You see?"

Ennis had the safe and its surroundings tested for fingerprints but there were none, not even Robinson's. The manager explained that when the outer door was shut one pulled at one of the dummy drawers to open it; the detective noticed that the fake was fairly obvious to an observant man. Ennis tried the handle of the safe and it worked perfectly, he looked at the outside and saw some deep and obvious scratches.

"Have you the key of this safe?"

"In my pocket," said Robinson, and gave it to him. Ennis shut the safe and tried the key which turned the lock without difficulty.

"Don't seem to 'ave damaged the lock," said Morgan, "that's one good thing."

Ennis made no reply, he straightened up and stood looking at the safe. Robinson explained exactly where he had put the notes and pointed out the silver which had not been taken; Ennis nodded absently and ran his fingers down the edge of the door where the jemmy ought to have left marks if a jemmy had been used.

"What is it, Inspector?"

"Very curious," said Ennis. "Very interesting."

"Why?"

"Because I have never before seen a lock forced with a jemmy without receiving damage. Like the door of this room. In fact, this safe was not forced with any instrument, it was simply unlocked."

"But . . ." said Robinson, and stopped.

"Where do you keep your keys?"

"In my pocket by day, in a locked drawer by night. At home, not here." He added, in reply to questions, that he had certainly taken them home the night before and that the only duplicates were at his bank.

"Now," said Ennis, "may I look through your desk, please?"

Robinson stalled at once; there were papers in his desk which it was most undesirable to show the police.

"Why my desk? There is nothing of any value—"

"I am sorry," said Ennis, "but I have a theory I want to verify."

The manager felt in his pockets. "This is certainly a most unfortunate day," he said. "I must have left the keys at home, a thing I haven't done since early in 1941, believe it or not." Ennis didn't. "There was a bad raid that night, this time I fear I have no such excuse—"

"I will send for a locksmith from the Yard," said Ennis. "He will do no damage, I assure you. May I use your phone?"

Robinson gave it up. "One moment—what is this," he said, fumbling. "I have them after all. Caught up in the lining—"

Ennis took them from him and rolled up the desk cover. Neat bundles of papers, docketed envelopes, pens and rulers meticulously tidy, nothing of immediate interest. He started on the left-hand column of drawers and though he detected a faint increase of anxiety in the manager's expression. The top drawer contained ledgers and account books, Ennis lifted them out, looked behind and under them and put them back. The second drawer down had bank passbooks in the front and behind that the stubs of exhausted cheque-books. Ennis raked them forward and pulled the drawer further out. Right at the back were two packets of notes fresh from the bank and an octagonal steel bar ending in a flat chisel edge, it was slightly bent four inches from the end. Ennis took hold of it with his handkerchief and drew it out, and Robinson gasped audibly.

"What on earth's that?" asked Morgan, staring.

"A jemmy," said Ennis. "Test for prints, please."

While his man was doing this Ennis picked up the packets of notes and looked at the numbers, there were seventy-five one-pound notes and fifty ten-shilling ones, one hundred pounds in all.

"Mr. Robinson," said the Detective-Inspector, "these are the notes which you reported had been stolen. How is it that I find them in your desk?"

"I—I haven't the faintest idea, I—"

Morgan looked hard at his employer.

"No prints, sir," said Ennis's assistant. "Wiped clean."

Ennis took the jemmy, walked across to the room door and compared the chisel end with the dents on the edge. It matched perfectly.

"This is, in my opinion, the instrument with which the door was forced. I have already said that the safe was not forced but unlocked; I think the scratches on it were made to give it the appearance of having been forced. This instrument was found in your desk, and so was some of the money alleged to have been stolen. Robinson, I am taking you into custody on a charge—"

"Blimey," said Morgan, "d'you mean to say as 'e's pinched the money 'imself?"

"On a charge," repeated Ennis, "of larceny."

Robinson threw down his hat and ran both hands through his hair in a wild gesture grotesquely out of keeping with his conventional appearance.

"But I didn't," he cried. "The stuff was planted there, I never put it—"

He stopped suddenly, looking at Morgan, and Ennis observed with interest the sly amusement on the commissionaire's face. Morgan had been surprised, no doubt of that, but the surprise was fast becoming derision.

"You will be able to consult a solicitor," said Ennis, "and bail will probably be granted."

Robinson's hands dropped to his sides, he glanced quickly about him and then looked at Ennis.

"I don't think I shall ask for bail," he muttered, and Morgan grinned.

Hambledon rose late, had a leisurely lunch and strolled in to Bagshott's office in the course of the afternoon.

"Well?" he said. "Did you find one large refrigerator?"

Bagshott nodded. "With the girl's fingerprints inside, poor kid. Since the manager has not been charged with murder he will be questioned about the 'frige. There's no doubt in my mind that that is how it was done."

"And how did they get the body away?"

"I have just sent for the man who was on duty outside the place yesterday evening and he will tell us. In the meantime, perhaps you'd like to tell me how you knew we should find the money and the jemmy in Robinson's desk?"

"I have recently made the acquaintance of an extraordinarily good clairvoyant," said Hambleton, lighting a cigarette. "She saw it in the crystal. No need to tell the Assistant Commissioner that—"

"I hadn't the faintest intention—" began Bagshott.

"Your man rightly considered that the safe-breaking was phoney. He looked for evidence and found it. 'What further need be sought for or desired?' Who was it? Ennis? He is doing very well, isn't he? Probably be Assistant Commissioner himself one of these days when you and I are laid up in lavender, Bagshott."

"Lavender," said Bagshott, and at that moment there came a tap on the door and a messenger to say that Crockett was there if the Chief-Inspector wished to see him.

"Send him in," said Bagshott. "Crockett's the man who was watching the Vavasour last night, he's pretty good as a rule."

Crockett came in and Bagshott said: "Now then. The dead body of a young woman was removed from the Vavasour cinema last night during your turn of duty. Tell me how it was done."

"There was nobody carried out or even helped out," said Crockett. "There was no big boxes taken out, or sacks, or anything like that. The only vehicle that stopped there later than the Vauxhall the girl came in was the van sent to collect the carpets."

"Carpets?" said Hambledon.

"Yes, sir. Just after the cinema closed and the audience had all come out, a van drove up with two men in front. They went in and brought out rolls of carpet, six or seven of them. I went across and spoke to the driver; he said the carpets had to be cleaned about once a fortnight and very often repaired too, owing to dropped cigarette-ends and so forth. They did the work at night and brought them back next morning."

"The body of Mary Gregory was inside one of those rolls of carpet," said Bagshott.

"But, sir, I spoke to him when he'd just come out with a roll and he set it down on the pavement and leant on it while he talked. It went flat in the middle and bent, as rolls of carpet do, sir."

"It wasn't in that one, that's all," said Bagshott.

"And they both went in together and left the van unattended with the rolls inside it."

"Cool hands, these," said Hambledon. "Can you describe the men?"

The driver was in no way remarkable a middle-aged man with dark hair going grey, brown eyes and a bulbous nose. Crockett gave a detailed description of him in the correct police manner, but it conveyed no recognized portrait to Hambledon. The driver's assistant was another matter; a broad-shouldered man with unusually long arms, his hands hung level with his knees. He was obviously immensely strong and took, without effort, most of the weight of the larger rolls which the two men carried out between them. He had a sullen stupid face and did not speak at all, in the detective's opinion he was mentally subnormal.

"I've met him before," said Hambledon. "Sam, the gorilla man. He did the strong-arm stuff when Robinson and the motorist fellow wanted to toast my toes at the gas-fire in David Arnott's room in Verbena Street."

"I remember," said Bagshott. "Was there any name on the van?"

"No, sir. I made a note of the identification mark," said Crockett, opening his notebook.

"You'll probably find it belongs to the Assistant Commissioner's family Austin," said Hambledon.

"You can look it up," said Bagshott, "but it's almost certainly false."

Crockett went out and Bagshott gave Hambledon the full story of the investigation of the Vavasour.

"So you're holding Robinson on a charge of fraudulent conversion while you look into the murder," said Hambledon. "And he doesn't want bail."

"The Vavasour gang think he was going off with the cash, of course. I think he's probably a lot safer in jail. What time was it when you entered that room, Hambledon?"

"What room?"

"The manager's office."

"Last night, d'you mean? I didn't go in, I only passed the door. It was shut then. That would be soon after two a.m. Why?"

"Only wondered when Robinson did the job."

Hambledon looked at him with faint amusement but only said: "D'you think he'll talk, Bagshott?"

"Not before the rest of the gang have been roped in, I think. He might talk then."

"Try the subject of aiding prisoners to escape, he might talk about that. Well, I must go."

Hambledon went to see Savory and told him that Robinson was in custody. "Morgan was in the room while the investigation was going on. Not one of our brighter citizens, but he can grasp an idea when it's handed to him on a sufficiently large plate."

"I was hoping he would be there," said Savory. "I hope he will spread the news all round the gang that Robinson was double-crossing them."

"Thank you very much for your telephone message this morning," said Tommy.

"I was pleased to be able to send it," said Savory. "A very bright boy, Peter. We really did very well out of it. Of course, he left the new notes behind for fear they might be traced to us; besides, how convincing they made the scene appear."

Hambledon laughed outright. "I have been longing to ask you how the trick was worked but I didn't like to."

"Quite simple. Peter had a jemmy with him to lever up the skylight. You pointed out the manager's room. Peter said that the cellar with the mournful detective in it made him feel as though he were intruding on someone's private orisons, so he came away quietly. Well, there was the tool and the locked door, and you can guess the rest. It was only when he'd got the safe opened and seen all the money inside that it occurred to him to put the blame on Robinson. As he said, if Robinson's going to be hanged for murder a little petty larceny won't make much odds. He won't even be asked to repay it."

"He's only got one chance to dodge the hangman in my opinion," said Hambledon, "and that is by turning King's Evidence."

Savory nodded. "A pity if he did, I think. Anyone who had even the smallest finger in that particularly revolting murder ought to be hung twice over."

"I couldn't agree more," said Tommy.

On the following morning Robinson was taken to the local magistrate's court to be charged with larceny by a servant under Section 17(1) of the Larceny Act of 1916. He was committed for trail. When the magistrate raised the question of bail he was told that the prisoner had not asked for it, and that the police would have opposed the application if it had been made. The prisoner was accordingly removed in custody. Two constables, one on either side of the prisoner, took him out by the back door of the building into a yard where a police car was waiting. The yard was a dingy asphalt square backed by a tall block of Council Schools, empty at that time because it was Saturday morning. When the prisoner Robinson was within a few paces of the police car the constables in charge heard a sound like a stick breaking; the prisoner lurched and fell heavily on his face. When they turned him over they saw that he was quite dead and there was a bullet-hole just above the right eyebrow.

XV

THE FIDDLER RETURNS

When Robinson's body was examined it was clear from the direction taken by the bullet that he had been shot from above. The school was immediately searched and in one of the upper rooms an ejected cartridge-case was found near an open window, but there was no sign of the man who fired the shot. A witness was found in the next street—that into which the school really faced—who said that she saw a man come out of the side door at that time and walk quickly away. He was a big untidy sort of man who looked like a plumber.

"Why a plumber?"

Because he had a long bundle with sacking round it he was carrying as though it was heavy, and there were the ends of a couple of iron pipes sticking out of the sacking.

"A neat way of concealing a rifle," said Bagshott. "It was a .303."

"They are working steadily through all the people who can tell us anything, aren't they?" said Hambledon. "Very soon there'll only be one left, and unless he talks in his sleep before a brace of credible witnesses we're sunk. You know, the only large untidy man in the gang whom I can imagine being mistaken for a plumber is Bates, from Verbena Road, and he'll have alibis inches deep all round him. Is anything known about Bates?"

"There are the particulars he gave when he applied for a license for his so-called hotel," said Bagshott. "He was in the Army. I looked him up the other day."

"Would it be worth while looking up his Army record, do you think? A man who could put a bullet one inch above another man's eyebrow at that range in that dark yard is a pretty fine shot."

Bates's Army record disclosed the fact that he was one of his regiment's picked marksmen and had in his day even glittered among the stars at Bisley.

"Relevant," said Bagshott, "but not conclusive. We are looking further into the matter. Our witness can't give a reliable identification, she never saw the man's face at all."

Hambledon was right about Bates's alibis for the time when Robinson died, he seemed to have spent the whole morning talking to one friend after another and always within the Verbena Street—Lobelia Avenue area. "It sounds all right," said Ennis, reporting to Bagshott. "If they were all lying it was extremely well done. There's one thing about Bates that is interesting, he's frightened. He was all over us. He wanted to know whether we were really satisfied with the search of his premises for the body of David Arnott because, if not, we were more than welcome to come and search again."

"I'm not surprised," said Bagshott. "If, as Hambledon suggests, the gang are eliminating all the people who could tell us anything about them, he must be pretty high on the list. If I were Bates I'd get myself arrested for something else."

"Unauthorized plumbing," suggested Ennis.

On the same Saturday on which Robinson was shot, Hambledon went to Cobden's lodgings to ask for news of him and found him still living there.

"No, I didn't move into other rooms," said Cobden. "Why should I? It would only arouse comment and this place isn't too bad. People always think you must have a good conscience if you don't run away. I have been keeping pretty quiet just as a precaution, and when I read in the papers about your arrest it seemed no use coming to look for you. Have you escaped again, or what?"

"Not exactly," said Hambledon. "I managed to convince the police I wasn't Hawkley so they let me go."

Cobden grinned, and Hambledon changed the subject by giving him an account of everything that had happened since they parted. "It's been a busy week, hasn't it?" he added.

"Arnott expired on Tuesday, Mary Gregory was murdered on Thursday and Robinson was shot today. Wonder whose turn it will be on Monday?"

"I suggest Sam, the gorilla," said Cobden, "but I suppose the boss keeps him under his own eye. They went off from Verbena Street together on Tuesday night."

"Oh, did they?" said Tommy. "You saw them, did you?"

"Yes. When you told me to get away out of Arnott's room I galloped downstairs and found a door at the back of the house. There are spaces behind, I suppose they were gardens once, and a path running along the bottom of them all. I ran along, too. You remember a gap in the row where there'd been a bomb? Yes, with Portal houses in it, but they didn't quite fill the gap, there was a sort of blind alley between them and there were two cars in it. When I arrived the Vavasour lot were getting into them. Robinson went off in a Morris Eight, but the tall man and Sam had a great big open tourer with a tonneau cover over the back seat. I don't know what make the car was nor the number, but it was certainly some car, Lancia or Bentley or something like that.

They started her up and went off with a roar that reminded me of Brook-lands. You must have heard it."

"I did," said Tommy, "with envy. That might be a help if anyone else no-ticed it. What did you do then?"

"Continued along the path till it came out in Petunia Street and then came straight back here."

"Turning to another subject, I have been commissioned to ask you for any information you can give about a man named Edward Stone who was a friend of yours and who was found shot in a lane—"

"Who commissioned you?"

"The police," said Hambledon frankly. "The case is still open, of course, and they think you might be able to give them a fresh start. There is a certain difficulty about their interrogating you personally, as if they actually saw you their consciences would compel them to arrest you. You couldn't expect otherwise, could you? I mean, one must be reasonable."

Cobden got up and walked restlessly about.

"In point of fact I can't think of anything that would help the police at all. I was in 'stir' myself when it happened and all I had was hearsay. The word was passed round that Ted had got his for threatening to split on the Vava-sour gang, and anyone else who thought that was a good idea had better remember Ted and think again."

"A sort of 'so perish all traitors' warning," said Hambledon.

"Yes. But you must see that though I believe myself that they shot him, I've no proof. The police must know a lot more about it than I do."

Hambledon nodded.

"And now the police have got several more recent murders to hang them for, why bother about that one? If I could help the police over this I would, but honestly I don't know anything."

While Hambledon was talking to Cobden in his shabby bed-sitting-room in the Paddington district, a certain policeman on his beat was walking slowly up Vauxhall Bridge Road. His attention was caught by the sound of a violin being played in the street and strolling violinists reminded him of the Masked Fiddler. The constable accordingly lengthened his stride and came within sight of the player. It was a man in a long dark overcoat, he was wearing a mask and he was playing "Silver Threads Amongst the Gold."

The constable blinked, looked fixedly at something else for a moment and then back at the violinist, but he was still there. What was more, other people saw him too, for several of them gave him coins. The constable walked up, touched the violinist on the shoulder and said: "Here, I want you."

The tune broke off in the middle of a note and the Masked Fiddler, with a gasp of astonishment, said: "What, me? Whatever for?"

"You come along to the station," said the constable. "There's some questions they want to ask you."

The fiddler sighed, packed up his violin and went submissively with the policeman.

Interrogated, he said that he'd been away in the country for a week, no crime in that, surely? No, he had not been playing in Verbena Street on Wednesday and Thursday of that week. He wouldn't have been anyway, even if he'd been in Town. Alternate Saturday evenings were his time for the Lobelia Avenue district, no use going oftener, the people who lived there weren't made of money. He never went to any street two days running, let alone a poor district like that.

At this point he was asked whether he would mind having his fingerprints taken as that would help to clear up the point, and he agreed at once. "You won't find them in your files, believe me." The prints were compared with those on the violin which the kidnapper had dropped on the pavement when Mary Gregory was abducted, they were totally different.

"What was done," said Detective-Inspector Ennis, "was to persuade you to go away for a week while somebody else impersonated you. Now, will you tell me all about it in your own words, every little thing you can remember?"

"What's behind all this?" asked the fiddler, no longer masked.

"Murder," said Ennis.

The fiddler whistled. "Well," he began, "it was like this—"

There was an old gentleman who had passed him twice in one day when he was playing in the Wigmore Street area, and each time he passed he put five shillings in the fiddler's cap. The first time he just said: "Thank you," the second time he said: "You can play. It's a pleasure to hear you. You must come and play to me at my little place in the country."

"When was this?"

"Tuesday. Yes, Tuesday last. Seems longer when you've been away."

The old gentleman went on to say why not then, at once? That very evening. Terms: board and lodging and one pound a day, just to play for an hour night and morning. Yes? Splendid, splendid. He paid the fiddler three pounds in advance and said he would send his chauffeur and the car into Wigmore Street to pick him up within the next half-hour. "'I am a man of impulse,' he says, 'and I can afford to indulge myself.' So off he goes and I went on playing. Half an hour later up comes a nice saloon car and the driver says he's been sent to fetch me. So in I gets and off we go."

"Just like that? You didn't hesitate, or think it a bit queer, or anything like that?"

"No. Bit unusual, that's all. 'Course, I thought he was bats but it didn't worry me. Country holiday and all paid, just my cup o' tea."

They drove out of London by the Great North Road, turned off into lanes at Welwyn and then dodged about his way and that. Darkness fell early and the fiddler did not know where he went. Presently they drove in through some gates, up a drive and into a stable-yard. The driver unlocked the back door and took the fiddler into a big kitchen. He lit a lamp—"very countrified it was, only oil lamps"—put a match to the fire and filled a kettle. They had a good tea with sausages and went to bed. Next morning they got up and had breakfast. "I said was it now I was wanted to play but the chauffeur said not yet, the old gentleman had one of his bad turns and we'd better wait. Tomorrow, perhaps." After that he spent the day in the garden or indoors by the fire, had supper and went to bed. "All the days were like that." On Friday night the chauffeur said that would be all and he would take the fiddler back to Town. "He paid me another couple of quid, I got in the car and he drove me up to Town and dropped me in Edgware Road. I just went home and went to bed. This afternoon I come out again and it being my day for Vauxhall Bridge Road, to Vauxhall Bridge Road I went. That's all. Except that I never did play my violin to the old gentleman after all. Queer, don't you think?"

"There may be an explanation," said Ennis, "Didn't you ever see your old gentleman again?"

"Not a hair of him, mister. He was upstairs somewhere."

"Ever hear him moving about? Did anybody take meals up to him?"

"No. The chauffeur said he was a bit of an invalid at times, like, and when he'd got one of his bad turns on he 'ad—had—to stay in bed. He'd got a manservant waiting on him, the chauffeur said."

"Ever see the manservant?"

"No. I reckon he must have had a sort of flat on the first floor, self-contained like, they didn't need to come down for anything."

"What was the rest of the house like?"

"Don't know, mister. Never went beyond the kitchen and the blinds was all drawn at the windows."

"Where did you sleep, then?"

"In the kitchen, me and the chauffeur. There was a couple of camp beds. Cozy it was, with the coke fire in the grate all glowing when the lamp was out."

"And the kitchen was the only room you ever saw?"

"There was a sort of scullery where we washed, and a coal-cellar across the yard. That's all."

"And what was the country around like? Was there a village?"

"Don't know. Never went out. You see, it was a big garden, awful neglected, with 'igh walls all round and the gate was locked. No, I didn't go out. Didn't want to, really."

"How did you manage for milk?"

"Tinned. All tinned food bar a few veges out of the garden."

"Newspapers?"

"Wireless."

"And you didn't see anybody but the chauffeur all the time? Not even the postman?"

"Not a soul, sir. The postman didn't come to my knowledge."

"Didn't you think it was rather queer?"

"Well, yes, but it didn't do me no 'arm—harm—it's nice to have a rest sometimes. Hard on the feet is playing in the street."

"I expect so. What did you and the chauffeur talk about all the time?"

"Oh, this and that. We didn't talk much. The wireless was on a lot and we played cards, evenings. The weather was dry, mostly, and I did a bit in the garden. Cleared up a bit and that."

"I see. Did you make a bonfire?"

"Funny you should ask that. I was goin' to, but the chauffeur said not, the smoke would worry the old gentleman."

"What was his name?"

"The chauffeur's? He said to call him Jim."

"I meant the old gentleman, really."

"Mr. Smith."

Detective-Inspector Ennis sighed.

"Are you quite sure you didn't see an address on anything lying about? On an old newspaper or a box used to keep something in?"

The fiddler's face lit up. "Ah, now. One night the B.B.C. was giving out the results of a voting competition for the twenty most popular tunes and I thought to myself I'd better write them down, they'd be useful to me. I looked round all in a hurry for a bit of paper—I'd got a pencil—and all I could see was a label on a packing-case the tinned stuff came out of. So I tore it off quick, it was nailed on, and wrote on the back."

"Have you got it?"

"No. No, I'm sorry I 'aven't. I put it up on the mantelshelf and in the 'urry of leaving, Friday, I left it behind. But I remember most of the titles."

"Well, that's something," said Ennis, "but can you remember the address on the label?"

"No. I can't recall even looking at it. Sorry, if you really wanted to know."

"What I am trying to get," said Ennis patiently, "is some sort of a hint as to where this house is. Can you remember any little thing, such as trains in the distance—"

"No, mister. No trains."

"Or traffic on a main road, or church bells, or a clock chiming the hours, or anything to suggest there was a town anywhere near?"

"Never heard nothing but cows mooing some way away. For all I 'eard we were fifty miles from everywhere. There was only one thing I 'eard, or thought I did, and I put that down to 'allucination."

"What was that?"

"The second evening I was there, that was Wednesday, just before the six o'clock news. We was just going to have tea and Jim asks me to go out in the scullery and rinse out the teapot. Well, I was just giving it a wipe round with the cloth when I thought I 'eard a siren blowing the 'All Clear.'"

Ennis cheered up at this for he knew, as the fiddler evidently did not, that the Air Raid sirens are still retained in many country districts and the steady note once used for the All Clear is sounded to call out members of the Fire Brigade whenever there is a fire in the neighborhood. Records are kept of fire calls and it would be possible to find out where such a call was sent out at a certain hour on a certain day.

"On Wednesday?" he said, making a note. "Sure of that? Good. And just before the six o'clock news?"

"I was still standing there," said the fiddler, "with the teapot in one 'and and the lid in the other thinking what a fool I was to think they still had sirens now, when I 'eard the six pips on the six pips on the wireless in the kitchen and Jim calls out 'Come on, here's the news.'"

"And that was the only bit of real help I got from him," said Ennis, reporting the interview.

"I wonder you got that," said Hambledon, from his chair by Bagshott's desk. "My own experience of musicians leads me to believe that they are—er—extra-mundane is, I think, a polite way of putting it. I wonder he didn't tell you that he'd heard G sharp on a wind-instrument. You'd probably have asked him if he saw bright spots before the eyes at the same time."

"Perhaps he's no so much of a musician as all that," said Bagshott. "Well Ennis, they've had twenty-four hours to clear their things out of the house and probably they did it last night, after dark. It wouldn't take them long; there's very little doubt in my mind that the furniture the fiddler saw in the kitchen was all there was in the house. A large empty house, probably, and I don't suppose they asked permission to go there. He was told not to play his violin, of course, for fear someone passing by might hear it; and the same reason applies to being forbidden to light his bonfire. Somebody might have seen the smoke. That's why they burned coke in the kitchen range, too. I expect the stuff is all out house ago, but I am hoping that when they were clearing up in a hurry by the light of an oil lamp they didn't notice a scrap of cardboard on the mantelpiece. Put an inquiry through about the fire-call just before six on Wednesday last and we'll see what we get."

The town of Bishop's Stortford, near the border of Hertfordshire and Essex, admitted to having sounded the fire-call on that Wednesday night just before six p.m. Asked further which way the wind, if any, was blowing at that time, they said there was a steady westerly breeze with occasional gusts. The fiddler's holiday resort was, therefore, probably east of Bishop's Stortford and might be five miles away or even more.

Ennis went to Bishop's Stortford and conferred with the local police. There were a fair number of biggish houses in the neighborhood which had been taken over by the military during the War; most of them had been released and many were still empty awaiting conversion or repair before their owners returned. Ennis, armed with the fullest details the Masked Fiddler could supply, was able to eliminate all but three, and a police car took him and the Superintendent on a tour of inquiry. The first house they came to answered the description, there was even the fiddler's unlit bonfire piled up on what had been a herbaceous bed. The back door needed no key for it was unlocked; they passed through the scullery with a pile of empty food tins in the corner into the empty but unswept kitchen. On the mantelpiece there was a piece of thin card torn on two sides where it had been hastily dragged from its staples. It bore a typewritten address, or what was left of it. "—ford, Grocers. High Street. Mark."

XVI

DAVID FROM MARY

Mark presented no difficulty since there is only one in England and that is in Hampshire. The grocer also was obvious since there was only one in the High Street, his name was Cinderford and his house adjoined the shop. When it came to identifying the last owner of the wooden case from which the label been torn it was quite another matter Mr. Cinderford arranged his spectacles carefully across his face and examined the card.

"Looks to me, by the typing, like a case from the Fray Bentos corned beef people, but when I had it is another matter altogether. We don't retain these cases now; as no doubt you know, Inspector, they are charged for if not returned, not like the old days before the war when we used to crack them up and sell them for kindling. Or sell them whole for a few pence if anyone wanted a box. You see my pint yes, we have a few in the shop we use for packing up the orders for outlying houses but we don't part with them, not if we know it. Too scarce. Besides, they haven't got lids and you say this label came off the lid. You see my point. If this box had a lid it was possibly— probably—prewar. Might be years old though the label isn't very dirty, if it had been kept in a cupboard or some such place. Might have passed from one person to another several times with different things packed in it. You see my point. Nice strong boxes, they were."

"I see," said Ennis. "Although this was certainly your box at one time, it may have been a long time ago and may have traveled almost anywhere in the meantime. Yes. But this was the only label on it."

"But if a case is taken away in a furniture removal with a family moving to another house," said Mr. Cinderford, "it wouldn't have a fresh label on it. Nor if it was taken somewhere in a private car. You see my point."

"Oh, absolutely," said Ennis. "Do you not then, ever send whole cases of tinned stuff, complete as they come to you, to any large establishments like schools or hotels?"

"Oh, yes, we have a few large customers who do take whole cases even today," said Cinderford. "But not wooden cases today. Cardboard. Reinforced cardboard like this, look, but still cardboard. Not wood. I am so sorry not to be more helpful—"

"I see your point," said Ennis thoughtfully, and went back to the mark police station where the Superintendent sympathized kindly.

"Not that old Cinderford would have had so many large customers, as he calls them, before the War," he said. "There was a very good-class grocery store in Unicorn Street in those days, just opposite the Unicorn Hotel. It was run by a nice old chap everybody liked and a good tradesman too, most of the gentry dealt there. Then he died and his daughter sold the business to one of these multiple grocers not everybody likes, and Cinderford got quite a lot of his business."

"I seem to remember, before the war," said the Mark Inspector, "that about the only big place which dealt with him was Quietude."

"Quietude?" said Ennis. "What's that?"

"It's a place where they cure inebriates," said the Superintendent, "or try to. It's a well-conducted place, only takes high-class inebriates."

"Old Cinderford," said the Inspector, "used to say he was one of the few men in England who made money lawfully out of drink without holding a licence."

"'If you see my point,'" murmured Ennis.

The Superintendent laughed. "Catching, isn't it? I said just now that Quietude is well conducted, so it is, but it's just given us our biggest puzzle for years, hasn't it, Murdoch?"

"It has indeed," said inspector Murdoch.

Ennis was not really interested since he had quite enough puzzles of his own to satisfy any reasonable man, but he had an hour to wait for his train and mere politeness dictated a show of attention. He asked what the puzzle had been, "if it's not confidential."

"Quite the reverse. It was last Wednesday morning early, soon after eight, when we were called out to Quietude on a case of sudden death. When we arrived there were two dead men in the garden, sitting side by side on a garden seat. At least, one was sitting up, the other was lying against him with his head against his shoulder. The p.m. showed that they'd both died from a narcotic poison and they were both quite stiff—it was a very cold night. One was easily identified, he was one of the inmates, but the other was a total stranger and we haven't so far, been able to trace him. There was a whisky bottle on the ground where it had slipped off the seat, it still contained a small amount of whisky heavily doped with one of the barbiturates. Of course, the case has only just started, but so far we've no information at all as to where they'd got the drink, when or by whom it was doped, or, as I said, anything about the stranger."

"I expect you've got some ideas, though," said Ennis.

"Possible suggestions but no proof to support them. You see, this place isn't prison, all the patients go there voluntarily for treatment just like a hospital for any other sort of disease. In fact, a Hospital for the Treatment of Alcoholism is its official title. So it's not impossible for the patients to slip out and have one at the local, and it does happen, though not so often as you'd expect."

"I should have thought they'd be always slipping out," said Ennis, "if it's as easy as that."

"I said as much to Dr. Grainger, who runs the place, but he said no. The treatment is designed to stop the craving for drink and he says he can do that while they're under his charge. They don't want drink while they're there. At least, that's what he says. It's the danger of relapsing when they are out in the world again that worries him."

"But apparently this patient wasn't so good," said Ennis, glancing at his watch.

"Hadn't been there more than a couple of days. Whether he slipped out, met the other man by appointment and brought him back into the grounds so that they could drink without being interrupted; or whether he was just someone the patient had chummed up with in some pub, we don't know. There's no evidence obtainable from any licensed premises within easy reach of Quietude that either of 'em had been served that night."

"Then I should think your first suggestion is right, and the stranger came from somewhere else bringing the binge elements with him," said Ennis. "The case certainly seems a bit queer at present, but no doubt you'll break it before long. Well, I must go and catch my train I'm afraid. Thank you very much for all your help."

Hambledon listened to Ennis's report with discouragement and Bagshott said that they didn't seem much further forward. "The blighter certainly covers up his tracks well, whoever he is. I've a good mind to bring in that fellow Morgan, the commissionaire, and grill him again."

"This unidentified corpse," said Hambledon.

"I suppose you could usefully look through the photographs of every unidentified corpse found in Great Britain during the past week," said Bagshott. "After all, there aren't so many of them."

"But this particular one comes from the place where the box possibly came from, which the Masked Fiddler sat on in that house near Bishop's Stortford, where he didn't play his violin—"

"That frightened the cats, that ate the rats, that lived in the house that Jack built," said Bagshott, "You think it may be Arnott—"

"Not think." corrected Tommy. "Hope. I take it there'll be a photograph of the deceased among your confidential papers?"

"Go and get it, Ennis, please."

When Ennis returned with the rather ghastly photographs of the dead men in the garden of Quietude, Hambledon looked at them carefully, threw down on Bagshott's desk and said: "Yes, that's Arnott all right."

"You're quite sure? Good. Well, I'm going down to Quietude to stir them up a bit, are you coming?"

They paused at the police station at Mark to pick up the local Superintendent. Once the police car had turned off the busy Portsmouth Road it passed through narrow lanes with trees meeting overhead and high banks on either hand. Presently they came to a couple of cottages with oast-houses behind them; a pond and a large barn; a small ancient alehouse, The Hampshire Rose, and a letterbox set into a well and still bearing the venerable initials V R. Bagshott pointed it out.

"Yes," said Hambledon. "We bain't 'asty in 'Ampsheer. Do you suppose the Hampshire Rose is where the inebriates illicitly repair?"

A garden fence enclosing an area given over to nettle and cow-parsley and backed by a small ugly brick house with a slate roof. The house looked neglected, but there were curtains at the closed windows and wheel-tracks up a short drive to a group of outbuildings. Hambledon looked at it in passing but his attention was at once diverted by the high brick wall of the adjoining property. They came to a white gate in the wall with a lodge beside it; on the gate there was a name painted: Quietude.

"Very appropriate," said Hambledon. "In fact, I suppose that unless the inmates let out a few whoops themselves nothing but the cry of a passing sea-gull ever breaks the stillness."

A woman ran out from the lodge to open the gate and the car passed up a long drive between grassy slopes planted with small trees. There were fixed seats here and there; the Superintendent from Mark pointed out one of these and said that that was the one upon which the dead men had been found. The house was a large and cheerful-looking red brick building with wide windows towards the south and a glassed-in verandah where several men were sitting, one of them rose to his feet and went indoors as the car slowly passed.

The police party were admitted at one and shown into an oddly-furnished room between office and consulting-room. Dr. Grainger came in almost at once, a fat short-legged little man with a rosy face and a bald head. The Mark Superintendent introduced Bagshott and Hambledon, and an expression of humorous concern crossed the doctor's face.

"Really," he said, "a terrifying posse. Whatever can have entitled me to this honor?"

"You had two dead men on the premises last week, doctor," said Bagshott. "You must have expected a certain activity on the part of the police."

"Well, yes, but I thought I'd told the Superintendent all I knew. However, if there's anything more I can do . . ."

Bagshott asked for every detail available about the patient whose dead body was found beside Arnott's. His name was Parkinson and he had only been there two days, he came from Cumberland. "An interesting case, if I had been able to persevere with it, gentlemen, but I expected difficulties. A very long-standing history of alcoholism coupled with a hereditary tendency that way. The poor man had spent most of his life in a remote part of the fells and for the last five years had never gone beyond his own garden gate. Increasing distaste for company amounting to reclusion—great difficulty was experienced in inducing him to undertake the journey—"

"Who identified the body?"

"I did," said Dr. Grainger, and his eyebrows went up.

"Did you know the patient before he came here?"

"No but I received an account of the case from his own doctor," said Grainger, and added the name and address. "He traveled here with poor Parkinson. May I be allowed to ask the point of these questions?"

"We are trying to find out whether there was any connection in life between the two deceased men."

"Do you know who the other one is, then?"

"We have an idea," said Bagshott. "It will have to confirmed, naturally."

"An exhumation, I suppose," said Grainger.

"Possibly." Bagshott asked for the list of the inmates in residence during the previous week and also of the staff employed on the property, but none of the names suggested anything either to him or Hambledon. "May we go over the house, if you have no objection?"

"Absolutely none. Look in every room—and every cupboard if you like. I'll take you round myself."

"Are all your patients on the premises at the moment?"

"I don't suppose so, by any means. This is not an asylum and I encourage healthy exercise such as walking, playing golf, and boating on the river. That's not so popular in winter, naturally. There is, however, an unostentatious list kept at the lodge of patients going out."

The doctor started Hambledon and Bagshott on a thorough tour of the house and into every room, including bathrooms, storerooms and linen-cupboard. Hambledon soon tired of it and said he would have a walk in the grounds if nobody minded. Nobody did, so he strolled out, leaving Bagshott striding slowly along corridors behind the doctor's pattering feet. When eventually the Chief-Inspector had convinced himself that the whole place was an honest concern openly run, in which nobody was trying to conceal anything and that he was wasting his time listening to the doctor's theories and methods of cure, he took his leave and returned to the car, expecting to find Hambledon there. He was not. The Superintendent was sitting in the car looking patient behind the police driver looking wooden, but that was all.

"Have you see Mr. Hambledon?" asked Bagshott, but they had not. "I suppose he's in the ground somewhere, I hope he won't be long. I've got to get back and I expect, Superintendent, you want to, too."

"I have a few jobs waiting for me," admitted the Superintendent. They waited some time and then instituted first inquiries and then a search. Hambledon had not gone out at the only gate and he was nowhere in the grounds.

Bagshott led the search accompanied by the Superintendent, with Dr. Grainger trotting voluble in the rear. As though a brace of corpses wasn't enough in itself to give the place a bad name without persons, doubtless of the highest importance, disappearing in this unaccountable manner—there was a toolshed behind the greenhouse, perhaps that—no—really, events were becoming almost met a couple too much—

Bagshott met a couple of patients and inquired if they had seen a man—he described Hambledon—anywhere about, and they said they had noticed him going quietly into the shrubbery beside the wall. Asked whether they had seen any more of him they raised their eyebrows and replied that, on the contrary, they had tactfully looked the other way. Bagshott worked his way into the shrubbery, an overgrown blend of rhododendron, laurel and aucuba running close to the wall like a screen. He knew well enough what Hambledon was looking for. Arnott was dead before ever he came to Quietude so he must have been carried in somewhere. One does not heave a limp corpse over a seven-foot wall with spikes on the top—at least, not without leaving traces. The gate as locked at night and was too near the lodge for anyone to take the risk of introducing Arnott that way. Therefore there was another entrance and eventually Bagshott found it; a door in the wall. He ducked under a laurel to reach it and his face fell. The door was fastened with a couple of iron bolts immovably rusted in place, moreover it and its doorposts and lintel were thickly coated with cobwebs in a manner which testified that it had not been opened for years, let alone within the last half-hour.

"That door," said Dr. Grainger, "yes, I'd forgotten that door, but it's never been opened since I've lived here and that is over seven years. I understand that at one time these properties were one and probably the adjoining house—"

"Superintendent," said Bagshott, and pointed with his finger to the joint between the doorposts and the brickwork against which they abutted. There were no cobwebs across that joint and the Superintendent's eyebrows went up.

"We'll have it open, I think," said Bagshott. "You and I, Superintendent, one two, three—heave!"

The two heavy men crashed their shoulders against the door which opened in one piece; posts lintel and all. They staggered in and found themselves in a narrow twisting path through just such a shrubbery as the one on the Quietude side. The doctor uttered exclamations of surprise and was imperatively hushed.

"Come on," said Bagshott, and ran along the path with the Superintendent lumbering behind. They came into a yard at the back of the house, the back door of the house was locked and all the windows bolted.

"You knock on that door, Superintendent, I'm going round to the front," said Bagshott, and ran round the house to the accompaniment of a loud tattoo from the back door knocker. A minute later the front door knocker added to the noise but there was no reply from the silent house.

"Superintendent!" called Bagshott.

"Sir?"

"Come on round."

He went, with Dr. Grainger trotting behind saying he did hope nothing had happened to the poor old professor.

"We'll see about him in a minute," said the Superintendent, and rounded the corner to find Bagshott looking at the stable doors, which were wide open, and down the drive to the entrance gate which was open also.

"That was shut when we came along," said Bagshott. "The whole place was shut up."

"That is so," agreed the Superintendent, and pointed to a patch of grass on the weedy drive. It showed the mark of a tire upon it and the stiff thin stems were slowly straightening themselves as the men looked at it.

Only just gone," said Bagshott softly. "I'm going inside that house, Superintendent. Who lives there? Does anyone?"

"Professor Jeremy Carnoustie," said Dr. Grainger. "A retired professor of physiology from one of the northern universities, I understand. Something of a recluse, I never meet him to speak to though I saw him in the distance once or twice. He may be a way from home, he often is."

"Do you know him, Superintendent?" asked Bagshott operating with a knife on one of the ground-floor window catches.

"By sight, only never spoken to him. Elderly gentleman, tall, stooping, white beard and whiskers. Very hairy gentleman. Can I give you a leg up?"

Bagshott stepped over the windowsill and a moment later opened the front door. "Come in, Superintendent. Dr. Grainger, if you wouldn't mind waiting outside a moment—"

The door shut and the Yale lock clocked into place. The two policemen made a rapid search of the ground floor and found evidences of a struggle in the kitchen in the form of wet patches on the floor, smashed crockery hastily swept into the fender and a chair with a broken leg. The house was shabbily and scantily furnished upstairs and down but was clean and tidy enough. Of Hambledon and the whiskered Professor there was no trace.

"Outside," said Bagshott, and led the way to the stable, brushing off, as it were, in passing, the plump from of the questioning doctor. "What was the number of the Professor's car, do you know?"

"No, I don't. He has been seen to drive an open sports car, rather a big one, a Lancia—"

Bagshott halted in his stride, stared at the ground a moment and said: "Dear me. You don't say so."

They went into the stable which was much more spacious than one would expect because the partitions had all been removed. At the further side there was a large object covered with a rick-sheet. Bagshott dragged it off and disclosed a big open Lancia with a tonneau cover fitted to the back seats.

"That it?"

"I believe so."

Bagshott began a quick but thorough examination of the car with the help of a pocket torch since the stable was obscurely lighted. There was a rug in the back of the car, under it the carpet was rucked as though something heavy had been dragged out. A small bright object slid from a fold in the carpet; Bagshott picked it up and looked at it.

It was a flat silver case made to contain book matches and inside the lid was engraved: "David from Mary."

XVII

QUIETUDE

Bagshott was under no illusions about the danger Hambledon was in, this gang were killers; if they had not hesitated to murder Mary Gregory because she knew something and might talk, and Robinson because he knew everything and still might talk, there seemed little chance for Hambledon. The neighborhood of Quietude was examined, cross-questioned and sifted. Bagshott himself was with the Superintendent of Mark when somebody came in with a small boy who had been in the road with a bicycle that afternoon at the moment when Professor Carnoustie came down the drive and opened the gate. Yes, the garage doors were open and there was a car inside, a dark-colored saloon car. No, he couldn't remember the number, seemed like it wasn't too plain. Muddy, like. Ordinary-looking car and he didn't know the make. Besides, he was looking at the old gentleman, especially after he asked him in to see the kittens.

"Kittens?" began the Superintendent, but Bagshott stopped him with a gesture.

"What did you do then, Sonny?" asked the Chief-Inspector.

"'Opped on me bike and rode away. I—I didn't want to go in."

Bagshott nodded thoughtfully and then asked the boy's mother if he had a money-box. When she said he had, the Chief-Inspector rose from his seat and gave her something that rustled to put into it. Mother and son prepared to leave in a haze of voluble thanks.

"Don't thank me, please," said Bagshott.

"Who should I thank but you?"

Bagshott started to answer and checked himself. "Listen, Sonny. If ever you see that old gentleman again anywhere, don't go near him, just cut straight off as hard as you can pelt and tell a policeman. Any policeman. See? Run along now."

"What's he done, mister? Murder?"

"Dear me, no," said Bagshott. "He just isn't a nice man, that's all. Good-bye."

As the door closed behind them the Superintendent said: "There weren't any kittens anywhere there. Not even a cat."

"There weren't, were there?" said Bagshott evenly.

The Superintendent looked straight before him for a moment.

"When that man's hanged," he said at last, "I'll take a day off to go and see it."

The only other item of helpful interest on the premises next door to Quietude was a case of Three Roses whisky, still half-full. Bagshott remarked that it was an American brand, one didn't often see it in this country.

"I have," said the Superintendent. "Once. That bottle with the doped whisky in it Quietude garden, that was a Three Roses bottle."

"Any fingerprints?"

"Only Parkinson's."

Two days after Hambledon disappeared there was a conference at Scotland Yard. The Assistant Commissioner, who was Bagshott's immediate superior, intimated firmly though reasonably that he would like to see results. So far they had had the man David Arnott poisoned, the Quietude patient Parkinson also poisoned, the woman Mary Gregory murdered, the prisoner Robinson shot dead and the F.O. Intelligence Officer Thomas Elphinstone Hambledon abducted. He—the Assistant Commissioner—had had a personal telephone call from the Home Secretary on the subject of Hambledon. He sighed and drew cats on his blotting-paper.

Bagshott said that all available lines of inquiry were being followed. He himself had interrogated the commissionaire, Morgan, twice in connection with the murder of Mary Gregory at the Vavasour cinema. He merely said he didn't know anything about it or about anything else beyond his duties, and he kept on saying it. It was a fact, on the evidence the van came to the cinema and removed the carpets and, presumably, the body of Mary Gregory. Actually, it was not likely that he had had any hand in the murder itself as he was not likely that he had had any hand in the murder itself as he was on duty at the entrance during the time it must have taken place. The police watcher said that Morgan had been on view almost continuously at the material time. It was just possible that Morgan was speaking the truth. He was merely and employee of a rather low grade of intelligence and might not have been told anything about it.

"Does he remember Mary Gregory passing through the vestibule?"

"He says not, sir. There are so many girls, he says. He was taken to view the body and said he didn't remember ever having seen her before."

"The other employees—the usherettes or whatever they call them?"

"They don't remember her either. But if she did not enter the auditorium but was taken straight down to the cellar, they may not have seen her."

"Didn't anyone see a man and a girl—or two men and a girl—go towards the cellar stairs instead of towards the auditorium?"

"We can't find anyone who did, sir. They probably waited for a moment when no one was passing."

"It's a nasty case," said the A.C. "Particularly beastly. I keep on trying not to call it cold-blooded because it's too damned appropriate. You did not interrogate Morgan about the concealed cupboard where the Capitol jewels were found?"

"No, sir. You said you thought it better that they should not know we had that line on them."

"Quite right. I still think so. Now, about that lodging-house keeper, Bates."

Bates had been brought in for questioning after the second corpse in the Quietude garden had been identified as David Arnott. "He expressed extreme surprise and, what is more, he looked surprised. I must say I thought he really was. He said he'd never heard of Quietude and that sounded like truth, too. He denied knowing anything about Arnott's death; that was a lie and sounded like it. He says he didn't see the three men who went up to Arnott's room and assaulted Hambledon, and he has no idea—he—says—who they could be. Of course the body of Arnott travelled down from Verbena Street to Quietude in the tonneau of the Lancia, with the cover over it; finding that silver case for book-matches in the tonneau proves that. But who put the body there is not so clear, because it was certainly taken out of the wardrobe while those three men were in the room with Hambledon. I mean, they could not have taken it out. Besides, they asked for him and Hambledon is sure they expected to see him."

"I suppose Bates put the body in the car," said the A.C., adding a row of kittens to the portrait of a motherly-looking moggy on his blotter.

"To incriminate the three men? Or because he knew he could rely on their help? Or in desperation, just trying to get rid of it, if they were strangers top him?"

"Of course, none of the other residents saw anything."

"No, sir. It's my belief that if a murder was committed in the front hall and not cleared up for two days, nobody there would see anything."

The A.C. drew a tall thin cat of hieroglyphic aspect and added a pair of horns as embellishment. The result was so horrifying that he pulled off the top leaf, tore it into small pieces and dropped them into his wastepaper basket. There came a knock at the door and a messenger entered with a paper from Ennis for Bagshott. It was a copy of the day's *Times* and an advertisement in the Agony column had been marked with blue pencil.

> "Daniel Deacon. Will Mr. Daniel Deacon please communicate with Dr.
> Grainger as there are letters for him. Quietude, near Mark, Hants."

Bagshott read this aloud and added: "Apparently one of the patients is missing."

"Do you think that will interest us? I suppose it will have to be looked into."

"Anything that happens at Quietude interests me," said Bagshott, and went away to talk to Dr. Grainger on the telephone. Grainger was very surprised to find Scotland Yard still taking an interest in the affairs of Quietude, and said so.

"There is no mystery about it. Quietude is a hospital, not a prison, and may patients can leave if they wish. Mr. Deacon has gone away somewhat abruptly on previous occasions and always returned. It is only that there are letters—"

"When did he go?" asked Bagshott, beginning to lose interest.

"On Sunday. The same afternoon that you were here, Chief-Inspector. In fact, the last time I saw him was when I was hurrying to meet you. He said he was looking for Sam."

"*Who?*"

"Sam. His manservant. He brought his own servant with him, an excellent idea in these days of staff shortage. I only wish they all—"

"Dr. Grainger," said Bagshott, "will you oblige me by describing this manservant as accurately as possible?"

"Dear me," said Grainger, with an irritated laugh. "No doubt I must expect the ways of Scotland Yard to be beyond me. I must remember my duty as a citizen. Sam is a very ugly man, to the unscientific mind reminiscent of Darwin's Missing Link. He is about my height, five foot seven, but looks shorter on account of his great breadth of shoulder. He has very long arms and is, to my personal knowledge, immensely strong. Why, once when I wished a large and heavy sofa moved from one place to another, he picked it up and carried it as you or I would a basket chair. He has reddish hair, a low forehead, small eyes, a snub nose and a prognathous jaw. I said he was ugly, Chief-Inspector, did I not?"

"He doesn't sound as though he'd win a prize in a beauty contest, certainly. Do you by any chance happen to have a photograph of him?"

"Photograph of Sam? Certainly not."

"Or of his master, Mr. Deacon?"

"No. There was a photograph taken of a group of patients but Mr. Deacon declined to join them. He said he didn't like photographs of groups."

"You are keeping Mr. Deacon's room for him, are you?"

"Most certainly! He will be back in a few days, no doubt."

"I hope so," said Bagshott, and rang off.

A description of Sam, supplied by Hambledon, had been circulated to the police ever since the murder of Mary Gregory. It had been something of a puzzle how a man so easily recognizable had managed to remain unseen ever since; if he had been acting as valet to a gentleman in an inebriate's home the problem was solved. Bagshott sent for Ennis.

"Go down to Quietude at once," he said. "Go through Deacon's room and get whatever there is. Get a description of Deacon, he's our man. Grainger says there's no photograph of him but one of the other patients might have one. You'll get fingerprints anyway, a man can't live in gloves."

Ennis started off and walked across Westminster Bridge at a slant, leaning against the rising gale. The train from Waterloo was delayed between Milford and Witley by a tree blown across the line; the carriages rocked in the gusts, the rain lashed against the windows and bubbled in above the door with a sucking sound. Ennis eventually reached Mark an hour and a half late when night was falling, and learned from the Mark police that the road to Quietude was blocked with fallen trees and that the telephone wires were coming down all over the countryside. "I suppose the high-tension cables will go next," said the Superintendent gloomily. He had hardly spoken before the electric light winked once and went out. "There now. What did I tell you?"

"Where do the Quietude people get their supply from?" asked Ennis. "Are they on the mains?"

"No. They make their own, they'll be all right. Wish we did."

"Then I'll be going," said Ennis.

By the time he had walked the four miles to Quietude, finished his business there and struggled back to Mark it was nearly midnight. He staggered into the police station and sat down heavily in the nearest chair.

"Superintendent says, sir, as he'll be pleased to put you up for the night if you'd care to accept," said the Desk Sergeant on night duty. "There's no more trains tonight, the roads are all anyhow and the telephone isn't working."

"Glad to hear it," said Ennis. "Now I can go to bed with a clear conscience. Gosh, what a night! These wooded lanes of yours are dangerous in a gale like this, Sergeant."

"No worse than slates and chimney-pots," said the Sergeant stoutly. "When you're rested, sir, I'll send a constable round with you to the Super's, it isn't far."

Ennis reached London late the following morning by an emergency route of trains and buses in relays and reported to Bagshott.

"I've got some prints, sir, but there was nothing else. A few Penguin and Pelican books with 'D. Deacon' written in them, some clothes without marks in any of 'em and no papers of any sort or kind. The letters Dr. Grainger talked about; there was only one, this is it."

It was a cheap envelope postmarked Turnham Green, with "Urgent, Deliver Immediately" across the top of the envelope. The address was typewritten by an amateur, the pressure on the keys had been uneven and there had been mistakes. Bagshott opened it; inside there was only a blank sheet of paper.

"Intentional, mistake, or practical joke?" he said, half to himself.

"More likely intentional, sir, I should say," said Ennis. "Prearranged."

"Test for fingerprints," said Bagshott, and the sheet went down to the Fingerprint Department while Ennis continued his report.

"Deacon. Description compiled from various accounts. Six feet tall or a little over, slim build, erect carriage, age variously estimated as from forty to fifty-five. Black hair turning grey at temples, grey or blue eyes, long eyelashes, dark eyebrows, forehead high, flat at temples, short nose, strong jaw, clean-shaven, well-shaped mouth, good teeth. Very good looking, I was told. Speaks in a cultured voice, is well-read and well-informed, has travelled extensively in Europe. Great charm of manner. No scars or other distinguishing marks noticed."

"And Professor Jeremy Carnoustie?"

"Nobody has done more than see him occasionally at a distance. Tall, slim, round-shouldered, carries his head forward. Thick white hair, whiskers and beard. Can't find anyone who has spoken to him except the small boy I told you about."

"Same man, Ennis?"

"I should think so, sir."

"So should I. Did you—"

A man came in from the Fingerprint Department. The prints on the blank sheet of paper were those of Harold Parker, convicted of smash-and-grab raid on jeweller's shop in Kensington High Street in 1944 and sentenced to—"

"That's him," said Bagshott. "He drove the lorry which carried and subsequently inflated the balloon in which the prisoners escaped from Northern Moor. He later attempted to abduct Hambledon in Marjorie Street, Soho. Something else you have to report?"

"The fingerprints brought in this morning by Detective-Inspector Ennis marked as from Room 28, Quietude, are the same as those from Rose Villa, next door to Quietude, which you brought in, sir, on Monday morning. Two sets."

"Yes, thank you. That settles it, Ennis. Professor Carnoustie is Deacon, and Sam is always Sam. Now then—"

A messenger entered with a report from the Thames River Police stating that a body left by the tide on the foreshore at Erith had been identified as the wanted man "Sam," surname unknown. He had been drowned not more than eighteen to twenty-four hours earlier.

"Drowned," said Bagshott. "Drowned, eh? Ask the Thames police whether—no. You'd better go and see them, Ennis. See the body, and particularly anything on the body. Also ask them whether—whether this was the only body found anywhere round there. Ask them whether they have any idea whatever how the body came to be in the water—no, that's wrong—how the man came to get drowned. Any particulars, however silly and irrelevant. Get on with it, Ennis."

"Yes, sir," said Ennis, and left the room. "And if there is another body," he added to himself, "and it's Hambledon's, I'd rather somebody else told him."

The body of Sam was no more informative in death than he had been in life. His pockets contained only the sodden rags of a packet of Woodbines, a box of Bryant & May's matches and a khaki handkerchief. There was also a wristwatch: Ennis picked it up. It was a Rolex Oyster and Hambledon wore a Rolex Oyster. Ennis laid it down carefully.

"Nothing else?" he said. "No knife, no letters?"

"If he'd had anything heavy like keys or a knife in his pockets it probably fell out. As for letters," said the Inspector in charge of the exhibition, "I suppose he could read? He doesn't look like one of the intelligentsia."

"He doesn't, does he? I don't know whether he could read or not."

"I don't know that I've ever seen a specimen quite like that," continued the Inspector. "Look at the hair on him. Give you my word, if he hadn't been wearing clothes like a human I'd have rung up the Zoo."

"I suppose he was drowned," said Ennis. "There's no doubt about that, is there?"

"Oh, no. None whatever. He was alive when he went into the water."

"Thank you. Now, can you tell me whether there were any other bodies washed up anywhere near here? Or anybody rescued unconscious? There is reason to think that this man may not have been alone."

"Nothing in our area; but, you know, bodies may not turn up for days or weeks—or ever. They may go miles downstream, rolling along in the undertow of a ship. But you want to ask headquarters, they'll be able to tell you if anything's been picked up anywhere else. Probably be able to offer you a choice," said the Inspector, and laughed cheerfully.

Headquarters had a choice of two, but both corpses had been so long in the water that obviously they could not be Hambledon.

"The only other report we have which is so far incomplete comes from the master of a tug, who says he ran down and sank a landing craft drifting without lights in the fairway just above Mucksand Spit. Apparently there was a man on board who was locked in and was yelling for help. Two of the tug's crew jumped aboard the sinking L.C. and managed to unlock the door, but just as it opened the craft rolled over and sank, leaving them in the water. They were pulled on board the tug but no trace could be found of the man who had shouted. Rotten luck," added the official, seeing Ennis's expression. "Have you any idea who he was?"

"I hope not," said Ennis. "Might the body still be in the cabin?"

"We don't know yet, but we soon shall. The wreck must be located and buoyed as it will be an obstruction. A diver will go down to investigate and he can be told to look, if possible, for a body. He may not be able to if she's upside down. She will have to be lifted, of course, and taken away; we shall be able to tell then, if not before."

"So it may be some time before we know," said Ennis slowly.

Rose Cottage, next door to Quietude, was being kept under police watch. It had been searched without result, but there might be something there of sufficient importance to induce somebody to go back for it. At all times of the day and night, therefore, a rotation of constables occupied the place.

On a brilliant moonlight night the relieving constable walked quietly along in the black shadows under the trees to take over at midnight. He rounded the bend till he could see before him the Rose Cottage entrance in the clear light of the moon. Even as he approached a man came up from the other direction, looked carefully about him, and turned in. The relieving constable broke into a run.

The policeman in the house heard quiet steps outside and thought it was his relief. He opened the door, saying: "You're early, mate," and immediately dropped across the doorstep because he had been sandbagged.

The relieving constable swung round the corner just as this happened. He put on a spurt up the drive; the man in the doorway turned and saw him and immediately bolted across the garden. The constable followed but lost his man almost at once. Reinforcements sent out from Mark searched the area but without success.

"There is something there," said the Superintendent. "It will be found."

It was found behind a false back to the copper fire, three thousand pounds in odd Treasury notes, a small bag containing assorted precious stones, and the diamond-studded wristwatch which David Arnott had kept back out of the loot from the Capitol robbery.

"I hope he's down to his last pound note," said the Superintendent.

"I hope he's down to fivepence ha'penny in coppers," said Ennis on the Scotland Yard end of the telephone. "If he can be induced to do something silly—"

Chief-Inspector Bagshott was not the only person who was in a state of fidgets about Hambledon. Cobden had arranged to meet him the day after the visit to Quietude. When Hambledon neither came nor sent a message, when another day passed, and another, without a word from him, Cobden became acutely uneasy. He went to Wimbledon to consult Salvation Savory.

"I don't like it," said Cobden. "I had a letter from him by the first post on Monday saying he had some news for me and was going to look for some more. I was to meet him that night. I went to the appointed place and hung about from soon after eight till nearly midnight. That was Monday: today's Thursday and I haven't heard a word."

"He didn't say where he was going? Nor whom he was going with?"

"No." Cobden smiled faintly. "He never said who his friends were and I never asked, but I'm sure he has some pretty useful ones."

Savory nodded. "I asked him point-blank once whether he was connected with the police, but he said he wasn't and I believe him. All the same, he has a terrific pull with the police, that I do know. That time he was arrested as Hawkley in that boardinghouse in Verbena Road, some big noise from Scotland Yard came down and proved he wasn't. I know that's true, he told me himself. Again, he had the police watch taken off the Vavasour while we broke into the place. A detective arrived in the middle of the show and said that Chief-Inspector Bagshott had sent him to say they'd found the Gregory girl."

"Chief-Inspector Bagshott," said Cobden. "If I wasn't an escaped prisoner I'd go to Scotland Yard and ask for an interview. I might be able to tell him something he doesn't know."

"I shouldn't," said Savory, "really, I shouldn't. I imagine the only thing our friend has not told him already is where you are. I could go, I suppose, but if this fellow Bagshott starts getting interested in me it would be damned awkward. Besides, it's pretty certain that the police know all that we know and a lot more. No, I don't recommend a visit to Scotland Yard for either of us. You'd go straight back to jail and I'd have to amend my life. Most undesirable."

"But what can have happened?" said Cobden. "He would have let me know if he'd just gone away unexpectedly. I'm sure of it."

"He may be ill," suggested Savory. "Or had an accident."

"Yes. And the silly part about it is that if I'd read an account of it in the papers I shouldn't be any the wiser because I don't know his real name. Do you?"

"No. Except that it isn't Hawkley although I used to ask for him by that name when I rang him up. He gave me a telephone number but asked me not to use it too often. I tried it yesterday and was told Mr. Hawkley was away."

"Try again now," urged Cobden, and Savory did so but the answer remained the same. No, they were sorry, it was impossible to say when Mr. Hawkley would be back.

"Is he ill?" asked Savory bluntly.

"No, oh no. Not so far as we know," said the pleasant voice at the other end. "Can I take a message?"

"Ask him to ring me up as soon as he returns, please," said Savory, and gave his own number.

"And that was all," he added to Cobden. "Nothing cooking at all. Let's get down to business. You're afraid the Vavasour gang's got hold of him, aren't you? Yes. So am I."

"What comes next?"

"All I can suggest is that I should put out all the lines I can and hope to pick up some news, if there is any. If Hawkley has been abducted, there'll be a buzz going round and we might hear it if the police don't."

"I can do that too," said Cobden, rising to take his leave. "The sooner the better. I'm not on the telephone where I live but I'll ring you tomorrow whether I've any news or not. Well, here's hoping."

"Watch your step," warned Savory.

"I always do. Goodbye, and thanks no end."

XVIII

THE DOOR IN THE WALL

Tommy Hambledon left Bagshott and Dr. Grainger to their tour of Quietude House and went for a walk in the grounds. Since the gate was locked at night and was too high to climb, the body of David Arnott was brought in somewhere else. The walls round the grounds of Quietude were topped with spikes; Hambledon walked all round the perimeter looking for signs of entry. Several thicknesses of rug or possibly an old mattress might have been used to muffle those rusty spikes, but even so something ought to have been torn in transit. Some shred of material somewhere—

He worked his way through the shrubbery, and was in the act of disentangling himself from a branch which had hooked his coat-collar when he heard someone else passing carefully between the bushes ahead of him. Tommy stooped down; one could see much further at a height of two feet from the ground. He saw a pair of legs in grey tweed trousers ending with feet in black leather shoes; they made their way to the wall, paused a moment and passed right through it. There followed a soft scratching noise as of a door grating on a pebble.

Hambledon waited long enough to ensure that whoever it might be was not returning immediately, and then made his way to the door. He was disappointed by the obvious appearance of disuse which the door presented, but solid legs with, no doubt, a body attached in the usual places, would not glide through two inches of old oak. He laid his hand on the doorpost and pushed and the whole thing swung inwards.

He went inside with considerable caution but could see no one. The door, together with its frame, was hinged on the inside and there were a couple of strong bolts not fastened. Hambledon closed the door quietly, leaving it unbolted as before. Actually, it had been left unfastened so that somebody else could follow, but he was not to know that. He advanced cautiously along the twisting path almost overgrown with bushes, stopping at every bend to reconnoitre before he turned the corner. A sound ahead of him—someone shut a door—stopped him to listen, and the next minute something round, hard and cold was pressed against the back of his neck. A hoarse voice behind advised him to keep going.

Hambledon had had much experience of violence though he always did his best to avoid it; he knew that a round cold thing at the back of the neck is not always the revolver it pretends to be. It is sometimes a short length of pipe or even a round ruler. He accordingly turned his head slowly and carefully to see what was behind him—and looked straight into the unpleasant face of Sam, even more like a gorilla than before. But gorillas do not as a rule carry 45 revolvers, and Sam did. Hambledon sighed and walked on up the path with Sam following very closely behind. They entered the yard behind the house; apparently they were observed from the windows since the back door opened as they came to it. Hambledon entered the kitchen and found there a tall man, clean-shaven, with dark hair turning silver at the temples and a lined intelligent face.

"Mr. Hawkley again," he said. "What a surprise."

"A pleasant surprise so far as I'm concerned," said Tommy.

"I am glad to hear it, but why?"

"You at least will have the sense not to fire off a .45 Smith & Wesson within earshot of several policemen. You know, I thought you must be somewhere about when I recognized your anthropoid playmate behind me."

"You are right, of course, about the revolver," said the tall man regretfully. "We shall have to find somewhere a little more private if we decide to use that."

Hambledon knew it would not be long before Bagshott missed him and decided to play for time. He sat on the edge of the kitchen table and said: "Do you mind if I take my cigarettes out of my pocket? Perhaps I may be allowed to offer you one. I am not armed."

"You may smoke if you like," said the tall man. "I have one or two preparations to make and then we are going a journey."

"To find that quiet spot? Tell me," said Hambledon, producing cigarette-case and lighter, "what is all this fuss about? Have you just taken an æsthetic dislike to my face or is there more in it than that? I mean, it can't be the Capitol jewels you're still worrying about because you must have seen in the papers the announcement that the police had got 'em back. I told you so, I remember, the last time we met, only you didn't believe me. Would you care for a cigarette? These are Egyptians."

"Not at the moment, thank you." The tall man picked up a small attaché-case and went out of the room; Hambledon pushed himself further on to the kitchen table with his feet dangling and grinned amiably at Sam, who was now holding the revolver by the barrel ready for use as a truncheon.

"You feel more at home with it like that, don't you, Sammy?" said Hambledon cheerfully. He put the cigarette-case and lighter back into his pocket and rested his hands on the table behind him. "Complicated things, revolvers, I always think, too many moving parts to—"

He broke off short and looked quickly out of the window as though he had heard something. Sam followed his look and in that instant Hambledon drew up both legs and drove his heels into the pit of the gangster's stomach. It was a trick which would have disabled most men; Sam doubled up but fell upon Hambledon in the same movement. Tommy hit him in the face with all his strength but failed to dislodge him, the next minute Sam lifted him clear of the table and threw him violently to the ground. Hambledon's head crashed on the brick floor and he collapsed into unconsciousness. The tablecloth came with him, together with a jug of beer, some crockery and an alarm clock; tall man dashed back into the kitchen and surveyed the wreckage.

"Let me kill him, boss," whimpered Sam. "He kicked me."

"Looks as though you had," said his master, "and anyway it serves you right for not watching him. What were you doing? Looking for dicky-birds in the treetops, you fool? Get a broom and clear up this mess, quick." The tall man bent over Hambledon, rolled him over, felt the back of his head and then his pulse. "He's not dead yet. Get a rope and truss him up, gag him and put him in the back of the Austin, on the floor, with a rug over him. I'm going down to open the gate; wait by the front door till I wave you on. Got that? Tie him up first. Then sweep up this mess. Then carry him through the house and out by the front door. Be quick."

Professor Jeremy Carnoustie, a tall man but for his scholarly stoop, his long white hair and whiskers blowing in the wind, opened his garage doors and went quickly down the drive to open his gate also. While he was swinging it back a small boy came along the lane, very wobbly on a bicycle too big for him. He dismounted and stared at the Professor who could cheerfully have killed him. The old man hooked the gate back and glared at the small boy, who merely looked at something else and did not move.

"What is it, boy, what is it?" asked the Professor in a high thin voice. "Have you got a message for me?"

The boy shook his head and began testing his brakes, pulling on first one lever and then the other and pushing the cycle a few inches back and forth. A hundred yards away, on the other side of the high wall, Bagshott tired of waiting for Hambledon and began to look for him. The Professor glanced over his shoulder towards the house and saw Sam come to the front door and look out.

"Come here, boy," said the Professor. The boy looked at him but did not move. "Do you know anybody who wants a kitten?"

"Kitten?"

"Yes. There's a litter of kittens in my stable and I don't want them. You can have them if you like. Come and look at them."

The small boy wheeled his bicycle across the road till he was almost within the drive entrance when he looked up into the Professor's face. What he saw there is not clear, for the face was smiling; or perhaps he was merely prompted by whatever agency looks after small boys. He turned his cycle abruptly, hopped on to it and pedaled away down the lane with his head down and his brown legs going like pistons, and never once looked behind him.

The Professor sighed with relief and signalled to Sam, who trotted across from the front door to the garage with a burden across his shoulders. Half a minute later the Austin slid quietly down the drive, out of the gate and away. Bagshott and the Superintendent threw themselves at the door in the wall and it opened.

Hambledon recovered consciousness by painful degrees with a splitting headache and flashes before his eyes whenever he moved his head. He was no longer either roped up or gagged, and it was some time before the soreness at the corners of his mouth and the red rings round ankles and wrists informed him that he had been so maltreated. He made an effort to sit up, the world swung round him and he was most violently sick.

He felt better after that though his head still ached abominably. He was in a steel-walled room, in plan the shape of a flatiron, it was all painted grey now streaked with rust, and the steel framing and plates showed the rivets which held them together. Hambledon was still very confused, he lay still and wondered how in the world he had come to join the navy at his time of life. When he became convinced that the slight swaying motion he felt was genuine and not one of his symptoms, the puzzle merely grew thicker. Why and where was he afloat?

Some time later a door opened in the wall which formed the heel of the flatiron, and a man put his head in. He had a round pale face not remarkable for intelligence, and a thatch of red hair. He saw Hambledon looking at him and called over his shoulder to someone outside. "Sam! Your patient's woke up?"

Sam pushed the redhaired man out of tile way and came in; he looked at Hambledon without speaking for a long time during which Tommy did his best to stare coldly back. Eventually he said: "Want a drink?"

"Yes, please."

"Get a jug of water an' a mug, Ginger."

Ginger came back almost at once with a jug and a cracked cup, he poured out some water and even helped Hambledon to sit up and drink it. Tommy thanked him and lay down again.

"Where am I?" he asked, but Sam merely grinned and the two men went out again, locking the door behind them. Tommy drank some more water, poured a little on his handkerchief to make a cold compress for his aching head, and went to sleep again. He was awakened some hours later when Ginger came with a plate of tinned stew and a spoon to eat it with. It was not very inviting to one suffering from the effects of concussion, but Hambledon persuaded himself to eat it and felt all the better for it. He even got unsteadily to his feet and made a tour of his prison.

It was plainly a compartment in the bows of a boat of some kind; there were no portholes and light entered only through two round holes about six inches in diameter high up in the bows. They were unglazed, the wind blew chill and Hambledon shivered, but they were the only means of ventilation so he made no attempt to block them up. The compartment had been intended for stores of some kind, never for men to live in; there was no furniture in the place but the mattress and pillow upon which he had been lying. The sun was setting outside but even so the light hurt his eyes; he groped his way back to the mattress in the gathering darkness, had another drink of water and went to sleep again.

When he woke up again it was morning; his headache had left him, he felt enormously better and ravenously hungry. Ginger came in with a tray holding a pot of tea, a tin of condensed milk, a slab of corned beef on a plate, and a thick slice of bread and margarine. Hambledon sat up with the tray on the floor beside him and ate up every morsel; the tea, strong to blackness, tasted like nectar. He felt so at peace with the world that when Sam came in and stood glowering in the doorway it was difficult not to greet him as man and brother. Tommy finished the last drop of tea he could squeeze out of the teapot, glanced up at Sam as though he had only just noticed him, and said sharply: "I want this place cleaned out."

There was a long pause before Sam answered. "Do it yourself," he said rudely. "Ginger! Mop and pail o' water."

Ginger brought it and set to work himself, Hambledon stood the mattress against the wall to keep it dry and Sam leaned against the doorpost and watched without a word. Hambledon looked out at the two holes for'ard and saw that they were on a river; on his right there was a bank covered with leafless bushes about twenty yards away, on his left there was a wider expanse of water with a continuous line of buildings beyond. He also saw a very stout post close to the bows with a rope round it; evidently they were moored to posts, probably fore and aft to obviate swinging. There seemed to be no one about anywhere within sight.

"You won't get out them 'oles, mister," said Sam.

Ginger took his pail outside, threw the contents overboard and came back with fresh water. A conscientious worker, evidently. Hambledon turned and faced the two men.

"I suppose you know what you're letting yourselves in for," he said sharply. "Kidnapping and unlawful detention—like this—are felonies, and when you're caught you'll go to prison for a long, long time. Years."

"Got to be caught first, mister," said Sam.

"Oh, you'll be caught all right; don't worry. Years and years in Dartmoor—"

"That won't 'elp you," said Sam.

"It will. It'll please me no end—"

"No it won't. You'll be dead."

"If you murder me you'll hang for it."

Ginger left off mopping and stood apparently engaged in thought, or merely in allowing these unpleasant ideas to sink in.

"You get on," said Sam, noticing this.

"That's all very well," said Ginger, "but I'm not 'aving no truck with murder."

"You mind your own business—"

"T'is my business, I know 'bout 'anging. My father was 'anged for murder. I ain't goin' to be."

"You shut up. Nobody's going to 'ang for 'im. We've only to keep 'im 'ere till the Boss comes and says what's to be done."

"I won't 'ave no truck with murder," said Ginger obstinately, "an' so I tells you. S' unlucky."

"Very unlucky indeed," said Hambledon with emphasis.

"Ah," said Ginger, and went on mopping. "You an' your murders," he added.

"Committed many, Sam?" asked Hambledon brightly.

"You mind your own business."

"There is a certain monotony about your conversation," said Tommy, and turned to look out upon the river again. "All the same," he added over his shoulder, "you'd better think over what I've said if you don't want fifteen years in Dartmoor."

"Fifteen years?" said Ginger slowly. "Fifteen years?"

"Get out," said Sam violently, pushed the redhaired man, mop and all, out of the room, and followed him.

"Fifteen years," said Hambledon in an awful voice just before the door shut. "It's what you deserve, anyway," he added, when he was alone.

Sam came back an hour later with a pair of blue serge trousers, not too clean; a blue jersey with a high collar, a serge jacket and a peaked cap. He threw them down on the floor and said: "Put 'em on."

"Why? Are we going—"

"Put 'em on! You've gotta come out of 'ere sometimes, 'aven't you?" said Sam.

"Oh, ah, yes. So people do pass near enough to see us sometimes, do they? I don't think I care about these clothes, they want cleaning. Besides, they're—"

Sam caught him by the wrist with one hand, his coat collar with the other and wrenched the coat off with one pull. His shirt collar followed—fortunately Hambledon had taken off his tie at an earlier stage of his discomforts or he might have been garotted. Sam, he felt, would not have minded. Similar treatment applied to his trouser-band removed most of the buttons with rending noises and the trousers immediately slid down.

"Nex' time," said Sam, taking coat and collar away with him, "do what I tells yer first off."

He went away, leaving Hambledon white and shaking with fury; only the fact that his head still felt as though one tap would burst it prevented him from attacking Sam with every ounce of his strength. Besides, it would be useless, the abnormal length of those simian arms could outreach him easily. Hambledon sat down suddenly, for his knees were trembling. "One of these days," he said, "one of these days—" and then laughed at a ridiculous mental picture he had formed of himself hitting Sam on the head with the sort of hammer men use to drive spikes into roadways. A three-foot handle and a five-pound head. . . . A pleasant thought, but silly. He got up and dressed in the seaman's outfit they had brought him, at least it was warm. If he were allowed to cross the deck it might be possible to jump overboard.

This also was a forlorn hope, for when he was conducted aft he was handcuffed. He did at least recognize what type of craft he was in: it was a landing craft, sold out of Government service like so many thousand others. It was pleasant to be in the open air again even though it was cold, gusty and raining. Hambledon looked up at the sky and said to himself that it would blow harder before the day was out. He was right, the wind rose steadily and moaned through various crevices in a most unpleasant manner, while the L.C. rocked in the gusts and jibbed at the mooring-ropes which creaked dismally.

When Ginger came in with the supper Hambledon remarked conversationally that it was a nasty night and Ginger agreed with him.

"'Orrible," he said. "This wind 'owling fair gives me the 'ump."

"Are you a seaman by trade?"

"Me? No."

"Nor Sam?"

"No. Why?"

"Only wondered what would happen if we broke loose," said Hambledon.

"Oh, I don't know," said Ginger miserably, and went away. The wind increased to gale force as the night fell and the moaning noises rose to howls. Hambledon switched on the one electric light in his prison; apparently Sam or Ginger had neglected charging the batteries for the light was dim and unsteady. Presently he heard voices outside and footsteps over his head, he went to one of the hawse-holes—if that was what they were—and listened. Sam and Ginger were looking to the moorings.

"Don't look safe to me," howled Ginger above the storm. "Sort of loose-like."

There were more remarks which Tommy did not catch, and then something about "tie that rope round there."

"Hi!" yelled Hambledon, "let the ropes alone, you fools! You'll have us adrift!"

The only answer was an impatient stamp with a heavy boot just above his head and some more talking. The wind had thinned and torn the rain-clouds and the moon was shining intermittently on writhing trees bending before the gale. As Hambledon watched a great limb broke from one of them, fell into the water and was blown towards the landing craft. It passed below the area of his restricted visibility and he could hear it bumping and scratching along the side of the boat. Sam and Ginger overhead were still scrambling about and arguing; Ginger's voice said something indistinguishable and Sam shouted: "What-say?"

"I said," yelled Ginger, "I don' like ropes. Give me the creeps, they do."

"Why?"

An inaudible answer from Ginger and Sam burst into a roar of laughter.

"This ain't the kind, they 'angs you with," he bawled. "You silly—, get on with it."

A few minutes passed.

"Now then," said Sam. "Got it? Right. Off with it!"

There was a slithering noise and an appalling yell from Sam. Hambledon, shaking with excitement, saw the mooring-post apparently move back with Sam, horizontally extended from the boat, clinging like an ape to the post. There was a rush overhead, presumably Ginger to the rescue, for he shouted: "I've got you!" Sam's hands were torn from the post and he fell forwards and down towards the water. For a moment his fall was checked, then a second body passed Hambledon's lookout and the two splashes merged into the roar of the wind. At once the craft swung round through a third of a circle, pivoting on the stern moorings; the post and the tossing trees behind it passed out of his sight. He listened till his ears ached with strain, but there came no sound of voices any more, not even a cry for help.

Hambledon, left alone on the landing craft, instinctively looked for his wristwatch, but of course it was not on his arm. Sam, he remembered, had been wearing it. Tommy guessed the time to be about eight o'clock. The boat was much steadier; no longer broadside on to the wind she did not heel at each gust. She only kept up a barely perceptible but incessant tugging at the remaining rope. Hambledon went to the door and tried it, but it was immovably fast.

"I have only to wait for daylight, when at the first sign of anyone moving anywhere I can help," he said. At a quarter-past twelve the moon set and the rain came on once more; it was as dark outside as a coal-hole with the door shut, Hambledon could see nothing at all, not even when he switched off his failing light. By half-past one the light had sunk to a red glow in the bulb; Hambledon stared at it till he could see a green loop wherever his eyes turned.

But at half-past two in the morning the last strand of the mooring-rope parted. The landing craft lurched heavily and drifted away in the howling darkness.

XIX

OSCAR

Presumably there was at one time some reason why Henry Billing should have been nicknamed Oscar, but whatever the reason may have been it was lost among the shadows of his dingy past. The name stuck as such names do; one might say that he was Oscar among his friends and Henry Billing to the rest of the world—the police, for instance. He owned a rowing boat and said he earned a living doing errands and suchlike. In point of fact most of his gains were the results of petty pilfering; an odd coil of rope, a sweater hung over the rail to dry, anything left within reach of an open porthole. On the night of the great gale he spent the evening ashore at the Six Bells, but the wind dropped towards morning and Oscar turned out early, before it was really light. There's pickings on a lee shore.

He was pulling downstream, letting the current and the falling tide do most of the work, making his way towards the point which ran out opposite the gasworks. Things which floated downstream were apt to fetch up on that spit, especially on a falling tide. Even deaders; there's a reward for deaders. He had eyes like a cat; from his low viewpoint close to the water he saw ahead of him a landing craft obviously drifting out of control. No lights, no sign of life. Broke adrift in the storm. Something might be made out of that. He put his back into his rowing and in ten minutes had come near enough to see the white identification number stencilled on the side, a familiar number to him, for he knew to whom that particular L.C. belonged. He lay on his oars and thought it over. Not people one interfered with, definitely not, but a helping hand might be kindly rewarded. If he could get aboard he could at least switch the lights on, possibly even start the engine and take her in somewhere.

He had been so busy watching the L.C. that he had not noticed the lights of a tug coming fast downstream behind him, till he heard the sound of her engines and looked over his shoulder to see her almost upon him. He uttered a loud yell and pulled out of her road; one of the men on the bridge ran to the side and looked down towards the sound and the tug altered course to miss him. The next moment she crashed into the landing craft wallowing broadside on in the fairway, hit it squarely amidships and all but rolled it over.

Hambledon, who had dropped off into an uneasy sleep, woke with the crash and slid across the floor as the boat heeled. He scrambled to his feet, staggered to one of the hawse-holes and howled for help at the top of his voice. He was relived to hear someone shout: "There's someone in there", and another voice addressing him personally: "Hold on, mate, we're coming. Where are you?"

"For'ard here, I'm locked in."

The matter was obviously urgent; the L.C. was very slowly heeling over towards the side on which she had been holed and the floor beneath Hambledon's feet was dropping, an inch or so at a time, in sickening jerks like a defective lift. There were a couple of heartening thuds overhead as two men jumped from the tug to the deck over his head and scrambled down to the well-deck outside his door. Hambledon rushed to the door and hammered on it; at the moment the boat heeled over so steeply that he had to cling to the door-handled to avoid sliding away from it. There was a scraping noise outside as the men from the tug crawled up the steeply-sloping deck, and the welcome sound of the key turning in the lock. The door opened, with Hambledon clinging like a monkey to the doorpost, exactly as the river lipped the sides of the well-deck and poured into it. The landing craft turned like a diving fish and sank, taking Hambledon with it and leaving the other two men struggling in the water.

Oscar, prompt to his cue, came out of the adjacent shadows to offer his help, but the tug's crew could manage quite well without him. Ropes were thrown and the two men hauled on board. The tug skipper asked who he was and what in the name of several strange gods he was doing sculling about in the fairway, and all the time keen eyes were searching the dark water in the hope of seeing the man they had tried to rescue. The tug skipper was afraid to start his engines again for fear the swimming man—if he were swimming—should be chopped up by the screws, and tug and rowing-boat drifted downstream together to the accompaniment of bawled questions and answers. More accurately, Oscar didn't know any answers. He said he hadn't seen the L.C.'s identification numbers, which was one lie, and had no idea who she belonged to—which was another—nor where she came from. The tug's crew had not been able to read the numbers as they were painted across the place where the L.C. had been stove in. At last eh tug skipper said that evidently the poor devil had gone down with her and there was nothing to be done but to report the accident to the authorities. In the meantime he must start up again if he didn't want to find himself sitting on the point of Mucksand Spit on a falling tide, so Oscar had better get away from the screws, quick.

Oscar pulled hastily away, the water churned white under the tug's stern as she swung out to avoid the point and went off downstream. By this time the day was beginning to break and the visibility was improving rapidly. Oscar thought that as he had come so far he might as well row along the spit just in case there was anything deserving of salvage dropped there by the falling tide. He pulled slowly along in the shallow water, occasionally pushing himself off the mud with one short abraded oar. No luck. A bit too soon, perhaps. Yes, there was a lump of something further along. He pulled towards it, it looked like a sack of something. No, it had legs and arms, it was a man. Probably a deader.

He came close in and ran aground, he was in the act of getting out the rope he used for towing purposes on these occasions when the corpse stirred feebly, tried to sit up, and fell back again.

"Ere," said Oscar. "Hi, you!"

The man on the mudbank made another effort and raised himself on his arms. He was so coated with mud as to be unrecognizable, and there was a cut on his head from which blood was mingling with the slime which covered his face. Oscar backed his boat in close beside the derelict and practically lifted him in. The man mumbled something and tried to wipe the mud out of his eyes.

"That's no sort o' use," said Oscar contemptuously, "smearin' more on is what you're doin'. 'Ere! Was you the bloke in that landing craft?"

Hambledon tried to speak, blew a large mud bubble, and nodded instead. Oscar watched him with interest. Since he came off the boat belonging to That Lot, he was either one of their friends or—since he was locked in—one of their enemies. In either case an object of interest. Oscar cheered up; the morning's work was not to be fruitless after all.

"What you want," he said kindly, "is a wash." He pulled the boat off the mud into clear water and took a piece of rag from a locker. "'Ang over the side," he said and washed his patient's head till the features rose like landscape from the primeval slime. The process was refreshing as well as cleansing and Hambledon was grateful, thought his teeth chattered and he shivered violently in his soaked garments.

"Water for yer outside," said Oscar, "but a drop o' somethink else for the innards." He took a flask from his pocket, opened it and passed it so Hambledon, who drank from it and nearly choked.

"What is it?" he gasped.

"Ah. That'll do yer good. Never paid dooty, that 'asn't. Now, look. You take one oar and I'll take the other, else you'll catch your death."

Hambledon did hid best, but rowing was not one of his hobbies and it was very hard work against stream and tide. He was near exhaustion long before they reached the slimy wooden steps where Oscar kept his boat; when at last they shipped oars and the boatman reached for the painter, Tommy had barely the strength to crawl up the steps on to the wharf.

"What you wants," said the philanthropist, taking his arm, "is to get them wet things off an' have a nice lay down. This way."

Across the wharf and up stone steps; along a narrow alley into a busy street; across the street into another alley; left, right and left again. Hambledon lost count of the turnings and was barely conscious when at last they stopped to unlock a door. Another flight of stairs, narrow wooden and something pressed against his knees, a bed. He fell upon it and was dimly aware of wet clothes being roughly pulled off and replaced with a blanket. More blankets over him—

When he woke up again it was dark except for some light coming through the window from a street lamp outside. He could not imagine where he was nor remember how he got there, but he was warm and dry. Too warm, in fact; hot and thirsty. There was a jug of water on a chair beside the bed, he drank greedily, threw off some of the blankets and shut his eyes again. Almost at once he was too cold so he dragged up the blankets once more.

Henry Billing, alias Oscar, had about as much connection with the Vavasour gang as the latest new boy at school has with the First Eleven. Less, in fact, for the new boy at least knows these gods by sight, but Oscar had not the faintest idea who the Boss was or what he looked like. He had had some dealings with Sam; otherwise he merely knew somebody who could get in tough with somebody else who could pass the word on that Oscar had something to interest the gang. Accordingly, he set the mechanism in motion, and it was a little like throwing a pebble into a pool in order that the ripple should reach one particular water-rat in due course. Naturally, all the other water-rats in the pool get the ripple also, and the message reached Cobden before it reached the gang. They were, through no fault of their own, a little disorganized. Cobden rushed off to see Savory.

"There's a buzz going round," he said, "that a man called Oscar at Purfleet has got somebody he's keeping under cover, and will somebody please tell Sam."

"Sam. Sam the gorilla, as Hawkley called him. It seems worth inquiry. You don't know where in Purfleet the good Oscar lives, do you?"

"No," said Cobden eagerly, "but I expect the police do. If we let them know—"

"Let's thing for a minute first. Let's assume that it is Hawkley he's got, it may not be. If so, telling the police might be taking rather a risk, mightn't it? I'm afraid that if the cops began to gather round, Hawkley might be removed somewhere else, or worse. Listen. Oscar is not a member of the gang, or he would know where to find them."

Cobden nodded.

"We know how careful the gang's leader is that nobody should know him," went on Savory. "Is it likely that Oscar knows him personally?"

"No."

"Very well. I am the gang leader and you and I will go to Purfleet in the largest car I can hire and see what Oscar is up to."

Cobden's face lit up. "You—you are—" he began. "But what about finding him?"

"Oh, I think I can get his address now we know whom we want," said Savory. "Just a minute, I am going to do some telephoning. Help yourself to the whisky."

It was nearly half an hour before Savory returned, rubbing his hands together and beaming all over his broad red face. "Things begin to move," he said. "I don't know now what Oscar's place is called but I have the most detailed directions for finding it. I have ordered a large Daimler limousine from a garage I sometimes employ, they know me so I shall drive myself. It will be here in twenty minutes and in the meantime I am going to make myself what I hope Oscar will consider imposing. Excuse me."

He came downstairs again just as the big car rolled up to the front door, and Cobden's eyes widened at the sight of him. Savory looked like a bookmaker who had been left a fortune by a jeweller. He wore a suit of tawny-orange tweed checked with green, a yellow waistcoat and suède shoes, and carried a light-brown bowler hat. In his cravat—brown with yellow horse-shoes—he wore a pin set with a diamond the size of a prize-winning green pea and another as big on the little finger of his left hand. Across the yellow waistcoat there passed a gold curb watch-chain with a diamond in every link; from one side of his mouth there projected a cigar at least ten inches long.

"Will I do?"

"Words fail me," said Cobden. "You look like Harounal-Raschid."

Oscar's home was actually the loft over a ship-chandler's store. The space had been divided by matchboard partitions into four small rooms; the addition of a pipe conveying cold water to a sink completed the amenities. Oscar cooked on a couple of Primus stoves, cleaned the place after his fashion and made the beds when he felt-fish energetic. There was a pawnshop on one side of his dwelling and a shop on the other; the Six Bells public-house was beyond the fried fish. After all, it is not granted to every man to have all he wants within twenty yards of his front door.

The great Daimler limousine, all mirrorlike black enamel and chromium plating, slid noiselessly down the street scattering the children from the roadway and the cats from the gutters. It stopped outside the ship-chandler's Savory and Cobden got out and the children gathered round. Savory looked them over and crooked his finger at a skinny little boy with bright red hair and abrasions on his knuckles.

"What's your name?"

"Terry Sullivan, your honor."

"Oh. Terry; if, when I come back, there are no fingermarks, scratches, mud or any other damage to my car I'll give you five bob. If there are, I'll give you a hiding instead. O.K.?"

"O.K.!"

There was a knocker on the door between the ship-chandler's and the fried-fish shop but savory ignored it and tried the handle. The door opened. Savory threw back his shoulders, elevated his cigar to an angle of forty-five degrees with the horizon, and walked heavily up the stairs with Cobden at his heels. There was another door at the top; it was locked so he kicked it impatiently. There came a voice from inside.

"Who's there?"

"I am," said Savory. "Open the door."

The door opened slowly and Oscar's face appeared, preparing to parley, but Savory pushed the door wide and stalked in, sweeping Oscar before him.

"You know who I am, don't you? You sent me a message."

"Y-yes," said Oscar backing towards the sink.

"Where's the man?"

"In there," nodding towards another door on the left.

"Go and get him," said Savory to Cobden, who sprang to obey as a gangster's henchman should. He turned the key and went in, shutting the door behind him in order that Oscar should not hear what was said. Only a low murmur of voices penetrated to the kitchen where Oscar still supported himself by the sink, and Savory stood straddle-legged in the middle of the room and stared at the boatman in unbroken silence.

Presently the inner door opened, and Cobden came out holding by the arm a Hambledon almost unrecognizable behind a five-days' beard and a close coating of grime. He was dressed in the seaman's clothing which Sam had given him, and even Bagshott might have passed him by. Savory looked at them and Cobden nodded, a prearranged signal which meant that Hambledon had been reasonably well treated.

"Pay this fellow," said Savory. He took Hambledon down the stairs and put him into the back car with a rug wrapped round him, while the redhaired boy hopped round on one leg.

"Not a scratch, mister! Nobody ain't to so much as touched it!"

Upstairs, Cobden took a packet of new notes from his pocket, flipped them rapidly with his thumb so that the delighted Oscar reckoned that there must be nearly fifty of them, and threw them down on the table. He then ran rapidly down the stairs and jumped into the back seat beside Hambledon. Savory, having rewarded Terry, immediately drove away.

"Quick work," said Hambledon hoarsely, "wasn't it?"

"I thought I'd get clear away," said Savory, "before he discovers that all those notes have got the same serial number."

XX

DANIEL DEACON

"Are you all right?" asked Cobden anxiously.

"Oh, perfectly, or I shall be when I've had a bath and a shave. I've had a foul cold but it's going off now. I say, what I owe you two fellows is quite beyond all reckoning, I don't know where to begin, I—"

Don't even begin," said Savory. "That was just good clean fun. Will you come to my place for a bath and a shave and a meal and a drink—especially a drink—"

"It's awfully good of you," said Tommy gratefully, "but I think I'd better go straight home. There are those who are beginning to wonder where I am, and what is even more to me at the moment, there is a wardrobe with a reasonable supply of clean underclothes in it. I can't describe how my soul yearns for a clean vest—at present I feel like a leper."

"I understand perfectly," said Savory. "Er—can I drive you home, or would you rather I dropped you somewhere where you can pick up a taxi.?"

Hambledon laughed. "I think all this secrecy is becoming rather obsolete between us three," he said. "My name is Hambledon and I earn my daily bread at Foreign Office Intelligence. I have a flat on the Victoria Street side of St. James's Park; if you'll drive down Whitehall I will direct you."

"Hambledon," said Cobden, "is a much nicer name than Hawkley, in my opinion. It has pleasanter associations."

"I always shy violently at asking questions," said Savory, "but is the Foreign Office really interested in the Vavasour gang?"

"Not a bit. All this business started over something else, the epidemic of prison-breaking, to be exact. The Foreign Office couldn't with any particular prisoner. No, I got dragged into this as a kind of sideline; actually I'm on leave from the F. O. at the moment."

"Do you mean to tell me," said Savory, looking over his shoulder, "that this—this enterprise is your idea of a holiday?"

"Not entirely. Oh, look out, Savory, that's Trafalgar Square. It's all right, I thought you were going to miss it and hit a bus instead. Left here."

Two hours later Hambledon, washed, shaven, changed and fed, walked along the passage in Scotland Yard which led to Bagshott's office. Just as he reached the door it opened and Ennis came out. He stopped dead, staring, still holding the handle of the half-open door in his hand.

"What's the matter, Ennis?" said Tommy cheerfully. "Do you think you're seeing a ghost? You're not, I'm quite solid. Chief-Inspector Bagshott in?"

Ennis threw the door wide open, stepped back into the room and said: "Mr. Hambledon, sir."

"Hambledon," said Bagshott, rising slowly from his chair: "Hambledon, still alive?"

"Oh, quite," said Tommy, "if nearly not, at one time. "Pass, friend," he added, punching Ennis amiably in the chest, "all's well. I gather you thought I was lost."

Ennis, grinning from ear to ear, went out of the room and Bagshott, red in the face and apparently speechless, shook hands with Hambledon, pushed him into a chair and brought whisky out of a cupboard all, as it were, in one movement.

"Tell me," said Tommy, sipping his drink, "first, where do you get this whisky, and second, why so sure that I was dead? It's not a habit of mine."

"Sam's body was cast up on the shore wearing your wristwatch—"

"Now that is good news. Not about Sam, the conger-eels are welcome to him, but about my watch. Presumably I shall now get it back—was it damaged?"

"Don't think so," said Bagshott. "I'll send for it. Now tell me—"

There followed an exchange of news to date which Hambledon summarized by saying that this was obviously a war of attrition. "They scored David Arnott, Mary Gregory, and Parkinson at Quietude. We've scored Sam and Ginger, poor wretch, I'm at least glad he won't be hanged. Robinson counts against them but not for us. I was being kept in cold storage till the Big Boy had time to deal with me. There remain Parker and Tetlow, lorry drivers, Morgan at the Vavasour and Bates in Verbena Street. Oscar is not one of the gang though I think he had ambitions that way. According to my information he knew Sam, but not where to find him." Hambledon repeated Cobden's story of the disseminated message from Oscar to Sam which Cobden had heard. "It's no good questioning Oscar, he doesn't know anything."

"It will be worth watching him, though," said Bagshott. "If the message reaches Daniel Deacon—"

"What a name for a murderer," murmured Tommy. "I suppose he chose it for its eminent respectability. You couldn't suspect a Daniel Deacon. You think he'll get in touch with Oscar. I've no doubt you're right."

"We are looking for Parker and Tetlow, and one of these days we'll find them," said Bagshott. "They are probably in Turnham Green, they wouldn't go far from home even to post a letter. The Vavasour has been shut down and Morgan has got a job bill-posting, he shows no sign of running away. I am inclined to think him a very minor rascal; Bates, on the other hand—"

"I wish we could pin something on Bates," said Hambledon wistfully. "He knows something about David Arnott; he must do. He may have shot Robinson—I think so, but I doubt if you'll ever prove it. It doesn't much matter, he's only forestalled the hangman. What I was going to say was that if you could convict Bates of something that would get him a couple of years in jug he might talk about Deacon. He probably would, too. Not that that would matter much actually; England can spare Bates, but it would be another mouth shut and we want one in working order. Bates is—"

The telephone rang and Hambledon kept silence while Bagshott answered it. After saying: "Yes. Yes," several times he ended with: "Very well. Send him up at once," and replaced the receiver.

"Talk of the devil," he said, turning to Hambledon. "Bates is here."

"Bates? What for?"

"He asked for Ennis but Ennis thought I might like to see him."

"Shall I remain," said Hambledon, "or do you think the sight of me will strike him dumb? Hawkley the convict here? 'Old Sir Richard—caught at last—'?"

"I'll leave it to you."

"Then I'll stay," said Tommy comfortably, and lit one of the cigars Bagshott kept for important visitors.

Bates shambled into the room and came to a halt in the middle of the carpet. He had been ill-dressed and untidy when Hambledon first saw him at the boardinghouse in Verbena Street, but then there was that in his carriage and the set of his shoulders which told that he had once been a soldier. Any such indication had entirely disappeared since then, as Hambledon noticed with interest. In the ten days since Arnott died Bates appeared to have shrunk; not only was he so much thinner that his clothes hung on him, but he also seemed to be shorter, and his red hair was turning a sandy grey. He looked at Bagshott first; after a moment he looked at Hambledon, his eyes opened wide and he stepped back.

"Well, Bates," said Tommy cheerfully. "I owe you some money, don't I? I didn't pay for my supper, you know."

Bates swallowed and then said it didn't matter, that bit of supper. He paused and then added with a rush: "Did they get the other chap too?"

"Who, the police? Not yet, only me. To tell you the truth, Bates, I thought I was safer in here than outside with you-know-who after me."

"Too right," said Bates, "that's why I'm 'ere." He appeared to draw comfort from the presence of a fellow-sufferer, for he drew himself erect and stood at attention to speak to the Chief-Inspector. "Sir, I 'ave come to tell you what's coming to me for that."

"You wish to make a statement," said Bagshott. "You understand, don't you, that whatever you say may be taken down and used in evidence?"

"That's what I want."

"Very well. I'll send for a stenographer." Bagshott touched a bell. "Sit down, Bates. On that chair, there."

Bates began his statement by saying that David Arnott had done the jewel robbery at the Capitol and brought the proceeds back to his room in Verbena Street. "I never saw any of it bar the diamond wristwatch 'e kept for poor Mary Gregory. I asked 'im where the rest was and 'e says: 'What rest? I got a present for my young lady and this is it.' 'E winks at me and puts the watch back in 'is pocket. So I says I wasn't 'avin' loot like that brought into my 'ouse, making trouble and maybe getting me in dutch with the police, it's my living, my 'ouse is. So 'e says that's all right, the stuff's where I'll never see it and I've only got to keep my mouth shut and everything 'll be all right." Bates said he was not satisfied and he went downstairs and talked it over with his wife. "She said as it had got to be put a stop to. Very particklar my wife is." They discussed means of persuading Arnott to return the jewel to the Capitol; at this point Hambledon's left eyebrow went up but he made no comment. No such means, however, occurred to them. "Be just like taking a bone from a lion, even Mary Gregory couldn't 'ave persuaded 'im to that. Very pig-'eaded, young David Arnott." So Bates went out for a stroll and remembered some tablets the doctor had given his wife to make her sleep when she was ill the year before. "She took two an' never no more, she don't 'old with drugs." Bates returned to the house and took the tablets from the back of a drawer in his wife's dressing-table. "I never said a word to 'er, see? She didn't know a thing till it was too late." Arnott was in the habit of drinking coffee when he could get it, "which means whenever we 'ad a drop of milk to spare from the ration." Bates made a cup of coffee and took it up to Arnott's room, debating on the way how many tablets to put in. The two his wife took had had little or no effect on her, and the doctor had told him she mustn't drink coffee when she took them. "So I reckoned as they weren't too strong and I tipped the lot in, six or eight there were. 'E said as the coffee was bitter and I said that was what passed for coffee these days and probably mostly acorns. I gave 'im some more sugar and 'e drank it. I went away, taking the cup with me and left 'im." Bates's idea, he explained earnestly, was to wait till Arnott was soundly asleep and then search his room for the jewels, pack them up and post them back to the Capitol. Hambledon's right eyebrow rose to join his left, but Bates was looking at Bagshott and did not notice it. "We 'ad people comin' and goin' and I couldn't get up to 'is room as soon as I meant. Then when I did go, so 'elp me 'e was dyin'." Bates described the symptoms. "I shook 'im, poured cold water on' is 'ead and tried to make 'im sick, no good. Then I rushed down for my wife and when we come up again 'e was dead. Can I 'ave a drink of water, please?"

"Certainly," said Bagshott, and poured him a glass with some whisky in it. "You can have a cigarette too, if you like."

"Thank you, sir. Well, that's where we lost our 'eads. I told my wife what I'd give 'im and she says: 'That's murder and they'll 'ang you for it.' I says I never meant to kill 'im and she says meanings don't matter, it's what I'd done." They argued the point for some time and were then interrupted by the voice of Mary Gregory calling along the passage for David. Mrs. Bates put her head out of the door and said David was not there and the girl went downstairs again. "Well, that finished it, somehow. We pushed 'im in the wardrobe and locked the door on 'im and went downstairs to think it over. 'Sides, it was time to serve the supper. Then this gentleman came and his friend."

"That's right," said Hambledon.

"They badly wanted a room and we 'ad no other night, so my wife says 'put 'em in there, I've locked the wardrobe and I'll tell 'em they can't 'ave the use of it.' Didn't she?"

"She did," said Tommy.

"So she cleared up 'is things and remade the bed and that was O.K. It was only for one night," explained Bates, "we 'ad another room coming vacant in the morning. Then that lot arrived." He stopped.

"What lot?" asked Bagshott.

"Those three men who went up to Arnott's room."

"You knew them, did you?" asked Hambledon.

"I knew 'em, yes. Deacon and his lot. Well, where they are there's trouble; they asked for Arnott and wouldn't believe me when I said he'd gone and I'd let 'is room to somebody else. So they went on up. Well, wardrobe doors won't stop the likes of them and I didn't want 'em pinning Arnott's death on to me, so my wife and I went up and got 'im out through the backs of the wardrobes into the next room which 'appened to be ours, and that was just an 'appening. We didn't 'ave that room as a rule. Well, then the row started next door and we thought next thing they'd be through an' on us. So we took round for somewhere to dump 'im and there was a great big open car in the vacant lot next us, got a canvas cover over the back seats, sort of buttoned down. So me and my wife put 'im in there and buttoned the cover down again." Bates paused and took another drink. "You see, we didn't know who the car belonged to and I thought as maybe the owner mightn't look in the back seat for days, perhaps, and by then he'd 'ave been dozens of places. 'Sides, I didn't know what the car was doing standing there, maybe the owner wouldn't want to say 'e'd been there at all. There's some funny characters in Verbena Street, you know."

"There are indeed," said Bagshott, and gave him another cigarette.

"Thank you, sir. Well, we'd 'ardly left the car and was back in our own garden when the shooting started and we 'eard police whistles and all that." Apparently this further excitement on top of a thoroughly trying evening was too much for Mrs. Bates who turned faint and collapsed on the garden steps. Bates was still fussing round her when hasty footsteps were heard coming round the side of the house towards the cars. He went to look over the wall and saw, to his abiding horror, the tall slim figure of Deacon and the broad squat figure of Sam leap into the sports car and drive furiously away. "I tell you, gentlemen, when I realized what I'd done I damn near fainted myself."

The next few days were not so bad because the place was full of police and even Deacon would not attempt to enter a house under those circumstances, but when the police were withdrawn and Mary Gregory was killed Bates and his wife were terrified.

"Sam came in one night, through the gardens and in the back. He didn't come 'bout anything special, only thought a man in the street looked at 'im a bit old-fashioned and maybe he'd better get under cover for a while." Bates told in detail about how Sam sat in the kitchen and talked and Mrs. Bates went out of the room because she couldn't bear the sight of him. Sam said that the boss, as he always called Deacon, was furiously angry with Bates for saddling him with the body of David Arnott. Bates asked what they did with it and Sam said they dumped it in the grounds of some sort of hospital with a bottle of doped whisky to make it look as though he'd drunk it himself and died there. Sam rolled about with laughter as he described how one of the patients had drunk out of the bottle and also died; he thought it a great joke and even the boss said it was a good thing, it would help to muddle the police. "Sam went on to tell me as I'd better look out for myself as the boss was goin' to 'tend to me when 'e'd got time. People didn't play jokes like that on the boss and get away with it, he said."

Sam went away at last; Mr. and Mrs. Bates went to bed and lay awake all night talking.

"Which night was this?" asked Bagshott.

"Last Friday night—a week ago to-day." The Bates decided at last to sell 5 Verbena Street as a going concern and clear out. She had relations in Glasgow, though she wasn't a Scot herself, and they would go up there and make a fresh start. "Well, it's a good time to sell 'ouse property, I 'adn't but just seen the agents about it when it was snapped up and the purchase price paid over." Mrs. Bates packed up and went off to Scotland and Bates stayed behind just to hand over and sign the final documents, after which he was going to follow her at once. "That was this afternoon, they was comin' at three. At five to three the door opens and who walks in but Deacon?" Fortunately there were people about, and Deacon just stood there in the hall waiting and smiling at him and not saying a word. At three o'clock punctually there came a knock at the door and Bates, with knees knocking together, answered it. There was quite a party on the doorstep; the new owner and his wife, a couple of friends of his, the solicitor's clerk and a man from the house agency. Bates asked Deacon to excuse him as these gentlemen had come to see him on business. "Deacon just kep' on smiling and says: 'Please don't trouble, Mr. Bates. My business 'll wait,' 'e says, 'I'm used to waitin' for what I want but I always get it in the end. I'll be seein' you later,' 'e says, 'don't worry, I'll be seein' you.'"

Deacon went away, Bates pulled himself together and transacted his business. When the visitors were going Bates asked if he might share their taxi as he had an urgent errand in the West End and taxis were hard to come by in Verbena Street. "So we all piled in, 'im and 'is wife and 'is two friends and me, the more the merrier for me I can tell you. I sat in the back, well back. The others got out in Oxford Street and I come straight on down 'ere. And damn glad to get 'ere alive, believe me. That Deacon, 'e fair gives me the creeps. 'E's a killer, that's what. Might 'ave shot me through the window same as 'e did Robinson. Deacon's a crack shot, I'll 'and 'im that."

Bagshott glanced casually at Hambledon whose idea it had been that Bates might have shot Robinson, but there was as yet no evidence to support it and a good deal against it. There was no object in raising the point at the moment and Bagshott let the reference pass for the time. He asked for the names and addresses of the new owner of 5 Verbena Street and the people who came there with him; Bates gave them readily.

"Now then," said Bagshott, "that is the end of your statement, is it? Very well. What you have done is to admit to an offence under Section 22 of the Offences against the Person Act of 1861," and Bagshott quoted it. "It is a felony."

Bates nodded. "I know what I've done all right, comin' 'ere," he said. "But I wants it all cleared up."

"Very well. Leaving that matter for the present and turning to another subject—this is not part of your statement—what can you tell us about Deacon? Is that his real name, for a start?"

Bates supposed so but had no proof to offer. He did not know where Deacon lived or anything definite about him. He had, actually, only seen him four times, on each occasion at Verbena Street. The first time, David Arnott brought him and took him up to his own room, "that would be about six or seven months back." On the second occasion Deacon called to see Arnott; the third time was on the night that Arnott died; "the last time was to-day an' I sincerely 'ope it is the last time. What d'you say, 'Awkley?"

"Too right," said Tommy Hambledon.

Bates had, however, heard a good deal about Deacon before he had seen him. He was said to run a gang, or several gangs perhaps. Robbery, blackmail, forgery, anything like that, and he wouldn't stick at murder either if he thought it necessary, so it was said. Men who weren't afraid of much were afraid of him. There was a lot more of this, but it soon became clear that Bates knew nothing that was immediately useful in finding Deacon, though he might be a help when it came to collecting evidence. Hambledon yawned and Bagshott apparently agreed with him, for he closed the interview.

"Your statement will be typed out. Please read it carefully, and if you are sure it is correct please sign it. You will be brought before a magistrate in the morning, formally charged and remanded in custody."

"Thank you," said Bates. "I don't want no bail. You'll be careful, won't you, taking me to court to-morrow mornin'?"

"Don't worry," said Bagshott with emphasis. "We shall."

Bates was removed, giving the thumbs-up sign to Hambledon who grinned in reply.

"Well, Bagshott? What will happen to him?"

"He will probably be charged with murder but a clever counsel will get it reduced to manslaughter. No malice aforethought if his story is correct. I wish he'd known a little more about Deacon, I'm sure he'd have told us if he had."

"Deacon is still extant because nobody knows anything about him. I had hoped for more from Bates but I ought to have known Deacon better. Reminds me of the story about the V.I.P. who summoned a taxi and said: 'Home!' When the driver asked him where, he said: 'Do you suppose I'd tell a fellow like you where my beautiful home is?' Deacon is like that even when he's sober. So far as I can see, the only door open to us at the moment is Oscar."

"Yes," said Bagshott, "I'll have a watch put on him. Where does he live?"

Hambledon told him, adding: "I don't know how many exits the place has got because I was shut in most of the time, but the place looked all doors to me and I suppose they lead somewhere. There are trapdoors in the floor, too, dating no doubt from the time when it was a storage loft. There was one in the room I had but it was screwed down."

"That reminds me," said Bagshott. "How did you manage to get away from there? You didn't tell me that bit."

"Oh, just slipped away, you know," said Tommy vaguely, "just slipped away."

XXI

THE MAN FROM PINKERTON'S

Oscar, alias Hendry Billing, watched from his window the departure of Savory and Cobden with his late guest. So that was The Boss, and just what one would expect a man with that reputation to look like. The car, too, just the car a man like that would drive. Cost a couple of thousand pounds, probably more. He sighed happily and counted his packet of notes, fifty of them, nice new £1 notes. They must be spent by degrees, or inquisitive people might wonder how he came by them. He counted them several times more out sheer pleasure and then put two in his pocket and hid the other forty-eight away in very secret hiding-place. He craned his head out of the back window to see the time by the local church clock; it was not yet two and there was just time for a drink if he was quick. He locked his door and almost danced along to the Six Bells.

"Double Scotch, Charlie," he ordered, and passed over one of his beautiful new notes.

"What's up, Oscar? Come into a fortune?"

"No," said Oscar prudently. "No such luck, I picked up a bit on the pools, that's all. Not much, but I thought as I'd 'ave somethink good for once."

"Ah," said the bartender, examining the note. "Don't blame you, beer bein' what it is. Just a moment."

He went out at the back of the bar, leaving Oscar staring after him with faint disquiet. Presently Charlie returned, followed by the innkeeper himself holding the note between two fingers as though it defiled his touch.

"Not out of this, Oscar," he said.

"Wh-why not? What's matter?"

"It's phoney, that's what. Look for yourself. Got on thread through it."

Oscar looked as through he were going to faint.

"Can't be," he gasped. "Impossible. My friend what gave it me—"

"Thought you said you won it on the Pools," said the bartender.

"So I did. Me and my friend, we was sharing and the money came to 'im so 'e comes round to me with my lot—"

177

"If I was you, Oscar," said the innkeeper, "I'd take it back to him, quick. Maybe there's been some mistake."

"I can't," said Oscar miserably. "'E's gone away."

"Ah," said the innkeeper with meaning; the bartender grinned and Oscar saw it.

"Nothin' to grin at," he said with dignity. "I'll see 'im about it all right when 'e comes back. 'Ere's another one, since you're so narky."

He took out the second note and passed it over the bar; the innkeeper took one look at it and passed it back again.

"You're right, Oscar," he said. "It is another one." The boatman leaned heavily on the bar and the innkeeper was sorry for him.

"Draw him a half-pint," he said to the bartender. "This one's on the house, Oscar. Sounds to me like someone's put a fast one over on you."

"I—I—you're telling me," said Oscar bitterly. "Thank you," he added, talking the glass, "you're a gent." He drank the beer at one draught.

"How many of these have you got, Oscar?"

"Fif—ah, I don't know. Maybe some on 'em's all right."

"Fifty?" said the innkeeper. "Now, you be guided by me, Oscar. You go home and look at them notes and if there's even one more you've got your doubts about, you take the 'ole lot to the police. You don't want to go getting into trouble passing them things at your age. You tell the police the 'ole tale and then you'll be in the clear, come what may."

"I can't," said Oscar.

"Oh, it's like that, is it? Look here, Oscar, it's closing time. You go home and fetch the rest of them notes and come round to my private door. I'll look through 'em for you and tell you if any of 'em's any good. I'm more used to handling money than what you are."

"Thank you," said Oscar unhappily, and tottered away. When the innkeeper pointed out that not only had they all the same fatal flaw but they all bore the same serial number, Oscar's wrath boiled over. He told the whole story, not only to his friend the innkeeper but to anyone else who happened to be about. He said in crude Anglo-Saxon what sort of a man The Boss was, to treat a man like that. He admitted that it served him right for having dealings with crooks for the first time in his life, at which some of his hearers were afflicted with coughing. He said if he ever saw The Boss again he'd tell him this and also that, together with much else which would be good for him.

Deacon ultimately received Oscar's original message about having something of interest to him, and almost at the same time, from another source, a sparkling résumé of the things Oscar was calling him for paying in forged notes. Deacon's thin eyebrows went up and the lines deepened round his mouth. There was something here which required investigation.

Oscar was sitting in his kitchen mournfully going through the notes for the twenty-seventh time on the remote chance that one—even just one—might be a good one after all. There came a knock at his door, he pushed the notes hurriedly into a drawer and went to open it. Outside there waited a tall slim man with a muffler round his throat and his hat over his eyes.

"Henry Billing—or Oscar Billing?"

"Henry Billing, that's right, an' Oscar's what I'm called, like."

"May come in?"

Oscar hesitated, but there was that about this man which made him obeyed. The boatman opened the door wider and Deacon walked in.

"May I sit down? Thank you. Now then, don't imagine for a moment that I wish to intrude into your private affairs but a little bird told me that somebody has played a dirty trick on you recently. Is that right?"

Oscar hesitated again, for he was naturally suspicious, and Deacon smiled in a friendly fashion.

"I quite understand that you wouldn't feel like talking to a total stranger about this business, let me introduce myself before we start." He pushed a visiting-card across the table and the name upon it was not Daniel Deacon. "You have heard of Pinkerton's, have you? The famous American detective agency?" The name rang a dim bell in the back of Oscar's mind and he nodded uncertainly. "Of course you have," went on Deacon, "who hasn't? Well, I am one of the British staff of Pinkerton's—"

"Not the police?"

"Certainly not the police, though I will admit with gratitude that I've often found them quite helpful, No, not the police at all. Now, I have been engaged by the—I'd better not mention names—a wealthy and powerful business house in America to investigate the doings of a certain international crook who has defrauded them of really large sums of money. The methods he employs are very similar to the trick which was worked on you." Deacon paused; the thought of a wealthy American firm being taken in for a moment by a handful of dud notes lent a real warmth to his naturally charming smile. "I cannot, so far, get any clue to the disguise he has adopted in this country, though I have come across his tracks here and there. When I heard of your misfortune I came at once to see you to ask you if you would be so very good as to help me with a description of the man, and so on. Besides, there might be a possibility that something might be done—" Deacon broke off artistically short of a promise, but Oscar jumped at it.

"Say no more, sir, say no more. A wink's as good's a nod to a blind 'orse. Listen now, I'll tell yer all about it from the start, seein' you're not the police." Oscar began with the night of the great gale and how in the morning he had found the derelict landing craft drifting with the tide. He said he knew who she belonged to, a man he didn't know personally but he did know one of his men, a man called Sam. "Queer lookin' bloke, pretty much like Tarzan only uglier. King Kong, then." Oscar said he'd had dealings with Sam in connection with a couple of cases of Three Roses whisky the boatman had come across when he was working round the docks. "Let 'im have 'em for three pound fifteen a bottle when I could 'ave got four pound five anywheres," he added bitterly. He went on with the story about the prisoner aboard the landing craft howling that he was locked in when the tug hit her, and Deacon sat at the other side of the table nodding sympathetically and having many things made clear to him which had been obscure till then. "I did 'ear as Sam was washed up drowned on the other side," said Oscar, with a jerk of his head towards the Kent shore of the Thames estuary, "but I dunno, I didn't see 'im myself."

When he came to Hambledon's rescue Deacon asked what the prisoner was like and nodded sadly when Hambledon was described. "I feared so," he said. "Another Pinkerton's man. A colleague of mine. He is still missing."

There was a small noise outside the door but neither man noticed it.

"Ave they murdered 'im, sir?" asked Oscar, in an awed voice.

"Go on with your story," said Deacon gloomily, and Oscar begged his pardon. "I do seem to 'ave backed the wrong 'orse, sir, but 'ow was I to know?" When the story reached the point where Savory and Cobden took Hambledon away, Deacon asked for more personal descriptions. Oscar was better at describing people than one would expect and Deacon knew Savory very well by sight; had even spoken to him though Savory did not remember it. Deacon nodded, saying: "Yes, yes. The sort of role he would adopt. That will be of immense help, I know what to look for, now. And the other man?"

Cobden's appearance had made less impression upon an Oscar completely dazzled by the magnificent Savory, but Deacon was half expecting to meet the ex-convict again in that connection and knew at once who he was. "I know the man, yes. They have been long connected. An illegitimate son, I believe."

"You don't say," said Oscar. "Not a bit alike, they weren't. The boss—the one you're after—'e did look a real gent. Suède shoes, 'e 'ad, and a diamond ring as big as a—a walnut," said Oscar, blinking rapidly, "an' a diamond pin and diamonds all along 'is Albert chain. I mean, 'ow was I to know? What a car 'e 'ad, too; big—oh, as a 'earse."

"One really cannot wonder if you were deceived," said Deacon gravely. "Is there nothing else you can tell me? No, well, I think you told your story extremely well. It will be of immense assistance to me in tracing the criminal. Without making any rash promises I think I can say that the great American Corporation of which I spoke will not prove ungrateful. In the meantime, a small acknowledgment of what I owe you—you won't find this one's counterfeit, believe me—"

The door opened suddenly and Bagshott walked in closely followed by

Hambledon. Deacon sprang to his feet, Oscar rose more slowly and Bagshott started off in the specified manner.

"Daniel Deacon, I arrest you on a charge of murder—"

Deacon thrust his hand into his coat pocket but the long muffler impeded him and Hambledon was quicker.

"Put up your hands, Deacon!"

Oscar saw the gun and was horrified.

"Stop, stop!" he yelled, springing forward, "'e's yer friend, can't you see, 'e's the man from the—"

Deacon grabbed him from behind, held him like a shield and backed away towards an inner door. Oscar's mouth opened but no more words came, and Bagshott dodged round the table to attack from the flank. Hambledon was trying to get a disabling shot at Deacon but he was too well covered till he put one hand behind him to turn the door-handle, when Oscar's eyes closed slowly and he sank down in a dead faint. Deacon leapt through the door, slammed it after him and turned the key. Before Bagshott could remove the impediment which was Oscar there was a shout from the street outside and the sound of a car starting and being driven furiously away.

"My car," said Hambledon, and turning, leapt down the wooden stairs into the street. There were two constables looking exactly like terriers who have missed a rat, and a bunch of excited children all talking at once but completely out-screamed by a skinny small boy with red hair.

"Jumped outa winda!" he shrieked. "I see him! Into car wid himself and away!"

Hambledon looked over his shoulder at Bagshott, and remarked: "Passed to you, partner." He then took out a cigarette, tapped it down thoughtfully and lit it.

"Where's the nearest telephone?" demanded Bagshott and one of the constables dumbly indicated the Six Bells. "You two will hear more of this," he added furiously. "Hambledon, what's your car number?"

Hambledon told him; he burst through the swing doors and rushed inside. Out in the street a crowd began to gather, the children asked questions which nobody answered, the two constables told them to pass along there, please, and glanced uneasily at each other, and Hambledon leaned placidly against Oscar's doorpost and smoked. Inside the Six Bells the proprietor and his clients kept as still and silent as a waxwork group, since only so could they hear through a closed door the voice of Chief-Inspector Bagshott ordering that all patrol cars should look out for a Vauxhall number so-and-so, not to stop it but to follow it, and to keep in wireless touch with the Yard and each other. Finally, a patrol car also fitted with radio was to be at a certain spot at a specified time and wait there until he arrived. Let no mistakes be made.

Bagshott returned to the bar, thanked the innkeeper and paid twopence for the telephone call. He then asked if there was a garage handy where a car could be hired and was directed to one round the next corner. He thanked the proprietor again and instantly disappeared into the street. There was silence in the bar for nearly a minute.

"Seemed annoyed, like," said the Corporation dustman.

"Hold on here, Charlie," said the innkeeper. "I'm just going to have a look at poor old Oscar. He's too old for this kind of thing, so he is."

Bagshott and Hambledon, side by side in the back seat of a hired Wolseley, proceeded towards London and their rendezvous. More than once Hambledon seemed about to speak but glanced at his friend and changed his mind. Presently Bagshott relaxed his strained attitude, leaned back in his seat and broke into a laugh.

"Thank goodness," said Hambledon. "I thought you were going to burst. But what's the joke?"

"Nothing much," said Bagshott. "Only that blighter going off in your car." He laughed again.

"Oh, really," said Tommy, pained. "Mind this, Bagshott, if one of your star drivers crashes that car you'll find me a new one, and I said 'new'. I've waited fifteen months for delivery and only had it three weeks."

"They won't, that's all right. You suggested bringing it, didn't you?"

"Yes. I have discovered, since living in London's so-called Underworld, that the number of every police car is known to interested persons and taught to their intelligent if scruffy children. 'Daddy dear, a Headquarters car has just passed the post office going east.' I thought a little more anonymity might help."

"Tell me," said Bagshott, "who was the diamond-studded gentleman whom Oscar was describing? A friend of yours, I gather, since he came and released you. By the way, I thought you said you just slipped away when Oscar wasn't looking?"

"Yes, he's a friend of mine and he turned up very opportunely. I'd like you to meet him some day. He doesn't always dress like that and he's been very helpful over Deacon. You know, we were very lucky over that visit up to the last moment. You said it was about time we went to Purfleet and interviewed Oscar personally, but even you couldn't have hoped to arrive at a better moment. I did love Deacon mourning his departed colleague in Pinkerton's—me—didn't you? Pinkerton's, too, what a nerve the blighter's got."

"He'll want it before I've done with him," said Bagshott.

"Now, now. You mustn't let these little things sour you, Bagshott, or you'll have to throw in your job and keep bees before your disposition is finally ruined."

"Why bees?"

"Honey. Sweetness. And a cure for rheumatism. Is this where you bade your chariot await you?"

"Yes, and there he is, which is just as well for all concerned. Stop here, driver, please, and how much do I owe you?"

They transferred to the police car; Bagshott immediately plugged in to the radio and was told the latest news. Hambledon's car had been picked up just where Barking Road becomes East India Dock Road and was being followed. It was now passing westward along Commercial Road East and the driver was showing signs of suspecting that he was under observation. At the junction of Whitechapel High Street another patrol car would therefore take over.

"He must have driven like blazes to get there in the time," said Hambledon. "How many miles behind are we?"

"About five," said Bagshott. "He had fifteen minutes' start. As fast as you can, driver."

"Very good, sir." But the traffic was heavy and congested with trams, and Hambledon's scalp tingled once or twice when the police driver slipped through gaps which looked inadequate.

"The other patrol car has taken over," said Bagshott after, a pause. "Deacon appears reassured, he is driving more steadily."

"I am delighted to hear it," said Tommy sincerely. "I want my car returned in good order, if possible. I was beginning to like it."

Even Deacon had to slow down passing through the City and Bagshott's driver managed to close the gap a little. Deacon turned along Queen Victoria Street and then along the Embankment, here he made up time a little. Past Waterloo Bridge he slowed down and stopped; the shadowing car had to pass him.

"He has gone into a telephone-box," reported the police.

He was in it for some time; when he came out the patrol car took up the chase once more, but Deacon no longer appeared to be in any hurry and pottered along towards Westminster. The day was gloomy and overcast, the light began to fade in the streets and a thin drizzle was falling. Deacon, whether to waste time or whether to make sure he was not being followed led his pursuers a pretty dance through and about the maze of small streets between Victoria Street and the river. The following cars—there were three of them in it now—even lost him for a few minutes; Bagshott, who by now was back in his own room at Scotland Yard, was drumming with his fingers on his desk before another report came in from quite another part of London.

"South Acton police station reporting. Constable on point duty in Rollo Lane recognized driver and passenger of Morris Ten saloon going towards Chiswick High Road as Parker and Tetlow." They added the number of the Morris.

"Now we know," said Hambledon, "to whom Deacon was telephoning.

Where is South Acton, now?"

"Just beyond Turnham Green, where the blank letter came from which was addressed to Deacon at Quietude," said Bagshott. He issued more orders about the Morris. "If those fellows have lost Deacon—"

But Hambledon's car was found beside the river at Chelsea while Deacon himself was standing on Chelsea Bridge looking downstream in the gathering darkness. At last he threw the stub of a cigarette over the parapet, looked at his wristwatch and strolled slowly back to the car.

The Morris, in the meantime, had also been picked up by a patrol car and followed along Fulham Palace Road. It stopped at one point and waited for nearly a quarter of an hour till a man stepped off a bus and came along the pavement to the Morris. He was apparently unwilling to get in when told, and Tetlow, who was beside the driver, got out of the car and fairly pushed him into the back seat. Still arguing hotly but in whispers, he was driven slowly away. He also was recognized, it was Morgan, once commissionaire at the Vavasour. The Morris went slowly on towards Putney Bridge.

At this news Hambledon sat up sharply and said: "What's Deacon doing now?"

"Driving along King's Road," said Bagshott, "I suppose they're going to meet somewhere and—"

"And I know where," said Tommy. "Let me use your phone, may I?"

He asked for Savory's number at Wimbledon, only to be told that the telephone was out of order.

"Hell and blazes," said Hambledon, putting back the receiver. "Come on, Bagshott, for heaven's sake, or there'll be another murder within the next half-hour."

XXII

CHIEF-INSPECTORS CAN'T BE WRONG

"We are going to Wimbledon Common," said Hambledon. "To a house just off the Common, actually. The road is called Parson's Close, do you know it?"

"No, sir," said the police driver.

"Never mind, I'll pilot you."

"And who is going to be murdered?" asked Bagshott.

"It isn't a joke," said Hambledon. "A man called Salvation Savory, if we aren't quick. I think Deacon has run out of money and he knows Savory's got plenty. He wants to go abroad which will cost something the way he'd go, and he wants to live comfortably there till he can get going again. Besides that, Deacon knows Savory has wiped his eye several times lately, most notably when he rescued me from Oscar's flat four days ago."

"So Savory is the man covered with diamonds," said Bagshott thoughtfully. "I suppose they are what Deacon is after."

"Well, not those particular stones," said Hambledon with a laugh. "Savory has got some nice ones, though. I think he deals in them in a mild way."

"Does he live alone in his house?" asked Bagshott.

"There's a manservant called Dick who looks like a retired jockey, but he wouldn't be much good in a roughhouse. Savory had a man staying with him the other day but I doubt if he's there still."

"If you're so sure Deacon's likely to kill him," said Bagshott, "I can order the patrol cars to stop him. They'll probably crash your car doing so."

Hambledon hesitated.

"It would even be worth doing that," he said, "if we were perfectly sure of getting Deacon. But he might escape; he's very good at it, and then we should have to start all over again. No, better let him get to the house. He won't shoot at sight because he doesn't know where Savory keeps his diamonds."

Bagshott, who had the headphones on, held up his hand for silence and then reported the news.

"The Morris driven by Parker has just passed over Putney Bridge, fol-

lowed by a patrol car. Your car, with Deacon alone in it, waited near the
bridge till the Morris passed and then followed it. There is a second patrol
car following Deacon."

"Complicated sort of sandwich," said Hambledon, "and here come we like
the jam on the top."

"I think it better not to tell them where they may be going," said Bagshott.

"Better not," agreed Tommy. "Improbable as you will naturally think it, I
may yet be mistaken. Such a thing has been known to happen."

Bagshott looked at him and seemed about to reply, but the radio interrupted him.

"Deacon has passed the first patrol car and is now on the tail of the Morris.
He is about to pass it. He has passed it and is now in the lead."

"Let him carry on," said Hambledon. "We are now approaching Putney
ourselves, I see; could we close up, do you think?"

Bagshott gave an order to the police driver and the car increased speed. "It
is getting so dark," added Bagshott, "we shan't recognize them until we are
on top of them."

"They can't go faster than the Morris," said Hambledon, "but we can,
which is so nice."

Crossing Putney Heath, where the road begins to drop again, the police
driver said: "That may be them, sir, those four cars together."

Four sets of headlamps in line astern showed ahead of them for a moment
until they swept round a bend and were lost to sight.

"They have taken the Wimbledon Road," said Bagshott quietly, and
Hambledon said: "Close up, please. Better tell the cars to look out for a turn
sharp left half a mile ahead, and a stop two hundred yards down the turning.
Are either of the patrol cars manned by men in plain clothes?"

Bagshott asked by radio and was told that the second car was.

"Tell him to take the lead," said Hambledon, "and pass the other two cars
when they stop. Deacon will probably leave a man with the cars; they will
secure him without fuss. Tell them not to follow too close now. The other
patrol car will wait short of the stop."

Bagshott transmitted the orders.

"And we needn't rush it ourselves now," added Tommy. "I want them to
get inside the house."

The car slowed down perceptibly and the radio said that Deacon's car and
the Morris were turning left.

"'I did not err,'" quoted Tommy, "'there does a sable cloud Turn forth her
silver lining on the night.'"

"Shakespeare?" said Bagshott. "Is this the turning?"

"Milton. Yes. We'd better have our headlights off, I think."

The driver switched them off and turned the corner into Parson's Close.

When the first two cars drew up at Savory's gate four men got out. Three of them walked quickly up the drive and the fourth stayed by the cars. He strolled along the pavement with the measured tread of one in the habit of spending hours on his feet, for he had once been a commissionaire. He paused to look over the hedge when the copper front door of Kuminboys opened to show a rectangle of light from the hall. A tall man appeared silhouetted against it and there was a suggestion of quick and even violent movement. Three figures passed inside and the door closed. Morgan smiled to himself and went on strolling up and down with one hand clasping the other wrist behind his back. There was a street lamp only twenty yards away and he could be seen quite plainly.

Another car came slowly up the road from the Common; when it was level with him it stopped, a window was wound down and a head appeared at it.

"I say," a voice called from the car, "could you possibly direct me to—" some name Morgan did not catch. He went across to the car; one must at all costs behave quite normally.

"I beg your pardon, sir?"

"Albemarle Road. I thought this was it but it isn't. I must have taken the wrong turning."

"This is Parson's Close, sir. I'm sorry, I don't know Albemarle Road, I'm not acquainted with their neighborhood."

"I'll get out and look at the map," said the man in the car, opening the door. "If we know where we are it ought to help us."

"Yes, sir," said Morgan, and stepped forward smartly to hold the door open. He had been opening doors for people for years, the action was automatic.

The man stepped out in the road, turned on Morgan and heaved him into the car before he realized what was happening.

"Inside, you! And keep quiet or I'll—"

"What—wha'—who?"

"Police. I arrest you on a charge—"

Morgan's mouth opened but the Detective-Sergeant forestalled him.

"One chirp out of you and I'll stifle you with the plush upholstery!"

"T'isn't plush," said Morgan, seizing upon familiar ground, "it's leather. And I've got handcuffs on!"

"Only just noticed them? Pull into the curb, Ted, and if he utters one word, brain him with a spanner."

"Pleasure, I'm sure," said Ted, and leaned over the back of the driver's seat with a spanner at the ready.

The Detective-Sergeant walked into the road and signalled to two more cars waiting further back. They came up; Hambledon, Bagshott and the driver got out of the first and two uniformed policemen out of the second. Hambledon walked across to Morgan, who saw him plainly and recognized him.

"'Awkley? What you doing 'ere? 'Ave they got you too?"

Hambledon thrust his head in at the window and said: "Where are Deacon and the other two?"

"But—"

"Answer me!" His hand followed his face through the window and Morgan saw that he was holding a revolver. "D'you want your head blown off?"

"They—they've only gone to see a friend."

"All three of them gone in?"

"Yes."

"Right," said Hambledon, and removed his face and gun. "He says they've gone in."

"We'll just make sure," said Bagshott, and gave rapid orders to his men. They trotted across Savory's lawn and took up stations round the house. No sound floated back to the watchers by the gate, it was plain there was no opposition.

"Now," said Hambledon to Bagshott. "Round the back of the house, I think. There are various convenient windows."

Daniel Deacon walked quite openly up the drive, followed closely by Parker and Tetlow, and pulled the ivory skull which rang the front-door bell. Dick, who was clearing the dinner-table, laid down his tray and opened the front door. He had no time to see who was there before something soft and heavy struck him on the temple and they caught him as he fell. Deacon stepped over him, Parker and Tetlow between them shifted him out of the way and shut the door.

Deacon paused in the hall for a moment, listening. He had never been inside the house before but it had been described to him. Savory had a sitting-room upstairs, he might be there and not on the ground floor at all. However, someone coughed inside a door on the left, Deacon opened it at once and walked into the drawing-room.

Savory was sitting in an armchair with his back to the door, reading a book. He heard the door open; without looking round he said: "Well, Dick? Who was it?"

Deacon made a swift rush forward and pinned Savory down in his chair from behind, while Parker and Tetlow ran round and seized him by the legs. Savory was a big man and powerful; though he had been taken at a disadvantage he put up a very good fight in the course of which the chair collapsed, Parker put his head through one of the glass doors of the Dutch cabinet and emerged bleeding, and Tetlow received a black eye; Deacon found Savory's big hands round his throat and was half choked before Parker hit Savory hard under the jaw and stunned him for long enough to permit them to lash him up and stand back, panting.

Savory opened his eyes slowly and stared hard at them one after another.

"Daniel Deacon, I presume," he said, "and friends. To what do I—"

"No time to waste, said Deacon shortly. "You've got in my way once too often and this is the end, Savory."

"What," said Savory thickly, "another murder?"

"Yes. But before you die, where is your safe?"

Savory laughed. "You come here and say you're going to kill me, and expect me to pay you for it. What a hope you've got."

"You can either die comfortably with a bullet through the head, or slowly and uncomfortably with the help of your nice fire," said Deacon, nodding towards the gas-fire which bubbled and hissed through cast-iron logs already red-hot. "An easy death is what you'll pay for, I think."

They heard through the open door the sound of someone running down the stairs and a concerned voice saying: "Dick! What's the matter? Savory, Dick's fainted."

Savory's cry of warning came too late, or possibly Cobden merely thought it an exclamation of dismay. He was still bending over Dick when Parker dashed out of the room and knocked him out before he looked round. Parker returned to the drawing-room grinning and dusting his hands together.

"Easy, he said. "He's gone bye-byes."

"Now then, Savory," said Deacon, "which is it to be?"

Savory was not at all inclined to help them to anything except perdition and said so, after which operations started. Bound though he was, there was an interlude of sufficient violence before the three intruders had their will. Savory appeared to think that he had protested enough, for the next moment he said: "All right. I give in."

"Wise man, said Deacon. "Where is the safe?"

"In this room, and the keys are in a safe upstairs."

"And the key of the safe upstairs?"

"In my pocket here."

Parker took out the key and received explicit directions for finding the upstairs safe. He left the room while Savory lay on the floor perspiring, Deacon prowled round the room and Tetlow lit a cigarette.

"Where is the safe?" asked Deacon.

"If you take down that azalea picture behind you, you'll see it," said Savory unwillingly. Deacon did so and uncovered a safe door built flush with the wall. Parker returned with a key in his hand and gave it to Deacon.

"There weren't nothing else in that safe," he said.

Deacon fitted the key in the lock and tried in vain to turn it.

"This isn't the right key," he said angrily.

"Oh, yes, it is," said Savory. "You have to push to the left when you turn it."

Deacon tried again, the key turned in the lock and the door opened a little with the faint gasp of an airtight safe. Parker and Tetlow abandoned Savory as harmless and went to look over their leader's shoulder as he eased the safe door slowly open. It came forward for five inches without trouble, Deacon said: "Ah!" and swung it wide.

Instantly an appalling howl broke the silence, it rose to a higher note, sank, and rose again; the once familiar and always terrifying sound of the Air Raid Alert. The three men stood paralysed for a moment till Deacon slammed the safe door shut again and the howl ran slowly down the chromatic scale and ceased, leaving the air quivering.

"My burglar alarm," said Savory. "Works well, doesn't it? It's up on the roof."

"Let's go, boss," said Parker, and backed towards the door. "The police know all about it," added Savory. "No doubt they are already converging on the house."

Parker disappeared into the hall, Tetlow opened the window nearest to him and scrambled out. Deacon, his face convulsed with fury, came and stood over Savory.

"You've won that trick," he said, "but mine's the ace."

He put his hand in his pocket and noticed that Savory was looking past him just as a voice behind him said: "I wouldn't. Deacon."

He turned sharply, Hambledon stood in the doorway covering him with a revolver. Chief-Inspector Bagshott, who was already in the room, immediately closed with Deacon, and a Police-Sergeant slipped past Hambledon in the doorway and handcuffed the prisoner.

"Good," said Bagshott. "Have you got the other one?"

"Yes, sir. Stepped out of the window straight into the handcuffs, as you might say."

"There was a third," said Savory, whom Hambledon was releasing from his bondage.

"Oh, we got him," said Tommy cheerfully. "Parker, that was. He walked out backwards, the silly chump. Sergeant, I thought he bit your finger."

"Yes, sir, but I had gloves on."

"What have they done to Dick?" asked Savory, tearing off the cords round his ankles.

"Only sandbagged him," said the Sergeant. "He'll be all right. There's another gentleman out there, he's just come round."

"That'll be Brown," said Savory, before Hambledon could speak. "You know Brown, don't you?"

"Oh, rather," said Hambledon enthusiastically. "Good chap, Brown. I'll bring him in."

He went out in the hall and at once returned supporting Cobden who appeared to have a headache. The Sergeant, seeing the two men together and remembering the details of two "Wanted" notices he had committed to memory two months earlier, stared with his mouth open. Bagshott looked at Cobden, hesitated, and said: "Who did you say this gentleman was?"

"Harry Ernest Brown, a friend of mine from Cape Town," said Savory. "He's got a job in my eldest brother's business out there and is going back in a few weeks' time."

The color came into Cobden's pallid face. He said that was right and looked gratefully at Savory, who added: "He's got an identity card somewhere if you want to see it. Do you still look at identity cards?" He finished tying his shoelaces and looked up at Bagshott.

"Sometimes we do," said the Chief-Inspector, "but I don't think we'll bother Mr. Brown."

The Sergeant transferred his gaze to a small spot on the wallpaper and regarded it fixedly. Chief-Inspectors can't be wrong.

THE END

About the Rue Morgue Press

"Rue Morgue Press is the old-mystery lover's best friend,
reprinting high quality books from the 1930s and '40s."
—*Ellery Queen's Mystery Magazine*

Since 1997, the Rue Morgue Press has reprinted scores of traditional mysteries, the kind of books that were the hallmark of the Golden Age of detective fiction. Authors reprinted or to be reprinted by the Rue Morgue include Catherine Aird, Delano Ames, H. C. Bailey, Morris Bishop, Nicholas Blake, Dorothy Bowers, Pamela Branch, Joanna Cannan, John Dickson Carr, Glyn Carr, Torrey Chanslor, Clyde B. Clason, Joan Coggin, Manning Coles, Lucy Cores, Frances Crane, Norbert Davis, Elizabeth Dean, Carter Dickson, Eilis Dillon, Michael Gilbert, Constance & Gwenyth Little, Marlys Millhiser, Gladys Mitchell, James Norman, Stuart Palmer, Craig Rice, Kelley Roos, Charlotte Murray Russell, Maureen Sarsfield, Margaret Scherf, Juanita Sheridan and Colin Watson..

To suggest titles or to receive a catalog of Rue Morgue Press books write 87 Lone Tree Lane, Lyons, CO 80540, telephone 800-699-6214, or check out our website, www.ruemorguepress.com, which lists complete descriptions of all of our titles, along with lengthy biographies of our writers.